Baby For My Dad's SEAL Best Friend

A Steamy Age Gap Forced
Proximity Billionaire Romance

"Billionaire Silver Foxes' Club" Series

Valencia Rose

Contents

Prologue: Madeline

I couldn't believe my own audacity.

I was slipping away gracefully from just a few feet away from my father's seat to have – what I knew would be – one heck of a mind-blowing orgasm in a room just a few feet away.

As much as I tried at that moment, knowing what my man's skillful hands and chiseled body would do to me, I couldn't resist a minute longer.

As we were sneaking out of the big reception hall, I saw familiar faces, my father's friends, in the crowd. Music was playing softly from the live band on the stage. Dozens of military men and their families were there to commemorate their fallen brothers.

I tried not to meet my father's eyes – I was carrying too big a secret to face him. I was falling in love...*love?* Yes, I was falling in love with the most off-limits man in the whole world... my father's best friend, and I couldn't help myself.

We'd been eye-fucking each other the whole drive over, as we put on nametags, and as we walked down the hallway. My eyes were exhausted after the past hour. My pussy needed to take over for them. My heart was racing in my chest, and my breasts moved freely in my sexy dress as I rushed to keep up with him.

We didn't go far. This was his hotel, so he knew exactly where to take me. Inside the smaller event room down the hallway, he locked the door. He kissed me, the taste of him as familiar as my own name, but I pushed away. We didn't have much time. Our absence would be noticed.

I pulled up my dress and took his hand, placing it on my naked thigh. He needed no prompting. I gasped as his finger slipped inside my thong. My hand moved to his cock – that massive, girthy cock that I knew would pleasure my pussy with each thrust. I moaned, leaning back into his kiss, grasping his length over his pants and stroking it.

"Cum for me, baby," he whispered, his finger flicking gently across my clit.

"We don't have time—" I started to say, but he silenced me by biting on my lower lip, quick and sure, just like everything he did. I closed my eyes, giving in to the bliss building in my body.

The thrill of so many people nearby, of being so easily caught, turned me on so much that I came moments later on his hand, riding it as my muffled cries filled the empty room.

I felt him kiss me, then his free hand was on my bare back, finding the zipper to my dress and pulling it down. Cool air caressed my skin as my dress slowly fell away from my body, my naked breasts revealed to Hudson's hazel eyes.

I undid his suit pants and eagerly reached for his length. I wanted this. I needed this.

His lips captured my pink nipples as I stroked his hard cock, naked and huge in my hand. I panted, and then whined, as his finger started playing with my clit again. He was always a generous lover.

He lifted me onto one of the small tables in the room. Then, his finger was back on my clit. I closed my eyes to relish every sensation. I felt his strong hands on my thighs, opening my legs for him.

And then, oh glorious bliss, I felt his cock as it slid into me. My eyes flew open as he kissed me again. I could feel that familiar connection between us. Each thrust felt deeper. Each moan felt less controlled.

"Yes, take me please…" I lost myself in the feeling of this god of a silver fox pushing his rod into me.

"That's my good girl," he said, in that dangerously deep voice.

The room was filled with the sounds of my quiet moans and his guttural groans as he thrust into me hard and fast.

"Cum inside me. I need it!" I was ready. I threw my head back and felt his warm seed as it filled me.

Minutes later, we were dressed and ready to return to the event before we were missed. Hudson stole one more forbidden kiss, nipping at my lip before pulling back to study me with his intelligent hazel eyes. He was unlike any other man I'd ever dated. My heart swelled with emotion.

"You are perfect." I saw he meant it by the look in his eyes.

He pulled open the door, and we stepped into the hall-way. The sounds of music and voices were distant. All was quiet in the hallway. He stiffened a bit when we walked down the hallway to the ballroom. I could feel the tension in the air the moment we stepped into the grand ballroom of the hotel, coming face-to-face with a large screen that showed images of days gone by when Hudson and each of these men here were SEALs in active service.

Hudson had been quieter than usual all morning, his brow furrowed in thought when he didn't know I was watching him. Even the event room sex hadn't seemed to calm his thoughts down.

I knew him well enough now to know he was mentally preparing himself for what lay ahead.

I stayed close to his side as we walked through the crowd-ed room, the noise of laughter and conversation filling the space. Men in their old dress uniforms and others in casual attire were scattered around, some already sharing stories and others catching up after a year apart.

I used to attend these reunions when I was younger with my dad, as strange as that seemed now, but it had been a while. There was a sense of camaraderie that was not to be dimmed by time, but beneath it all, I could feel the undercurrent of bittersweet nostalgia that each man carried.

Hudson squeezed my hand discreetly as we moved through the crowd, and I squeezed back, letting him know I was there for him. I glanced up at him, catching the way his jaw was set as if he were steeling himself for what was to come. "Are you okay?" I asked, softly, trying not to draw too much attention. I knew this was hard for him, and I wished I could do more to help.

Hudson nodded, but his eyes were distant, scanning the room as if he were searching for something—or someone. "I'm fine," he said, his voice steady but lacking its usual warmth. "Just... a lot of memories all at once. I will be fine, though. I just need to remember the good times, right?"

"You're doing great." I stepped away from Hudson's side when I spotted my dad across the room, talking to a group of men. He was laughing, his shoulders shaking with enthusiasm, but as he turned and saw us, his expression shifted. Had he seen us standing too close together?

I looked around for my mother and spotted her at the appetizer table, talking with a few ladies. I stepped even further from Hudson and instantly felt the absence of his closeness. I felt my heart skip a beat, realizing Hudson and I had become way too comfortable around each other. We could not act like lovers tonight. When we came clean to my dad, it would need to be private, not here.

"Dad," I called out, trying to keep my voice light as we approached him.

But I shouldn't have worried. Dad was in his element. He whisked Hudson away jovially, and the men began sharing jokes, Hudson joining in. I slowly drifted away, happy for his moment of connection. I found my mom and gave her a hug.

"That looks delicious!" I said about her plate of appetizers. As I glanced up, looking for a table for us to sit around, I blinked in surprise as I saw a familiar face.

I gasped.

Was that Jon? What the fuck?

My blood ran cold at the sight of my ex-boyfriend, Jonathan fucking Wright.

One
Hudson

TWO MONTHS EARLIER

As a former Navy SEAL, I was always aware of my surroundings. But today, my real estate team surprised me in a big way.

I stepped into the tall, glass building on the north side of Miami and smelled a perfume I'd never smelled in my offices before. That should have been my first hint that something was different about today. It was exotic and heady, a blend of jasmine and something musky, yet distinctly feminine.

I walked toward the elevators when my assistant, Trevor, called me over to one of my conference rooms. This wasn't unusual. The huge projector that shone on the bare wall along the side of the room was perfect for assessing commercial real estate properties. I didn't make a billion dollars in the industry to skimp on our technology.

"Anything new on the oceanfront condo property we are looking to buy?" I asked him.

He tried not to grin at me, another hint that something was unusual. Trevor is the picture of calm on most days.

I noticed the scent of the perfume was stronger. It was arousing and I fought to ignore it.

Trevor walked quickly by my side, spouting off some numbers about the finances of the new deal we were working on with the condo property. Then, he pushed open the doors to the conference room.

"Surprise!" Everyone on my team shouted out as I walked inside.

Given my background, I was not a fan of the unknown or of surprises. I worked out six days a week and remained in tip top shape so that I would be ready in the event of an emergency. Even now as I stood facing my delighted team, beaming under the ceiling lights, a small cake on the table along with some sparkling juice, I could feel my core tense up and my biceps flex, ready for action.

PTSD was never far away, it seemed, even after years of therapy. I tried to force my body to relax. I tried to stop my mind from planning my escape, and I tried to keep my hands from instinctively balling into fists. This wasn't war. This was my office. These were my people, my team.

Trevor cleared his throat beside me. I forced a big grin on my face.

"What a pleasant surprise. You went all out for today." I shook Trevor's hand to show my thanks and everyone broke out into chit-chat and heartfelt, "Happy Birthday" greetings to me.

"There's more!" my office manager Linda said, beaming at me. She turned to pull a petite woman from behind the people standing next to her.

The moment I saw her, my breath caught in my throat. She was slender with curvy hips and beautiful, expressive blue eyes. They flashed over to me, a small smile playing on her full lips.

There was something familiar about her face, her features. Had we met before? As a businessman and billionaire, I meet new people almost every day through my businesses and network. It's possible I'd run into her before but just forgotten.

It wasn't lost on me that she was sexy, more than sexy. Her full breasts bounced as she was slightly jostled by my team, shifting and chatting around her.

I caught a glimpse of her narrow waist under her thin silk blouse. Her dark hair was thick and fell to her shoulders, classy and sexy all at once. If I were to have met her out somewhere... I would not be able to keep my hands to myself.

I tore my eyes from her young face, asking Linda, "And who is this?"

As far as I knew, we were not hiring any new staff or real estate agents. Maybe this was a new hire for our mortgage company and not the real estate company? I was not hands-on with the other parts of the business outside of buying and selling properties.

Linda patted the girl's arm, encouraging her to introduce herself. I was distracted by people filing by to grab a slice of cake and juice. Her voice jolted me back to the present moment.

"Hi. I'm Madeline. I'm Harry's daughter."

It hits me, then. This is little Maddie! I have known Madeline her whole life, though her dad and I have mainly kept in touch the last few years through phone calls and our annual SEALs reunion. Wow! Madeline Carter, Harry's daughter. I stare at her with tortured eyes. I had just felt the first hints at arousal from her beauty moments before, but if she's Harry's daughter, that is never going to happen.

I think back to the day that Harry told me he was going to have a child. We were both so young, early 20s, and gone overseas. He got the call from Julie, Madeline's mom, and when he told me, I could see an emotion in his eyes that I felt so distant from. I'd hugged him, both of us dirty and sweaty, and told him that it would be all right, that he'd be able to get leave. But of course, he couldn't. We had a war to win. Julie gave birth alone, Harry on speakerphone, her screams echoing through the barracks.

Our friendship had hung on for a long time. When Kenzie's mom left me without a word, a single note on the coffee table, and her side of the room empty, I'd gone straight to a bar and gotten drunk. I'd kept the note in my pocket. I was afraid to read it. When I got so drunk that the bartender wouldn't let me leave, I called

Harry. He'd come to pick me up, and I'd resisted, almost fighting him that night. When he finally got me into the car, I'd slipped him the note, begging him to read it first.

It wasn't good, of course, and I only got worse, drowning myself in liquor. It was around that time Harry decided he needed to take a step back from our friendship to take care of his family. He said he couldn't keep coming out to save me if I wasn't willing to put in the hard work to get sober. It was the right choice, but it had stung. He kept up with the occasional phone call, and he remained my best friend, but I didn't remain his. That much had become clear.

"She's here to redesign your home. You were just talking to Trevor about not having enough time to update your beachfront mansion, so we figured we'd get it started for you as a birthday gift." Linda looked pleased with herself.

"You were taking interior design classes at university a few years ago, right?" I asked Madeline, trying to piece together the past.

She nodded, her smile growing. "I was lucky enough to land a job with Johnson and Withers after I graduated and finished my internships. J&W is a top design firm in

New York. They'll be overseeing my work here remotely. So, you're in good hands."

I can't tell her that I'd love to be in her hands – to feel them brush against my skin, teasing my cock...

What the fuck, Hudson?

I cleared my throat. I wished she were anyone's daughter but my best friend's little girl.

"Welcome. I'm sure the project will go great. How is your dad, by the way?" I was wondering if he knew she was here, in Miami, about to start work on my house.

We were interrupted by my marketing VP asking me to gather with the executives for a group photo. I turned from Madeline with a little smile. I couldn't come across as too friendly... or too rude. I felt tense all of a sudden. I needed to talk to Harry. He needed to know that Madeline was here, if he didn't know already.

Then, I remembered that as far as Harry knew, I'd never had a moment's attraction to Madeline ... his daughter; the one who was an innocent little bookworm the last time I visited Harry a few years ago. He didn't know that I could have had a hard-on for her less than five minutes ago if she had been anyone else but Madeline Carter.

I dutifully smiled for the camera then made my rounds, shaking hands and thanking my team. One thing – out of many – that I learned from being a SEAL was that leadership was about connection. I made a point to be accessible and connected to everyone who worked for me. I found that people worked harder and thought more creatively in a safe, friendly environment where the CEO – me – wasn't hiding away in an office and unavailable.

It took me a full twenty minutes to talk to everyone. When I was done, I saw Madeline seated with Linda and a few other of my staff, chatting and laughing.

Her face tilted up as if she could feel my eyes on her. Then, she turned ever so slightly to me, adjusting her full hips on the chair and flashing her blue eyes at me. I fought my arousal as those eyes trailed down my body, resting on my muscled chest and then moving down my torso to rest again just below my belt.

Shit. She was checking me out – and she was doing it knowing I was watching her!

She was going to be a handful; I could see it already. She wasn't the little girl anymore. She was a woman in her mid-twenties, by my recollection, and she was unafraid to let me know she liked what she saw.

Her gaze was innocent by the time she met my eyes again, but the little quirk of her eyebrow let me know her mind was anything but innocent at that moment.

I forced myself to turn away, walking into the hallway and toward my office. I needed a cold shower. But instead, I closed the office door and pulled out my phone. I called my best friend, Harry.

"Hudson, did your surprise make it to you yet?" Harry boomed out in his deep voice.

I guessed that my question was answered, then. Harry definitely knew his daughter was here in Miami about to start working for me.

I strode to my windows that overlooked part of a small wildlife preserve, my office located in a very affluent part of Miami.

"She did. I was just calling to see if you knew. I hadn't realized Madeline was already working. I guess in my mind, she was still a teenager with bangs and her learner's permit, begging to drive your car." I smiled at the memories.

Those were simpler times, before I got married. My face fell into a frown. Before my seven-year-old daughter's mother walked out to pursue her dreams of modeling... leaving Kenzie behind in my care.

"She's good at what she does, Hudson. J&W has already put her up for a design award and she has a few big projects to her name with the firm already."

"I'm sure she's very talented," I said.

Before I could say another word, Harry's voice changed. His tone became serious. "I'm glad she got the assignment from J&W, Hudson. The truth is, I'm a little worried about her."

I straightened up from my casual slouch. Harry sounded stressed. "What's the matter?" My mind flicked back to the beautiful young woman in my conference room – what could she possibly have going on in her young life to warrant her father's anxiety?

"Her ex-boyfriend. His name is Jon. He's not a stalker or anything, but he did drop the ball with their breakup a few months ago. Look, I don't know all the details, of course. I know enough to know it shook Maddie up pretty badly."

My posture relaxed again. Is that all? A bad breakup? I thought Madeline was in real trouble. "How can I help?"

"Will you keep an eye on her? Just make sure she's not going out or doing anything crazy to burn off steam."

I chuckled low and loud at that. "She's a girl, Harry. She's not like how you or I were back in our SEAL recruitment days. You remember those early days, right? When the single guys would go out and find a quick rebound when their wife or girlfriend left them."

We shared a friendly laugh. Harry and I had so much history. I wished now that I'd done a better job at staying in touch the last several years.

"She told her mother that she'd be staying at an extended stay hotel or some other short-term housing while she was in Miami for your project, so I know you won't be able to have eyes on her twenty-four seven. Just, she's pretty vulnerable right now, so look out for her, will you?"

I thought back to the confident and sexy young woman I just saw in my conference room. She didn't look vulnerable to me – especially when she was checking me out.

I made my obligatory promises to Harry then made the excuse that I had to get back to my team. After I ended the call, I sat on the edge of my desk, feeling more and more uncomfortable with what I just agreed to.

I had no desire to play babysitter to a grown woman. And based on what I saw of Madeline, she wouldn't want that, either. But I did gather one interesting piece of data from my conversation with Harry – Madeline was single, and her last relationship ended several months ago. I wondered how soon little Maddie would be back in the dating ring. And if it would happen here in Miami right under my nose when I was supposed to be watching her.

I felt a headache tease my temples. I had a feeling my organized, calm life had just been turned upside down by Madeline's arrival.

Two
Madeline

"Yes, I am waiting for the rideshare to come pick me up now," I said into the phone.

Justin, one of the senior designers at J&W, was my boss. I was lucky to report to him with his twenty-plus years of design experience. He always provided timely and good feedback.

"If you need anything at all, just tell me. I'm looking forward to seeing your initial design ideas once you scope out the house."

I glanced out the front window of the extended stay hotel's lobby. For a long-term hotel, this one was nicer than most. It reminded me how much money J&W had and how much they were taking a chance on me, sending me here alone to start the project. Of course, once I had the designs worked out and the contractors lined up, another team member would come to wrap up the project. Unless we were spread thin. Then, I would stay myself.

All my life, I wanted to be in design. I thought I'd go into fashion for a while, but interior design seemed more complex to me and, therefore, more interesting. With J&W, I got to do a bit of both sides of interior design – residential and commercial. I loved making peoples' spaces feel like home to them. Even if it was a commercial space, I still thought the eight plus hours they spent there should be comfortable.

And now, I found myself working on a complex project – a man who, like my dad, was a former SEAL and who had found success in the business world after leaving the military. I had to figure out what Hudson valued and then dream up ways to bring that to life in his home. I was more than a little curious to see how his home looked. Personal spaces revealed so much about a client's mentality.

My mind zoned out as I thought back to seeing Hudson yesterday. His handsome face lingered in my mind long after I left.

I had had a crush on him when I was young, but no one knew. He was always so funny and friendly back then. I didn't see any of that in him yesterday. But the brooding, mysterious attitude he had yesterday that simmered under his smiles at the surprise party his team threw suited him.

If I hadn't been up to my ears in design ideas last night, on a video call with my team in NYC until after midnight, I would have pulled out my vibrator and sought a release. He had me turned on with just the way he looked. And now I had to work in his home, day after day.

I shivered at the thoughts I was allowing to cross my mind, but I wasn't that little girl he knew from back then anymore. And the crush I thought was only a childhood thing just hit me back, stronger than ever.

I was desperately going to need a release soon from the sexual tension I felt in my body. Why did my dad's best friend—his military friend—have to be so damn handsome? He was completely off-limits. Dad would lose his mind if he ever thought his daughter was ogling his best friend.

"You there?" Justin asked.

I blushed a bright shade of red, being caught lost in my thoughts of Hudson and my need for an orgasm.

"My ride just got here," I said, seeing the car pull up. "I'll text you if I need anything! Thank you so much, Justin. You're the best boss ever."

That last part was over the top, but my cheeks were not the only thing that was flustered from thinking of Hudson. I squirmed, rubbing my inner thighs together.

"Okay," Justin drawled out. "Look, Madeline. This is your first unsupervised job with us. Just...remember that you have a lot riding on this. You have talent, so don't mess around. I say that to you as, apparently, the best boss ever."

His tone was serious, though he tried to lighten it up at the end. He's right. My other three big projects with J&W design firm were either fully or partly supervised. My mind sobered instantly, thoughts of being attracted to Hudson gone in a flash. This was inappropriate and I would not do it again.

"Thank you. I will not let you down."

I ended the call and made my way outside into the dense, humid heat of Miami. I had a job to do today and no sexy man in this world would keep me from doing it.

"Ride for Madeline Carter," the woman in the rideshare chirped out to me.

"Yes," I said, slipping into the back seat.

She took a look at the GPS and then let out a whistle. "Oh my. This is a gorgeous part of Miami. Most of the celebrities who live here choose South Beach with their big houses and bigger parties on the beach. But the truly rich in the city go north to this neighborhood."

I pondered her words. Just how wealthy could a former Navy SEAL like Hudson Packard be? I knew he had made smart investments because it came up here and there in small talk with my parents, but I'd never paid much attention to it. My crush on him was lost as I grew up and faced the real world myself. Plus, he wasn't around as much when I got older.

He remained a very close friend to my father, though, even as their wealth and life choices took them in very different directions. My father had made a decent living. And now, I was on track to make a good salary each year with J&W. But to live in one of the wealthiest neighborhoods in Miami? I was not even close to being able to dream about that, let alone make it happen.

"Really? It's my first time in this part of Miami." I waited for her to talk more about the value of the homes in the area where Hudson lived, but she just smiled at me politely, choosing instead to talk to me about my life, asking where I was from and my job.

I was going to have to get a rental car. The thought of making small talk like this every day to a different rideshare driver was not appealing.

Soon enough, we pulled up to a beautiful, large estate in a long line of mansions. Mature palm trees swayed in the breeze and the sun beat down relentlessly on the white stucco of the home. The area looked very upscale with gated driveways, luxury vehicles, and square footage to die for.

The gate opened for us and she pulled up to the large front terrace. I thanked her for a pleasant ride and stepped out as the front door opened.

The landscaping was a bit austere for my taste, but it was likely chosen because it was low maintenance.

The front terrace was huge...and empty of anything warm or inviting. The door opened wider and there he was, Hudson. He stood like a wall of beautiful muscle and strength before me. He was tall, probably a little over 6 feet. His polo shirt was fitted and obviously designer quality. His khaki pants were very well fitted to the point that I could see the faint outline of his bulge underneath.

I dragged my eyes up where they belonged while my mind lingered on thoughts of his body. My eyes trailed up his thick neck to a jawline that was perfectly square and masculine. He won the genetics lottery, no doubt about that! I couldn't believe he was in his late forties. His face looked rugged but not a day over thirty-five. I finally looked at his lips. I shouldn't have. The places I wanted them to be on my body are sinful, wicked... I felt aroused at the wild thoughts that flashed through my mind.

Oh my God! I'm actually blushing. This is ridiculous. I hastily looked back up to his eyes. His eyes were shining at me as they moved up my body, making me regret the lightweight, thin day dress I wore to ward off the heat of Miami. I can feel my nipples harden under his gaze. This is all wrong! I shouldn't be feeling this for him.

"I'm glad to see you," I said.

"It's good to see you again," he said at the same time.

The tension was broken, then, and he ushered me inside with a smile. Unlike the fake smiles of yesterday, this one was real.

The inside of his home was, well, definitely minimalistic. And organized. And devoid of any warmth or color. I actually shivered as he began walking me through the rooms in his eight-bedroom mansion.

The last room we entered on the first floor was the master bedroom. I felt a rush of heat when his fingers brushed against my arm to draw attention to a painting of a brooding ocean underneath a dark, stormy sky.

"This is the energy I was thinking about for my home." He looked at me, his soft gaze turning haughty as I shook my head right away.

"I think we should avoid strong colors, Hudson," I said, my tone not leaving room for disagreement. "Most people think they like a strong color until it's on their walls and reflected in their furniture. We want to choose colors and designs that are not trendy that will stand the test of time. Do you understand?"

He crossed his arms. "It's my house. And I want what I want, Maddie."

"Madeline, please." I fixed my gaze on his, standing my ground. "And the colors you already have on your walls and the dated tiles throughout the front of the home need to go. You'll love the result—" I trailed off.

I saw it, then. The same thing I saw in my dad's eyes when his PTSD was triggered. No one seemed to have the same triggers, but the resulting look of panic and little nervous ticks were obvious to people like me who were used to living with people who suffered from PTSD.

"I'm not sure this design project is such a good idea. I don't change things in my home ever because I like things the way that they are." He reached for a stretchy black band around his wrist and flicked it gently over and over again.

He looked tense, like the idea of changing any part of his safe space, his home, was going to upend his entire existence. To his credit, he did try to soften his words with a frosty smile.

I tried not to panic myself. I needed this project. It was the first one I was doing on my own for J&W. I let him calm himself with the black band for a moment. I looked at him earnestly.

"I promise we will never do anything you're not comfortable with." I reached out and placed a hand on his wrist, where he was flicking the band. I felt him relax slightly. "I want you to feel safe and comfortable here. I promise you."

The terse set of his lips softened. This was good. Typically, my dad needed a moment alone after a trigger, whether large or small, that made him feel unsafe.

To buy myself some time to figure out how to make this design update work, I meandered toward what I thought was an empty closet in his master bedroom. But when I opened the double doors all the way, I saw it was actually his walk-in closet with his personal items on the right and down the long closet on the left...was nothing. It was empty with the shelves looking brand new and the soft carpeting looking like no one had set foot on it before.

I rushed away from Hudson's personal items and pretended to care about the empty side of the closet. I needed to think fast. I needed to figure out how to convince him to not give up on the project before we even started. But honestly, if he was that quick to quit after disagreeing on colors in a painting...maybe this project was already doomed. Maybe he wasn't ready for a big life change.

I felt his presence behind me. I had to face him, like it or not. I turned around and came chest to chest with him, the warmth of his body making me feel hot, and turned on. His eyes were the most attractive blend of colors—hazel, with flecks of green in them.

My old crush on him resurrected itself, building up to be something far more mature than what it used to be. Where before I longed for him to give me any attention at all, now I wanted his strong hands on me, those full lips to press against mine, and that cock I saw a hint of earlier growing hard for me.

"Hudson," I whispered, my voice strained. My hands moved on their own, up to his shoulders, my fingers playing with the lapels of his polo shirt. I'd imagined kissing him a million times when I was a teenager, and now I felt my heart racing with a need to make my long standing fantasies a reality.

I saw the guarded look in his eyes melt away for a moment. My arousal started building between my legs and I took a chance by pressing my hips up toward his, throwing out in that instance all promises of caution I had made to myself. I could feel his cock hardening as I moved my hips, needing to feel him, needing to know this man I hadn't seen since I was sixteen.

I could feel he wanted this as much as I wanted it. And to be honest, it felt damn good knowing that he saw me as a grown woman now.

I tilted my head up as his hands circled my waist. *Yes,* everything in me was screaming out. *Kiss me now!*

I parted my lips, ready to finally kiss Hudson after years of daydreaming about it. But he pulled back just before our lips met. I flushed red. He looked sternly at me.

Then, he stepped away, telling me that there was a special room upstairs I would need to see before I left that day.

Fuck, this day just got weird, fast. And it was all my fault.

I just risked my job, my reputation, by trying to kiss Hudson Packard. I bit my bottom lip as I trudged out of the closet and walked quickly to keep up with him as he headed toward the double staircase in the entryway.

31

My heart felt like a fist clenched around it as I thought of something else—I just risked everything because not only is Hudson a big client, he's also my father's closest friend.

I felt like such a fool.

Three
Hudson

I stared at my computer screen in my home office. My surroundings are pristine, the dark paneling of my bookshelves standing out from the pale blue of the walls. The wall behind my desk was a dark navy blue, making the room feel closed in just the way I liked it.

But Madeline had made it clear yesterday that lighter colors throughout the home and doing away with my favorite dark cherry wood paneling and bookshelves throughout the home was basically not negotiable.

I didn't get to where I am today by letting anyone tell me how to live my life. After the SEALs, I made several lucky investments in real estate, making myself a multi-millionaire quickly. From there, it seemed I had a knack for flipping huge commercial properties and my wealth grew fast. My personal life at the time was a mess with Kenzie's mom getting fed up with me and my PTSD. The glitz of modeling and glam pulled her away.

I wondered if Madeline was drawn in by the allure of fame the way Kenzie's mom was. I drummed my fingers on the desk. I should not think about Madeline. I blinked, trying to focus on work. My real estate development company had tripled the size of its portfolio in the past few years. I should focus on current projects. I should focus on anything but Harry's gorgeous daughter.

The email on my computer screen remained as unwritten now as it had an hour ago. I knew that Madeline would be arriving any minute to begin working on her design ideas.

Yesterday she gathered data, asking me a million questions about how I lived...and feigning not being shocked upon the discovery that I have a daughter.

Kenzie's room was of special importance to me. Kenzie's favorite colors may not be in alignment with J&W's vision for my home, but her happiness matters more than that.

I tried to focus on the email again, but I couldn't think of a good reply. In fact, the more I tried to think of a reply, the more anxious I felt.

My life existed with a series of preplanned activities and schedules. Everything had a time slot and everything was planned in advance.

Every guy who served in combat that I knew had their own way of dealing with the aftereffects of war. Some guys drank. Other guys hid away in their houses. And still others, like Harry, relied on therapy every week to cope. For me, it was order. Consistency. As long as everything was the same, I was barely triggered.

But this email upended my calm life. Every year, my fellow SEAL buddies organized a party to celebrate the year that we all graduated bootcamp. It was a tough few weeks of will-breaking exercises and activities, and we all made it through. The guys always hounded me to join them in the reunion. Out of respect for Harry, I would show up, but I never stayed long and I never enjoyed it. I didn't like reliving the past with all its horrors.

This year, the reunion was going to be here, in Miami. This was not in my plans. I felt my temperature rise and my heart start to race. It was the twenty-fifth anniversary, a huge milestone. And they wanted to plan a little ceremony to honor our brothers lost in battle.

"Fuck," I said, feeling like everything was out of control. Those men should not have died. I hated remembering their lives cut so short. I hated the survivor's guilt that I felt.

Suddenly, my breathing was short, as if I'd been sprinting away from a bear and couldn't catch my breath. I gripped the arms of my office chair, trying to find my willpower to fight through this.

Faces of my friends, my fellow soldiers who died, flashed through my mind.

"No, no!" I cried out. I shouldn't have stayed home today. It was out of my routine. I should have gone into the office. I had to stick to the routine. That was the only way to not be triggered.

More faces haunted me in my mind as the office around me disappeared. I tried to open my eyes, to focus on something real, just like my old therapist had taught me to do. But my mind had already run away with me. It was too late. I would have to ride this out.

Then, a small, soft hand was on my chest, rubbing soft circles there. I felt another hand on my shoulder pushing me forward. The counter pressure of hands on my chest and back, both rubbing, made me feel grounded. I smelled her perfume. I groaned. I needed her.

"Madeline," I said hoarsely.

"I'm here. You're safe. You're not alone, Hudson," she said in her strong, melodic voice. "Relax into my touch. Relax into me."

I felt her pull me toward her chest, resting my head between her full, soft breasts. The fabric of her dress was soft against my face. I felt my hands clutching her as if she was my only lifeline.

"Let's breathe together. Breathe in with me, Hudson. Slow. Slower," she prompted me, again and again, edging me back toward reality.

We breathed together for who knows how long until I was able to open my eyes. I couldn't believe what she just managed to do to me. No one had ever been able to navigate me through one of my panic attacks so skillfully.

Now, back in the moment, I saw that she had somehow made her way onto my lap, her hand stroking my hair. It felt so damn good that I forgot she was Harry's daughter, but just for a moment. When I remembered, I pulled my hands away from her waist as if she were lava and I was getting burned.

Her blue eyes were relentless in the way they looked at me, all desire and sexual need. I could see it and feel it coming off of her lithe body. She wanted me. And I'll be damned for thinking this—but I wanted her, too.

No! my brain yelled at me. *This is wrong.*

Yes! my body retaliated, my cock waking up in my pants.

I could sense her breathing changing as she shifted in my lap, the curve of her ass pressing against my cock. She hadn't even straddled me...hadn't done anything sexual but already I was hard as a rock for her.

This is Harry's daughter, you moron! my brain said.

This is an adult female who wants what you want, my body replied.

"Hudson," Madeline started, her voice husky, an earnest glint in her eyes. "I want—"

My lips met hers in a kiss of fiery bliss, my body exploding with need, my mind turning to mush.

I had no idea how much sexual tension I'd been building up for her since I saw her in the conference room. I felt it all erupt now, my lips longing to kiss every inch of her young body, my hands needing to rip off her clothes, my cock needing to be buried deep in her pussy. Already, I was twitching, thinking of coating her walls with ropes of my cum, thinking of her pretty little face screwed up in ecstasy. I needed to see her mouth open and her eyes rolling.

This was crazy. But more than crazy, this was wrong.

She moaned and straddled me, her dress riding up to reveal the softest, milkiest, naked skin as my hand moved up her thigh. I felt her tongue enter my mouth in an explosion of intimacy and need, and my hand squeezed around her upper thigh, my thumb threatening to poke inside her panties. I could feel the hem, and my hand longed to rip the crotch to the side and take her. I knew she would say yes, the way her hips rocked up and down on my cock that was straining against my pants told me as much.

I couldn't resist rubbing my thumb against her pussy as I gripped the top of her thigh, my other hand cupping her face as we kissed. That brush of my thumb against her pussy lip stilled her. Our eyes locked together in a reality check that I didn't want and couldn't take...but somehow turned me on more. *Would we really do this, knowing who we were to each other? And what was wrong with me that who we were to each other made my cock even harder?*

Her blue eyes darkened as I stretched my thumb under the fabric of her thong, watching her face to see how it changed. She closed those stormy eyes and scrunched her nose, letting her head fall back toward the ceiling as I let my hand follow my thumb. I brushed against her wet pussy lips, feeling how slick they were already as I massaged them. I pulled them apart and held her open, letting the air hit her clit and her wet core. She moaned quietly, letting herself feel it all the way, her legs opening to take in the sensation.

When I used just the very tip of my index finger to circle her clit, she gasped wildly and snapped her head back to face me, her eyes opening wider than I'd ever seen them.

I'd shocked myself, and I'd shocked her.

"Yes," she whispered gutturally, the whisper turning into a moan.

There was no going back now. I stood up, lifting her as I did, delighting in the masculine feeling of holding up a woman like Madeline, my arms around her back, my hands holding onto the back of her neck, her legs wrapped around my waist, and her wet crotch grinded against the bulge in my pants. I could cum at any moment if she kept going.

I set her down on my desk, and her hand shot out to catch herself. I kept one hand on her neck, pressing her mouth into mine, our kiss as wet as her pussy, while my other hand explored her core. I held my thumb still against her clit, letting the pressure build for her. Her chest flushed as I pumped my wrist, using my shoulder to thrust my finger into her as deep and fast as I could, and she braced herself against my shoulder. Her knees bent as she pulled her legs into her body, opening her entrance for me as much as she could with her mouth still on mine, and I pulled my mouth away so that I could say, "Hold your legs open for me."

She gave me a girlish look, her eyelids halfway closed, and with a sly look, she held her legs underneath her knees nervously. I watched her from where I stood and commanded her, "Now open them." Slowly, she pulled her legs apart, showing me her beautifully pink pussy, the slick juices running from her opening to the surface of my desk. A thought passed through me that if I didn't clean it, it would dry there, and I might smell it days from now, and I shuddered as my cock grew impossibly harder still.

The dirty thought combined with seeing Maddie holding her legs open for me, the look of her gaping pussy and her engorged clit, brought me to reality. She seemed to sense it and let go of her legs to reach for me instead, scooching forward to the edge of the desk. Her small hand was moving toward mine, and I resisted, instead resting my hands on her knees and looking into her eyes.

"Madeline," I started to say, my brief moment of good sense needling at my conscience.

"No," she groaned, begging with just one word while I knew what she meant: *don't stop. I want this.* She opened her legs for me, her eyes unsure but her mouth in an open pout and her hand inching toward her own clit, touching herself in front of me. *Well, she's insistent.*

I tried to think and rubbed my face with one hand, pulling my lips down as thoughts of how wrong this was flew around my head. *Harry trusted you with his child,*

Hudson. His child. I felt Madeline's warm hand on my wrist, pulling my own down from my face.

I looked down at her as she sucked on my finger, the very finger I had just played inside her with, tasting herself off my digit. When we made eye contact, she leaned back on her elbows, showing off her curves.

I couldn't help but notice how perky her breasts were. I liked all breasts, but hers were really something else, pushing up against the thin fabric of her dress, her nipples like the beacons on a lighthouse, calling me home.

So, I answered the call.

I gripped her hip with one hand and sank to my knees, settling down in front of her glistening lips. My other hand moved to her breast, tweaking her nipple through the thin fabric before I felt her pull her dress down, exposing a perfect breast to me. It was soft, more than a handful, and jiggly. I cupped it in my palm like a treasure I just dug out of an abandoned mine, letting her breast spill out over my hand, positioning her nipple perfectly to pinch between my finger and my thumb.

While she sighed in contentment, I shocked her with my tongue on her clit, licking just beneath the hood, tasting

everything she'd built up just now in being turned on by m
e.

"Oh, Hudson," she cried out, her voice strained with the kind of pain that only pleasure can give someone. Hearing my name out of her mouth in that way made my cock twitch, and I scooped my tongue through her slit before burying it deep inside her, tasting the depths of her.

Her body rocked against my face as I took my time, savoring every drop and intending to clean her up. I flicked her clit and felt her thighs clench and then release on either side of my head, letting me know what she liked.

She was so responsive and vocal, but it didn't feel performative. It just felt like a woman who knew what she wanted and didn't worry about how her face looked or how her voice sounded. She simply felt and existed, and it was a joy to make her feel good. I didn't want this to end. I didn't want to come back to reality.

I inched my fingers into her pussy along with my tongue, using every tool I had at my disposal to fill her thoroughly until she arched her back and cried out, signaling to me that she was close. I used my fingers to inch my way into her pussy, arching them and thrusting into her. Her smooth thighs parted wider than before as her beautiful body shuddered, an orgasm rippling through her.

I heard her gasp and cry out again. I felt her core clench my fingers, and I felt her arousal spill out as she surrendered to her own pleasure. The room grew quiet, her breathing strong and steady.

"That felt so good," she moaned.

I looked up at her, her breasts two perfect peaks between us. I could see her eyes shining down at me.

I had an urge to pleasure her again and then again. There was something so liberating about her, about the way she gave in to her pleasure, the way she surrendered to me.

It hit me in waves...who she was...why this was wrong on so many levels. My hard cock grew soft in my pants as I stood. I didn't let my sudden guilt stop me from pulling her to my chest, feeling her face rest against my pecs, her legs wrapping around me. I would never just walk out after exploring her body, but I felt like I had crossed a line that would change everything.

A different kind of panic than what I felt an hour ago consumed me. *How would I ever look Harry in the eye*

45

again after what I'd just done to his daughter? And how could I not do what I had just done to her again and again?

She sensed the change in me because she pulled back to look up at me before unwrapping her legs from my waist and pulling her arms from around me. She stood, put herself back together and stared at me, waiting for me to speak.

"Hudson, I," she started to say.

"No, it's alright. I loved what we did…" It pained me to look at her face, so full of honesty and raw emotion.

She kissed me softly. "Good. Then don't ruin it by saying anything else."

The sound of a door opening and closing in the house ruined the moment before anything I said could. The unmistakable sounds of my seven-year-old coming home with the nanny filled the space.

"Dad!" Kenzie drawled out. "We had a half day at school! I'm home!"

Madeline placed a hand on my chest, kissing my cheek. "Looks like we can spend the afternoon talking to your daughter about her color choices for her bedroom. Maybe she'll be more flexible than her dad."

She winked at me and waltzed to the door, leaving me to rush to catch up to her, the content of my unwritten email response about the annual SEAL reunion still unknown.

On my way out, my eye landed on a framed photo of a few of my fellow SEALs, including Harry. I quelled my guilt by assuring the photo—and myself—that I didn't have sex with Madeline. I could have, but I controlled myself.

How much longer I would be able to control myself, I wasn't sure. The door had been opened, and it would be a hell of a battle to try to close it now.

Four
Madeline

"Kenzie is such a sweetheart," I said on the video call to Joanna. Despite being my ex Jon's sister, she was actually my closest friend. I met her through Jon and honestly, she was the best thing that ever came from my time with Jon.

"Sounds like you were able to convince her that using neon green in her bedroom along with purple might not be the best design choice," Joanna laughed. She was in NYC in her modest town home making a pizza while we spoke. "I'm glad she's talking to you since you said her mom sort of walked out on her and her dad years ago."

I nodded, remembering the very brief information the nanny had given to me about Kenzie's mom. My heart broke for Hudson. Someone who already had PTSD did not need to go through the pain of being abandoned by someone the way Kenzie's mother had abandoned him.

"Yeah." I changed the subject. "I can't believe I've been here a week already. Miami is said to be a fun city, but I haven't gotten out at all! Too much work to do. Hudson's house is huge."

"I'll come down and visit you soon," Joanna promised me, sprinkling cheese on her dough. "God, I can't believe you're going to be there for months and months! Is that how long design projects really take?"

I wrinkled my nose, thinking of being stuck in that house with Hudson all that time. He'd been the perfect gentleman since the day he gave me an orgasm...which I wish he wouldn't be. I've wanted his hands on me again so many times since then, but it was like we had an unspoken agreement that we couldn't cross that line again.

"Sometimes they take forever. But if it's a commercial property, those go fast. Anytime we work on a person's home, it takes a long time. The owners always have opinions and they want to approve every little detail."

"And this owner is your dad's best friend, right?" Joanna said casually, completely unaware that Hudson and I had gotten a little beyond that boundary. I couldn't tell her. I could barely even admit to myself that I was all but fully naked in front of Hudson, letting him do all sorts of delightfully wicked things to my body.

"Yes."

It's the brevity of my answer that caused her to stop putting diced peppers on her pizza and stare at the phone long and hard. "Madeline Carter! You're holding back. What are you not telling me!"

I thought quickly, and said the first true thing that came to my mind. "Um, he has PTSD like my dad and lots of other combat vets. So, he hates that any part of his house is changing. It makes things, well, slower than they should be."

She relaxed. "Oh. Is that all? Well, just use your powers of persuasion on him. I want you back in NYC sooner than later."

I chewed on my bottom lip. "Sorry to ask, but have you seen Jon lately?"

She snorted. "My workaholic brother? No. Why?"

"He was texting me like every week since the breakup months and months ago, but he stopped a few weeks ago. I never replied to him. I was just wondering what changed."

She made a face into the camera. "Jon is such an obsessive asshole. Honestly, I can't believe he's even related to me, let alone my brother. If he finally stopped texting you to try to get you to give him another chance, well, that's a good thing."

I nodded slowly. Jon left me for the woman I caught him cheating with. It was an age old story and a tired one. I could look back and see the signs now, but in the moment with graduation and starting life as a career woman, well, it wasn't so obvious then. I didn't leave him right away after I found out about that other woman. I couldn't. I'd given so much of my life to Jon, so much of myself. I pretended things were perfect for months. Then I confronted him. Even though I knew he wouldn't fight for "us" that day, it still hurt to see him turn cold and distant.

I sighed, giving Joanna a smile. I could see why she thought it was a good thing he's left me alone lately. But I knew Jon differently than Joanna knew him. So for him to just suddenly stop texting me was weird. I didn't want his attention. And I knew my parents were relieved that the relationship was over, but I was worried for him. He had compulsive tendencies, and that made him seem unstable to anyone who didn't really know him.

My phone buzzed, letting me know my dad was trying to get in touch with me. I'd been avoiding him for days, ever since Hudson's fingers were pleasuring me and his lips were on mine.

I blushed red at the memories. It was so difficult not to! I wanted him. I wanted so much more of him, but we couldn't do it.

"I better get going. I have to head over to the client's house," I said, not referring to Hudson by name since the smallest thought of him sent my arousal into over-drive.

"Okie dokie; oh, hey! Don't forget Nancy's bachelorette party coming up! I'll get to see you there and then, after that, I'll fly out to Miami for a weekend!"

I promised to see her at the bachelorette party soon, and then hung up the phone. I saw the missed call from my dad but ignored it. I'd have to call him back, but it didn't have to be right away. I needed another day or two to let my conscience settle back down.

It was Saturday and I was due to be at Hudson's place by one, so I had an hour to spare. I poked around in the small kitchen in my extended stay room, but nothing looked appetizing. I gave up on trying to be productive on my computer and ended up getting in my clunky little rental car and driving to Hudson's place.

When I arrived, I saw some of the furniture for Kenzie's room being delivered. It wasn't ideal since the paint hadn't been put on the walls yet. Her room was one of the first places in the mansion we had started the work on. We had just decided on the color scheme a day or two ago! I couldn't keep the smile off my face, though, when I heard Kenzie's voice bouncing around the walls of the house in excitement.

"Maddie!" she called out, using my old nickname entirely on her own. "Come see! Dad says I can't put any of it in my room yet, though, because we have to paint the walls. Can you make him change his mind?"

I laughed as she ran from the spare bedroom down the hall on the first floor. I saw the deliveries being put in there. She took my hand and yanked me down, letting go to run inside just as Hudson was stepping into the hallway.

My breasts brushed against his chest, reminding me of the day I wanted him to kiss me in his master bedroom's walk-in closet...but he didn't.

The effect he has on me is...unbearable. With just a look and an accidental brush against his chest, I felt my nipples already grow hard under my blouse. I was very sure he felt it, too. His hazel eyes darkened into a pretty shade of brown and his hand reached out to my waist to steady me. I felt him grip my skin like a man starved before he let go, pressing his lips together.

His self-control was far more advanced than mine. I wanted to jump into his arms and demand that he make love to me, pushing that big cock of his deep into me.

We must have stood there, looking at each other with hungry eyes for a minute too long. One of the delivery guys cleared his throat, a humorous look on his face.

"Sorry, need to grab the last few boxes from the truck." He tried not to laugh as he walked between Hudson and me.

I felt a cold rush of air between us, missing his warmth and the feel of his hand on me. Every touch left me wanting more. I couldn't seem to help myself.

"The paint swatches are upstairs. I took Kenzie this morning to the hardware store to pick up samples." Hudson coughed and cleared his throat.

He was right to keep things professional between us, but it was killing me inside. Using my vibrator at night only helped so much. I wanted him.

I forced a cheery smile on my face as Kenzie bounded between us.

"Come on, Maddie! Come look at all the paint we got! Dad said we couldn't open any of them until you got here. And now you're here. Let's go!" She ran in a bundle of energy to the double staircase in the foyer.

I turned at the same time that Hudson did, our arms brushing.

This was too much. I turned to him, eyes pleading, needing to feel that he wanted me, too. We'd been so well-behaved. I was over it! I wanted to give in to this tremendous desire I felt for him.

"Hudson, I need...please," I said in a low voice.

Something in his eyes softened, their green flecks shining beautifully as he looked at me. "Madeline, I know. And I want—"

I was hanging on to his every word when the damn delivery guy rounded the corner, boxes in hand. The moment was lost. Whatever Hudson was going to say would remain unsaid.

I pouted at the unfairness of it all as I dutifully went upstairs, where Kenzie was waiting for us. Of all the men in the world to start to fall for – why did it have to be Hudson, the one man my dad considered to be his best friend!

I pasted a smile on my face as little Kenzie bounced up and down just inside her large bedroom. I would not ruin this moment for her. She was too precious, too sweet, and too deserving of a happy life full of wonderful moments, just like this one.

I took the hand she offered me and we approached the paint cans that her father, no doubt, had lined up perfectly on the tarp he'd spread across the floor.

Each can was labeled in black marker in bold hand-writing that I'd come to love the past week since it was Hudson's.

Everything about the man was meticulous. I knew it was his way of dealing with the trauma from war, but I loved that about him. Even if it did make every part of this home renovation slow.

Hudson joined us in opening the paint cans and putting a long streak of paint down the wall. I smiled, my heart leaping within me as he helped Kenzie paint some of the sample colors on the wall, too. The father and daughter moment was so pure and sweet. It reminded me of my dad and how patient he had always been with me.

I remembered Dad's missed call today and felt a pang of guilt. That feeling was washed away when Kenzie suddenly held her paintbrush out to me. I realized then that Hudson had been looking at me in that careful, detailed way he had about him.

"You do it, too, Maddie," she commanded, a wide grin on her face.

I took the paintbrush in my hand and stood to my feet. Kenzie gave me a little push, giggling. It sent me straight into Hudson's side, his arm coming around me. She laughed again, shyly, and I hazarded a glance up at Hudson to see how he would take his daughter's obvious attempt to put us together. Kids were so intuitive. I wondered how much she had noticed in her own seven-year-old way.

The nanny walked in just then, and I started to move away, cautious about appearance for Hudson's sake. But Hudson didn't remove his hand from my waist. Instead, he let his eyes drop to my lips oh too briefly before he covered my hand with his own. Together, we drew a straight line of paint down the wall.

With Kenzie and the nanny's voices behind us and the sensation of Hudson's hands on me, I couldn't help but think how absolutely perfect life was right now. What more could I possibly want than this?

Five
Hudson

I had never brought any woman into my house since Kenzie's mom left us both seven years ago. I planned to ride out the rest of my life, focusing on my work and on my daughter. Sure, I enjoyed the company of women to get my sexual needs met. It was fun at times and boring at other times, but it was just sex. There weren't any feelings involved, and I certainly never 'dated' anyone. I thought that was all I wanted. I thought I was okay just going through the motions.

But now, with Madeline here, literally in my arms, I was rethinking everything. It was turning my perfectly ordered life upside down.

Kenzie had pushed us together. I knew she had taken to Madeline, but this felt different than the way she liked Linda or any other woman who had been in my life over the years.

I could feel my grip on Madeline's hand tighten. I could feel my chest tighten. I could feel a surge of panic hit me.

I had organized my life so well that my panic attacks were down to only once every month or two. Now, I was having them regularly.

I looked at Madeline, feeling her energy reach out to mine somehow. Her eyes were telling me I was okay. I believed her.

My therapist had warned me that by making my life a safe place instead of working through my triggers, I was essentially building a cage around myself. He was right. And here was Madeline, breaking me out of that cage just by being her vibrant and confident self.

I need you, my brain screamed out at her, wishing I was able to tell her that. *I want you.*

Instead, I relaxed my grip on her hand and rubbed a thumb up and down her waist, where I still held onto her. I had to let go. I had to stop these feelings.

I removed my hands. I had been resisting touching her at all since the day in my home office. I knew if I kept touching her in any way, I would lose the battle between my mind and my body, and we would end up having sex. I needed to avoid that at all costs.

Her father would never approve of me, a much older man with a child in tow, dating his daughter.

I knew Harry better than most people did. He was a very protective father. He was very strict on boundaries. He would never in a million years even listen to me if I attempted to make a case for Madeline and I dating.

I could make a case for it, couldn't I? I was stable now. Since Harry and I knew each other for so long, shouldn't he consider me an appropriate partner for his daughter? And since I was sober...my thoughts stopped cold, the weak case I was building in my mind dying a quick death. Harry and I had not spent quality time together since I got sober six years ago. He knew I was in therapy after my ex left me and our daughter. He knew I sank so low as to turn to the bottle. And then he knew I was trying to get sober and getting help. But the last time we spent one-on-one time together was when I was a very heavy drinker.

He doesn't know that I *am* actually stable now. I put a smile on my face as Kenzie and Madeline ranked the paint colors from one to five to determine which one should be on the walls of the room.

I wondered then what Harry thought of me as a man. I felt my heart drop as I realized that, because of my ways of dealing with past trauma, I had cut all my personal relationships down to the bare minimum. I should have put effort into seeing Harry, into keeping our friendship as close as it used to be.

I felt a hand on my arm and it sent a jolt of desire through my body. Madeline. Her blue eyes were on me and she tilted her head toward my daughter.

"Hey, you. You were a million miles away. Come join us. Kenzie thinks she knows which paint color she wants. But let's see what you think."

Madeline was so thoughtful and kind that I could have reached out and pulled her to me that instant, kissing her like she was my lover, my girlfriend...my wife.

I shook my head. *No.*

As rosy as those thoughts were, that would never happen. Harry can't possibly trust me. He would never approve.

I swallowed my desire for Madeline and joined the two of them in picking out the perfect paint color.

I had just gotten a hold of my attraction to Madeline when my phone rang. I pulled it out and felt Madeline's eyes on me as I stared at the screen.

It was her dad calling. I felt the attraction between us die a sudden, painful death as I reluctantly took the call, putting it on speaker.

"Where is my daughter?" Harry teased loudly. "Being the hard worker she is, I bet she's not taking my calls because she's busy working for you, Hudson."

Madeline and I exchanged guilty looks. In a way, through that connection, I was glad I was not the only one feeling guilty. I was the older one, though. I should be the one to keep our boundaries in place.

Madeline and I each played our roles as two colleagues working together on a project. She updated her father and I could sense the tension in Harry's voice at the beginning of the call start to fade away as he learned that I was not alone with his daughter in my house. Two other people were with us. Was his voice suspicious at first, or was that just my guilty conscience?

"Well, I'm proud of you," Harry boomed out to his daughter. "I'll have to make some time to fly out there to Miami to check on you. Oh, that reminds me. I'm calling to talk to you, Hudson, about that reunion. It's coming up, you know. We want to hold the reunion in one of your hotels. What do you say? The date is set in stone. We just need to lock down a venue."

Madeline looked at me with concern in her eyes. It made me wonder if she'd seen the email pulled up on my monitor the day she came into my office. Did she know what had triggered that panic attack?

I hesitated before answering, but Madeline jumped in. "Why not let Linda work with my dad on this? She's so capable and she told me she loves social projects. That way you can just focus on your work." Her smile set my heart on cloud nine. She was right – my office manager, Linda, would love to lead the reunion project. And she'd do a great job with it, too.

I mouthed "thank you" to Madeline and made quick work of sending an intro email between Harry and Linda right there on the spot.

"Very good," Harry said. "Well, Hudson, I am so looking forward to coming out with the boys and all their families to Miami. This year is the big two-five! Let's make it the best yet."

The call ended and Kenzi asked her nanny for a snack, leaving me alone with Madeline. She rubbed my arm but didn't make another move.

"I remember that Dad was trying to plan the reunion location two months ago, Hudson," she said quietly. "I didn't know he wanted it to be here, or that it might be hard for you. Is everything okay?"

I placed a hand over hers, then tilted my head toward the door. "It's just something to get through," I said.

She opened her mouth to speak, but thought better of it and just nodded, her hands falling to her sides. It killed me to have to constantly pull back from her. But it just had to be that way. I had to be the one to keep our boundaries in place, like it or not.

After a kid-friendly snack of cheese sticks and Goldfish crackers, we did a little unboxing of Kenzie's new bedroom set just to make her happy, then it was time for Madeline to go back to her hotel.

"Oh my," she said as she rummaged through her purse. "I know I left my car keys here."

Kenzie and her nanny had gone upstairs to start getting Kenzie ready for bed. I had a sudden and very strong notion that my feisty little daughter had hidden Madeline's keys. She clearly did not want Madeline to go back to the hotel tonight. She had done more than hint at the two of them having a sleepover here.

I bit back a laugh. I would make sure the keys were found tomorrow. But for tonight, I wouldn't disrupt my daughter's bedtime routine over something like that. Plus, I wasn't ready for Madeline to leave either. I mean these were all the excuses I could think of at that moment to keep Madeline here for the night.

She looked at me. "Can you drive me to my hotel?"

My heart constricted. Oh. She didn't want to stay the night here? I forced a smile.

"Of course. I'm sure the keys will turn up."

Madeline smiled at me and walked by my side to the garage where we got into one of my luxury vehicles. She laughed once we were a few minutes down the road. I felt her hand grasp my arm and suddenly, all was right in my world. I found myself craving those little touches even as I tried so hard to not let them linger. The fact that she kept touching me was enough. It had to be enough, even though I wanted so much more.

"Oh my gosh. I just had a thought! What if Kenzie hid my keys, thinking it would be a fun little game to make me go searching for them? But I guess she forgot to give me a heads-up before bedtime."

We shared a chuckle. The drive to her hotel was far too short but, by the time we arrived, her fingers had moved down to my hand and then intertwined with my fingers. My cock grew hard at the off-limits touching. *Damn!*

I put the car in park and looked at her. I was a goner, then. And I could tell she was, too.

"I need it," she said cryptically, though we both knew what 'it' meant.

"Madeline, we can't have sex," I said, my voice strained, tight. That was a line we just could not cross.

She ignored my words. "Come inside."

She led me to her hotel room, my mind trying in vain to convince me that this was not a good idea.

The room was cool and dark when we stepped inside. Her lips were on mine before the door could even latch closed behind us.

"I need this so bad, Hudson." Her voice was full of hunger. All the pressure of saying "no" was on me. How could I say no to something I so desperately wanted?

Her hands were on my belt, then she took my pants off, letting them fall to the ground. She kissed me while stroking me with her hand, my length hard and ready for her. Being with her this way felt different from any other time I'd hooked up with women. It felt intimate, like I didn't want to rush anything. I wanted to see her, feel her, know her.

"Madeline, I...we..." I stopped as she dropped to her knees.

I felt a sharp inhale at the sight of her blue eyes looking up at me, her face so close to my erect manhood. She was so sexy. So in control. Her lashes fluttered against her pale skin as she closed her eyes, as if she were about to enjoy herself immensely. Her lips pressed against the hard head of my rod in a kiss before she opened her lips and slowly sucked me into her mouth. I almost lost it then and there. I growled, making her eyes open and snap up at me. Their bright blue had darkened into a lustful storm of dark gray.

"You are so damn hot," I said, in a voice so husky I barely recognized it. "Open up, take me deep."

I felt her breath on my skin and her hand gripping my thigh as she took me in deeper...and deeper still.

"That's it. That's my good girl." My breathing grew shallow as she stroked me with her mouth. Fuck. I wasn't sure how long I could stand there and take it. I wanted to pound myself into her body. I wanted so much more. I thrust into her mouth, matching her intensity and earning myself sexy sounds from her.

Then she pulled back and I grew still. She kept my tip in her mouth. I felt her tongue swirl around my swollen head, then pause before flicking under it, stimulating every damn nerve ending that I had. I loved it. I grabbed her silky dark hair, losing myself in the sensations.

She moaned and pushed her lips off and then back on my tip, as if she was sampling a new flavor of ice cream. She looked so horny for me with her flushed cheeks and glazed over eyes. Those eyes looked up at me again.

"Madeline," I groaned out her name like she was my queen, a goddess, my hand caressing the back of her head, my body responding to her every touch. This was beautiful torture. I couldn't let it continue, but I couldn't end it either.

She didn't stop taking me deep in her mouth and then pulling back again until I came. I came hard and long as I groaned out her name, and God knows what else, as pleasure filled my body. I felt invincible. I felt strong. I felt like I could take on the world, all because of this woman there with me, wanting me, seeing me and accepting me with all my flaws.

"You did so well. So good," I said, as I pulled her to her feet.

Her dark lashes framed her beautiful eyes perfectly and her look was coy, as if she were pleased with herself. She ran a hand over my naked chest, feeling my muscles one by one.

"You liked it?" she purred. "There's more we can do—"

I didn't let her finish. I didn't want to say no to sex. I kissed her hard, biting her lower lip until she yelped. I placed her on the bed, pulling every bit of her clothes off.

She was a wonder. All soft skin, pink rosebud nipples, and delicate little center that was glistening wet as she lay there.

"So beautiful." My words could never do her justice. She was fit and curvy. So pale and exquisite. I kissed her hardened nipples, hovering over her, wishing I could slide my cock into her, but knowing that I would not make love to her in that way.

"Fuck me, Hudson," she said, with a burning intensity in her eyes.

I knew she wanted it the way I did.

"I want to make you cum," I growled out, hard again for her.

She pouted and then surrendered to our reality. I saw the look of hurt flash on her face at my words, followed by resignation.

"My beautiful, sexy..." I tried to let her know I wanted her.

She interrupted me with a wicked gleam in her eyes. "Don't tease me. I need you now." She sounded desperate, breathy words escaping from lips swollen from my kisses.

I slid my length up and down her wet lips, tempting the last shred of my willpower, never entering her, just pleasuring her. I felt her beautiful arousal on my shaft and I thrust myself along her slit, so turned on, I could have come if I continued. But this was about her pleasure, about giving in to that wanton pleading in her blue eyes.

"Patience. We have all night."

I used the head of my cock to tease her clit a moment longer, loving the little sounds of bliss she was making. Then, I kissed my way down her soft skin, loving the feel of her hands on my biceps. I licked each nipple, flicking my tongue and sucking, before moving down to her hips, then her inner thighs.

I had to pull back to look at her, my hands taking hold of those lean thighs to spread them for myself. I felt a possessiveness grip me at the sight of her fully open to me, aroused for me.

Mine, I thought, not bothering to remember that this could never be. I looked at her. "So ready for me."

"Take me." She was insistent. I resisted.

It was a powerful feeling that consumed me in that moment, a protectiveness that transcended lust. I stared at her, chest rising and falling as she waited for me to make love to her with my tongue.

I dropped down to my elbows, brushing my lips on her wet lips, moaning with hunger. I used my tongue to take her to orgasm, flicking and sucking on her sensitive bud of pleasure. She gasped and cried out as she came, filling the room with the sounds of her bliss. I gripped her thighs after she came. I wasn't even close to being done giving her pleasure yet.

I slid a finger inside her while my thumb played with her clit. I relished the look of her giving in to her pleasure, her legs falling open, her back arching. Soon, her hands were in my hair and she was crying out my name before sinking into the bed, reaching for me to lay beside her.

I loved everything - the taste of her, the smell of her, and the feel of her body curled up next to mine. *Why, of all the women out there, the only one who could elicit these feelings in me was my best friend's daughter, was beyond me!*

And through it all, I convinced myself that this was okay – this wasn't sex, so that made it okay. Right?

We laid silently for minutes, my hand caressing her naked body, her ass pressed up against my cock. The moment was perfect. Until her phone rang. Somehow it had landed on her bed, face up.

We both saw the name on the lock screen. She froze. I felt more than a little awkward – and jealous. I recognized the name because it was the man Harry had told me had mistreated his daughter!

Her ex, Jon.

She clicked the phone off, shaking her head. I pulled my clothes on and left, reading her energy as 'I want to be alone.'

Whatever games that guy 'Jon' had played on her, I could see that they still hurt her. I could relate. When Kenzie's mom left it was after months of her playing games with me. Lies about where she was and who she was with. Lies about her intentions with me and our daughter. And more lies about the career she was secretly trying to build in the modeling industry.

It wasn't easy to just get over that type of manipulation.

I wondered what I could do to make Madeline feel better. Then, for the first time since I almost kissed Madeline in the closet, the memory of my promise to her father to look out for her came to me without guilt – I knew how to keep that promise now in a way that Harry would be pleased with. I grinned as a little plan started to hatch in my mind.

Six
Madeline

When Hudson texted me about going out to dinner the next night with him and Kenzie, I had no idea he meant taking Kenzie to an arcade that had a restaurant inside. The inner child in me delighted in the idea of it as I settled into the car while Hudson drove us there.

Kenzie had miraculously found my car keys and they were now safely back in my purse. As we pulled up to the arcade, Kenzie shouted out that she absolutely had to play mini golf with Hudson and me. It was adorable the way she looked at us with big, hopeful eyes. Of course, we both said yes.

As we piled out of the car and went inside to buy tickets to use at the various parts of the arcade, I could feel people's eyes on us, looking at us with smiles as if the three of us were a sweet little family. In my heart, I couldn't deny that I wanted that. It didn't make logical sense, since I didn't know Hudson that well yet and I was still bonding with Kenzie, but it felt right.

I felt a sour taste in my mouth as I remembered the five missed calls from Jon last night. Based on his social media pages, I pieced together that he had stopped calling me lately because he was back together with that girl he'd cheated on me with. Their relationship had fallen apart right after he and I broke up, but I guess they recently tried again...only to have that fail, too.

Now, he wanted me back. That was why he kept calling and texting me. It hurt to know he thought I could be used like that, that he really thought I would go back to him.

"Penny for your thoughts," Hudson said kindly. He held out a mini golf club, letting our fingers brush. The touch comforted me and made me feel closer to him than ever. He read my heart, knew that I needed comfort and gave it to me. At least, that was how I interpreted that brief moment.

I couldn't keep the smile off my face as my eyes met his. I shook my head as if to say, 'not here'.

He placed a hand on my lower back as we followed a very excited Kenzie to the mini golf course.

Lots of other families and children were there and I couldn't imagine a more wholesome way to spend a weekend. Certainly different from how Hudson and I spent part of the previous night.

I shot him a sultry look and he held my gaze. But he removed his hand from my back, reminding me that while we both clearly wanted the same things, we couldn't have them. We couldn't have sex. We couldn't date. We couldn't be together. It was eating me up inside.

I wasn't sure how much longer I could hold back. As a man, I'm sure it was even harder for him.

Kenzie aced each hole at mini golf, sinking her golf ball in with just a few strokes. It was then that I learned that she and her dad came here a lot. I found myself watching the two of them, admiring what a great father Hudson was and seeing how obviously close he was to his little daughter.

I had to look away. My heart was getting way too attached to him, so much so that I almost felt that I was falling for him, beyond the physical attraction. And that wasn't allowed.

We headed inside for a dinner of Kenzie's favorite foods, her insisting we order a pizza, chicken fingers, and then a hot dog. Hudson and I laughingly agreed to the odd combination of foods.

When the server asked if we wanted drinks, Hudson declined. I decided not to indulge either. But I was curious why he didn't seem to be interested in alcohol. Most men I knew – certainly Jon – enjoyed a good stiff drink.

As if reading my mind, he said over Kenzie's head as she had placed herself between us, drawing on the kids' menu with bright crayons in the most sophisticated way a seven-year-old could, "I gave up alcohol seven years ago."

We shared a long look, and so much was shared in that look. I thought I understood, seeing the pain in his eyes as he spoke. When someone says they "gave up" alcohol, from my observation, that meant it was causing them trouble, so they had to give it up.

I reached over and placed a quick hand on his cheek, discreetly but hoping to communicate my feelings of understanding to him.

Kenzie was too sharp to miss our little touches, though. She ducked under the table and popped up again on the other side of her dad. "You like Maddie, don't you Dad?" she announced, without shyness on the topic.

But instead of laughing and going with it, Hudson turned serious. It felt like a knife to my heart to see him respond the exact opposite of how he was to me last night.

"Sweetheart," he said to Kenzie, "it's not always nice to say the things we think inside our minds. Especially about other people's feelings. Do you understand?"

Kenzie was undeterred. "Well, do you like her or not?"

I saw the look of distress on Hudson's face and I decided to try to help, even though I was a little peeved at him for not even trying to act like it was hard for him to say he wasn't into me.

"What arcade game should we play first? I love the big basketball game they have. The net is so high up. Can you get any basketballs in it?"

Kenzie was off on another topic, then, the awkwardness that she created was long gone for her. But for Hudson and me, it started to fester. By the time dinner was finished, he and I hadn't attempted any under the table touches or any special looks at each other at all. It felt cold between us.

We drove Kenzie home where her nanny was waiting to take her inside and get her ready for bed. In Kenzie's arms were two huge stuffed animals that she won. I hugged her good night and waved back at her as she walked inside.

"She's such a precious little girl," I said, with my heart full of love for her.

To my great and utter shock, Hudson pulled me to him for a quick, warm hug. He rested his chin on the top of my head and then pulled away, his arms by his sides.

"You are so good with her, Madeline. Don't think I haven't noticed how kind you are to my daughter. It means everything to me."

I felt the tension in his voice as he spoke to me. I missed that tension – the sexual build-up that existed between us every day. The same energy he had squashed over dinner.

"I've never let any woman in her life before. I never wanted her to go through another woman walking out on us like her mom did." His voice was firm, full of conviction.

"That's why you pulled back at dinner." I understood a little better.

I hazarded a touch on his arm. He didn't pull away.

"I was cheated on by Jon. I was manipulated. I should have walked away sooner, when I suspected he was cheating, but I so wanted to make things work. Not for him, but because I wanted my happily ever after. My dad was right, though. I would never have found that with a man like Jon."

Hudson took my hand and brought it to his lips, kissing it. "We are so similar, you and I." His eyes darkened with something like jealousy. "I saw he was calling you last night." His grip on my hand tightened. "Tell me everything is over between you two, Madeline."

I felt my breath catch in my throat at his intensity. The warrior in him was showing, and I loved it. I knew in that moment that he would fight for me; that if we were ever able to date, that he would give me absolute loyalty – and demand the same.

I stepped into him. "I did not take Jon's calls. I am completely finished with that chapter in my life. His sister is my closest friend," I added, for full transparency, "but they are not close, so there is no reason for me to ever see Jon again."

His eyes studied me then he nodded once, as if to say he believed me. "I think you should block his number."

I quirked a smile up at him. "Do you block all of your exes' numbers?" I asked, interested to know how many women he had secretly dated without Kenzie knowing the past few years.

He placed his hands on my face, his eyes intense again. "There are no exes. There are only mistakes. Hookups. But no emotional attachments. And yes, they are all blocked. I gave that lifestyle up when I got sober. There have only been a few since then, and with them it was just a practical arrangement."

I could understand why his past relationships were free of attachment considering what he went through on and off the battlefield. He was a handsome man in the prime of his life, of course he would want to feel alive. It didn't stop the jealousy in me though.

The type of information we were exchanging was the exact type that two lovers would share with each other as they were walking toward the label of 'dating' and 'girlfriend/boyfriend'. I wish I could let myself believe that was what Hudson and I were doing, but it wasn't. Our attraction was forbidden.

"If he ever gives you any trouble, Madeline, just tell me. I'll see that he's taken care of."

I smiled at him, then leaned up to kiss him. His lips brushed against mine and he said, against them, "I can't keep saying no to you, to us."

I pulled back half an inch from him, looking at him, needing him. "Hudson Packard, I am a grown adult. I am making my own decisions. Let's not live in fear of what my dad would think if he knew we were into each other."

The primal look on Hudson's face at the thought of giving himself permission to take me, to have me, and to love me took my breath away and gave me chills the rest of the night as I tossed and turned alone in my hotel bed.

There was no doubt in my mind anymore– I wanted my father's best friend. If I could even have him just once, I could make the itch go away.

Unless it was good... And I had a feeling it would be good.

Seven

Hudson

I couldn't sleep the night I let Madeline go back to her hotel by herself. She had awakened the lion in me and I needed to claim her, to mark her as mine. I wanted to keep her close, to make sure she was safe and felt cherished.

I felt almost emasculated, knowing that I couldn't do that. My respect for her father was too great, our history was too deep, and our brotherly bond was too close for me to do that.

So, I tried avoiding her as much as possible. I kept myself busy at my office, letting Madeline work Monday and Tuesday at my house without me. The truth was, I had let myself get behind with my work by staying at the house with her during the day the previous week. It was time to return to leading my team, closing deals, and building wealth for my real estate company.

I was not planning on being triggered at the office when I was far away from Madeline on Wednesday morning. Linda knocked on my door in her cheery way, breezing into the room where I was with Trevor, my personal assistant, going over our upcoming projects.

"Knock knock!" she said.

Trevor and I looked up at her expectantly.

"I just need a few signatures from you, boss." She held out a few forms to me, tapping her foot impatiently as I started to read them.

"Oh, it's not an expense or anything. It's for your annual SEAL reunion. They are using one of your hotels' ballrooms and they are paying. A reduced rate, of course."

Trevor got a phone call and stood up to take it, leaving me to deal with this touchy topic on my own. I tried not to think of my brothers-in-arms who died in combat.

"I hope you read all the fine print," I attempted to joke with Linda, putting my John Hancock on the documents. "Anything else?"

She paused, then said, "No, I think if you really meant it when you said that I could make all the decisions with

Harry, then I am okay. I'm literally planning your entire twenty-fifth SEAL reunion, though." She laughed. "It's fun!"

She grinned at me as if expecting me to join in her enthusiasm. But all I could remember in that moment was that it was Madeline's idea to ask Linda to take over the project. It was Madeline who talked me down from my last few panic attacks. And in that moment, it was the thought of Madeline that kept me from seeing images of war in my mind that I never wanted to see again.

I met Linda's gaze, feeling confident, holding on to the good energy that Madeline was bringing not only into my life, but into my mind.

"I have full faith in you, Linda. You can make that reunion into anything that you, Harry, and the entire planning committee want. I know the reunion's budget is vast."

She interrupted me, "Thanks mostly to you, or so Harry tells me. You know, boss, you're a funny man. You supposedly, according to Harry, hate the reunions but you donate more than anyone else to the planning budget every single year." She cocks her head. "I think you only pretend to have a cold heart but underneath your gruff exterior, you're a good person."

She nodded at me as if she had just passed judgment on me and found that I was innocent. Then, she picked up her papers and left.

I sat in my chair, thinking about her words. Did I really come across as gruff or cold? Who was I kidding – that was the exact feedback I always received. Until Madeline came into my life.

I resisted the urge to pick up my phone and text her. She was at my home working. I didn't need to insert myself into her work. Plus, with Kenzie at school and her nanny off most of the day, if I did go home, it would lead to Madeline and I all over each other in that big, empty house.

I let my mind wander to thoughts of all the things we could do to each other in my big house...all the positions I could put her in and all the ways I wanted to hear her scream out my name. The next thing I knew, my cock was raging hard for her.

I got up and locked my office door, closing the blinds along the wide windows that separated my office from the hallway. I had to get off thinking of Madeline, since I couldn't have her.

I pulled up every memory of her that I could as my hand wrapped around my length. Madeline with her blue eyes looking at me as if I were her hero. Madeline comforting me. Madeline demanding that I kiss her, that I fuck her...*Oh God!* I groaned. I wanted to make love to her. I imagined it then, my strokes on my cock growing faster and harder. I pictured every detail in my mind.

I wanted to take her in my shower, with her lifted up in my arms, her beautiful legs wrapped around me as I buried myself deep in her body. I wanted to suck on her nipples as the hot water ran over both of us, as she held onto my shoulders and gasped as I filled her with my seed. I imagined how tight she would be, how she would surround my girth with her wet pussy.

I groaned as I came in my office. This was becoming too hard, too much, to say no to her. To try to find relief in my own hand. I needed more. And I knew by the way she kept looking at me, day after day, that she needed more, too.

Just last night, she had lingered in my home until long after Kenzie's bedtime, chatting with the nanny on the couch downstairs until I came in. She'd stayed with me while I ate a hurried and late dinner, and she'd looked at me with such longing as I allowed myself only a hug and brief kiss with her before she drove to her hotel.

I cleaned up my desk, suddenly feeling like a terrible human being. She would never force anything on me. Nor would I with her. Why was I relegating her to that hotel room when my own home was so large? Why was I torturing us both by not allowing us to spend any time together – chastely, of course – after my daughter went to bed?

"I can handle it," I said, to my empty office. "I can control my urges when she is around."

I slapped a hand on my desk in decision. I was going to do it. I was going to ask Madeline to move in with me and if anyone wanted to know why, I would say, logistically, it made more sense for the project. I hoped she would say yes.

I was just congratulating myself on my very good decision when I received a call from the nanny.

"Yes?" I said.

"I am so sorry – but I'm two hours away visiting my mom and I got a call from the school. Kenzie is running a fever and wants to go home! I wish I could pick her up but I thought I was free until four o'clock when I usually pick her up. Is there any way that you can get her, sir?"

My heart started pounding at the thought of my little girl in pain. I furiously flicked the black band on my wrist as I sounded far more confident than I felt. "Of course. Don't rush back. I will go get her and stay with her today. I hope everything is okay with your mom."

By the time I arrived, the school nurses had taken her temperature again and it had gone down already. I breathed a sigh of relief as I pulled my child into a hug. Kenzie gave me a smile.

"I don't want to go home, Dad. Today is show-and-tell and I wanted to see all the cool things my friends brought in today!"

I managed a relieved laugh as I led her to the car. "Well, I am sure that you, Madeline, and I will find something fun to do today instead of show-and-tell. What do you think about that?"

She smiled and then coughed, her face dropping into a sad expression. I was instantly on guard, ready to take her temperature, give her water or candy or anything she needed to feel better. In moments like these, I wished she had a mother. I wanted her to receive the best care, but I struggled with panic when those I loved were in danger.

I drove us home, making her laugh with terribly silly jokes that only Kenzie found funny. By the time we were home, her little eyelids were drooping closed, reminding me of when she was a toddler and needed daily naps. I scooped my daughter up in my arms and carried her inside, where Madeline waited for us, looking anxious.

I settled Kenzie on the couch with Madeline, smiling as my daughter snuggled up next to Madeline, completely happy and content. This was everything I wanted – a safe home for my child and me, and a woman by my side who loved my little girl and who loved me, even with all the baggage I still carried emotionally, both from combat and from Kenzie's mom leaving us the way that she did. It was just crazy to me that I would find the exact things I wanted with the one woman in this whole world that I could not have as my own. Harry's daughter. Madeline.

With Kenzie fast asleep between us, Madeline's hand found its way along the back of the couch toward mine. As our fingers touched, the weight of a million words unsaid lingered in the air between us.

"I'm glad you're here," I said to her, my tone gruff with emotion.

Madeline smiled at me. "There's no place I'd rather be."

I locked eyes with her, seeing the truth of her words, and the emotions of her heart, in their depths.

"Move in with me."

It wasn't sexy or romantic, but it was what I wanted.

"What?" she asked, her eyes wide.

"Please. Just while you're here in Miami. I have plenty of space here. And I know Kenzie would love it."

She smiled at me. "And you?"

"Me? Would I love it?"

Her fingers played with mine, tearing down every wall that I still had built up in my heart. If she'd asked me for sex then and there, I'd have thrown all caution to the wind and taken her to my bedroom, worshiping her body for hours. There was something so open in the way she was, so unlike other women I'd been with. It was capturing me – my body and soul. I couldn't escape. I didn't want to.

"Yes, Hudson. Would you love it?"

We shared a smile. "I'd love nothing more." I paused. "Say yes."

The moment that she looked at me with those big blue eyes and said that one word, "yes," I knew that what I felt for her was love. How could something so strong within me be anything less than that?

Eight
Madeline

I couldn't sleep a wink last night after I returned to my hotel. The idea of moving into the same house as Hudson thrilled me far more than I should have allowed it to. I sat in the small chair next to the round table that was in my extended stay hotel.

I was waiting for my boss, Justin, to join a video call. Moving in with Hudson was not as easy as just deciding to do so. I had to get the buy-in on the idea from Justin and, if he deemed necessary, from the founders of J&W.

His face appeared on the screen. "This better be urgent. It's barely nine o'clock and I just got into the office." He couldn't keep the good natured look he always wore off his face for long, though. His expression softened. "Your text just said the call was about a change in where you're staying. Is the hotel a dump or something equally tragic?" he teased me.

I swallowed hard, forcing a fake little laugh. "It's not the hotel – I mean, it's not bad and that's not why I'm asking to move." Out of his line of sight, my hands twisted in my lap.

He looked off camera and then brought a coffee cup up to his lips, waiting for me.

"I know designers on site at a property out of state work long hours, and I have no problem with that," I started, "but the drive time to the residence is over thirty minutes and almost an hour if there is traffic."

I had to be careful. I couldn't afford to come across like I wasn't able to handle the workload or was exhausted before we were even a month into the project.

Justin looked nonplussed. Okay. So that angle was not going to work.

"We're entering hurricane season and there are a few big storms brewing off the coast. You know how badly south Florida gets hit every year, right?" I saw concern on his face and knew this was the right way to approach him on the topic.

"Yeah, actually, I do. My grandparents kept a place there – snowbirds are what we called them. They flew there every winter. Is the hotel lacking on their safety protocols? I can give them a call or look for a place closer to the residence."

I laughed in a high pitched tone, feeling like my next words are going to be the exact same as if I were admitting to him that I was sleeping with the client. Well, sort of sleeping with him. Certainly exploring the client's body. I grew warm between my legs. The memories were as hot as the sexual touching had been.

"The client is a good friend of my family. I grew up knowing him."

Justin frowned. "I think I knew that, or you told me... I forget now. There are so many new projects we have coming in at J&W." He focused on his phone for a moment and said, "You want to move in with the client? That's going to sound strange to anyone who hears it."

"The client is my dad's best friend, a former SEAL, so they have a brotherhood, you know, and all that..." my voice trailed off. "It would be easier if I was staying there. That's all."

Justin sighed. "You want me to go to the owners to ask, or are you expecting a rubber stamp 'yes' here from me?

I have a lot on my plate already. I'm not sure I feel like asking for this on your behalf, honestly."

His tone was light and friendly, as if we were friends instead of boss and employee. But that was his way, part of what made him a good boss to work for. I gave him time to think about my request, crossing my fingers and toes.

He shrugged. "Sure. Why not? Just do it and if anyone asks I'll tell them the guy is part of your family, right, since he basically is? I trust you to keep yourself to yourself while you're there, if you know what I mean."

I gulped. I knew exactly what he meant. And I had no intention of listening to him.

"Right. Cool. Thanks." I relaxed slightly. I was getting what I wanted. What Hudson wanted. And, I think, also what was best for our strange, forbidden connection.

"If anything goes south, just tell me. You can go back to a hotel or Airbnb. Oh, maybe we should look for one of those nearby, if distance from the client is an issue. Hold on, let me look for one close by. I have to pull up the client's file to get the address." He clicked around on his computer, looking more alert after his coffee.

I'd anticipated he might say that, so I had already checked. The only ones near the ritzy part of town where Hudson lived were huge six or eight bedroom homes, totally expensive and too large for just me.

"Hudson – Mr. Packard – has safety measures in place for heavy rainfall or storms," I said, as Justin completed a quick due diligence on whatever options I had for where I would stay.

He made a face. "Well. J&W sure is growing and landing big deals, but not big enough to justify a two grand a night stay for you in any of these Airbnb homes near the client. Oh well, we will hope things work out for you and that you stay safe."

"Thanks, Justin. Honestly. You just took a load off my mind."

"Anything else? We expect progress photos and video—"

I cut him off, eager to prove myself. "By the end of the week. I've been texting you updates every day. Is that too much?"

He shrugged. "I look at them when I can. It's your first solo project so I expected you to be a little eager to show off." He winked good naturedly. "Okay, lady. Go get your work done. Text or call me anytime. Your plans looked good. You got those points of feedback I put in the shared file drive about the living room?"

I nodded. Personally, I already knew Hudson would not agree to anything as bright and cheery as what Justin was suggesting I change about the living room. Hudson wanted darker colors and what I had designed included his preferences. What Justin suggested was technically correct and with any other client, I would have done the same, but with Hudson, it just wasn't going to be approved.

"And?"

"Mr. Packard was hoping for a more," I paused, "masculine look. Think about a room that Ernest Hemingway would be comfortable in. Dark wood. Big, leather chairs. That sort of thing."

He grimaced. "Sounds depressing. And he has a kid? No. You have to convince him to go lighter and brighter, Madeline. It's good for one's mental health and it makes kids feel happier. Studies prove that. I'll send you links to a few studies. Maybe you can show him the data."

Justin's desk phone rang.

"Great. I'll look through the links. Anything else?" I asked.

"Nope. Doing great, Madeline. Talk soon." He ended the call with me while picking up the call at his desk.

That was Justin, a prime example of multi-tasking. I knew in order to succeed in the industry, I'd have to become better at that myself. I felt motivated again, the way I did the first day or two on the project. There was an inner drive I felt when working on new projects that I didn't feel a few weeks into them. I wanted to harness that passion and approach Hudson about the living room again.

But first, I needed to pack and head to his house. My house, for the next four weeks. I felt different when I pulled up to the home. Hudson had told me he needed to go into the office today, and Kenzie was at school. I would have the place to myself. That part wasn't unusual, but pulling in my huge suitcase through the front door and down the hall to the bedroom on the first floor that Hudson and I had agreed on for me last night felt, well, lonely.

A house as huge as Hudson's had a museum-like quality to it, with sounds that echoed around when I was there without him and Kenzie. I forced my mind to think only about my work. I had deadlines with J&W and milestones that they were tracking for the designs. Before I knew it, four o'clock had come and Kenzie was home with her nanny.

I grinned at her from where I was standing with swatches of materials for new curtains in the living room.

"Look who is feeling so much better today!" I said, holding out the fabrics. "Want to help?"

"I'm not sick at all today," she sang out, dropping her book bag on the floor and instantly forgetting about it the way that all kids do after school. "Sure. But first, I want a snack. I'm starving!"

She ran into the kitchen, leaving me alone with the fabric. I brought a vision board with me that allowed me to put physical pieces of fabric and paint cards that showed the colors of paint as well as pieces of metal like grommets on it to visualize the entire color palette for each room. I kept trying to make the curtains work, but every shade was just a little off.

"Need some help with that?" Hudson's deep voice sounded from the foyer.

I jumped a little as Kenzie darted into the room, granola bar in hand. I handed her the vision board since she liked to pull off the pieces and then stick them back on. She laughed and used her sticky fingers from her snack to rearrange everything over and over again. I smiled at her indulgently.

"Hey," I said softly, my eyes flickering up to meet his hazel gaze. "I am a little stuck on the curtains. But I'll figure it out."

Hudson came toward me, stopping so close beside me that our hands were brushing against each other. "Any luck with work?" he asked, and I realized that I forgot to text him that Justin had approved my moving in with Hudson today.

I couldn't keep the happiness off my face when I nodded.

"Good. All moved in?" he asked, hopefully.

"Yes. Justin said yes and I put my bag in the guest room just down the hall from... your room."

"Look!" Kenzie said, holding up the vision board with every single sample stuck to it that would fit. "Looks cool, doesn't it?"

Hudson and I shared a laugh and the moment of connection between us was put aside.

"Hey, I was thinking we could use the grill outside tonight?" Hudson asked his daughter.

"Pool party and hot dogs?" she asked.

"Pool party and hot dogs," he confirmed. He glanced at me. "To celebrate Madeline being our guest here for a little while."

Kenzie nearly lost her mind with excitement, planning a girls' fort building night, popcorn, a movie, and all the fun things that kids like to do. I said yes to everything, knowing it would make her happy. But there was a very different sleepover I wanted to do, even though I wasn't sure her dad was going to let that happen... a sleepover with him.

***

I tossed and turned in the luxurious bed in the room next to Hudson's master suite. He had been extra cautious with me that night, giving me a chaste kiss on my cheek and turning in so early that Kenzie hadn't even gone to bed yet.

"Message received," I grumbled, flipping onto my other side.

I knew he would never do anything to compromise me or my position at work, but having him so close to me, just one room over, and not even being able to touch him was too much. I finally sat up and pulled out my phone. I would watch a few videos online about the latest designs being done by the experts and hopefully learn a thing or two.

I was so lost in the show I was watching, taking mental notes on how the designers convinced homeowners to be more open minded that I almost missed it. Then, I listened closer. Was that Hudson? Was he having a nightmare? I sat up in bed, turning off the video on my phone. All was quiet. I must have imagined it.

I didn't know Hudson had nightmares. I heard it again, a muffled shout. I slipped out of bed and opened the door to my bedroom. Once outside his bedroom door, I paused. All was quiet.

"Hudson," I called out softly. No answer. I pushed open the door and saw him tossing and turning in bed. He was crying out for everyone to fall back, to take cover. My heart broke for him. PTSD. He was having a flashback dream of his time in combat. My dad had those sometimes, he'd told me.

I was by Hudson's side in his bed before I even realized it. I pulled this tall, muscled man into my arms and held him, stroking his hair and feeling his biceps flex as he held onto me. He was awake now. I was there. I hoped it was a comfort to him.

"Thank you for being here." His voice was muffled against my thin silk pajama top. The feel of his breath against the fabric sent a shiver through me, hardening my nipples. Guilt plunged through me. It felt wrong to want him while he was going through this.

But fuck did I want him. I felt him pull me down until I was cuddled up beside him, lying with my body pressed to his. I put my head on his chest, my heart racing. *I'm in Hudson's bed.* It felt like the universe was conspiring to tempt me to have sex with him. But this was his moment of need – for comfort, for compassion, for support. I wouldn't come onto him when he was vulnerable.

I felt his body relax and his breathing even out. But it took me hours to finally fall asleep in his arms, my body too wound up with a yearning for something more than just his arms around me in slumber.

Nine

Hudson

I woke up to a warm body and soft silk pressed up against me. Without even thinking, I pulled her closer and allowed myself a few minutes of peace while she still slept. I remembered her coming in last night and helping me after my nightmares.

They were always the same ones. Bodies and screaming for each other at the atrocities. Indiscriminate screaming that filled a dark space. When I was in therapy and quitting my drinking habits, my therapist had said that they might get worse in therapy before they got better.

Unfortunately, I was stuck on the "worse" part, having a few a month. But I didn't have to think about that now. I was with Madeline. She had helped me a few times already with my difficulties. I felt like I owed her a lot. She didn't have to support me, but she always chose to be there for me. I ran a hand down her arm and kissed her hair. Her head was on my chest, and she was breathing deeply and evenly. I could feel her mouth against my skin. I wanted it on other parts of me so badly.

I let my hand drop down to rub her back and then caress the swell of her ass. Memories of the times I had allowed myself to give in to my all-consuming desire for her flooded my mind, and my body responded. I felt my crotch stir with a hard-on.

I couldn't let that happen. I tried to think of the bright paint Madeline wanted for the living room to distract myself, to turn myself off, but the feeling of her in my arms was too much to deny. I wanted to explore her body.

She mewled a little in her sleep and I heard the unmistakable sounds upstairs of my daughter and her nanny getting up and moving about. Who was I kidding? Real life left no room for Madeline and me.

Harry is her father, you idiot. I grimaced as a wave of guilt and shame crashed into me. Harry still thought I was the same man I used to be, struggling with alcohol, struggling to regroup after Kenzie's mom walked out, just struggling day after day. He would never want any of his friends, men much older than Madeline, to be with her. He especially wouldn't want me.

I pulled my hand back up to Madeline's shoulder. I wouldn't touch her. I wouldn't tempt her or myself. I felt like I had already let Harry down by doing what I'd done with his daughter. Harry wasn't a visionary like me. He wasn't a big picture thinker or an entrepreneur willing to take risks professionally – I certainly didn't take them personally – to double or triple his wealth the way I did. He was a traditionalist. A work hard until the day you die type of man with an old-school mind.

There's no way in this world he'd understand why Madeline and I were attracted to each other. There's no way he would see it as anything other than me taking advantage of his daughter. Even if she shouted it from the rooftops that she wanted me, too.

I'm sorry, Harry. I'm sorry that I'm deceiving you.

Madeline stirred in my arms, slowly waking up. I looked down to see her eyelashes flutter as she opened her eyes. Her blue gaze disarmed me instantly, temporarily sending my thoughts of guilt, and the burden of that guilt, far away.

"You feeling better?" she asked me as she yawned, burying her face in my chest and then sitting up, propping herself up on an elbow.

"Yes, I am. Thanks to you coming in last night." I brushed some hair out of her face.

"I'm glad we picked the room next to yours for me to use." She laughed in her sweet, carefree way. She was so beautiful. It took my breath away.

Something about that statement reminded me that I selected the room. That I purposely put Harry's daughter right next to me, knowing that sooner or later, I'd give in to my desires. Never had I felt this way before. Never had I betrayed a friend by secretly seeing his daughter before.

Madeline's feet moved to touch mine, playing footsie under the blankets. Her thighs intertwined with mine, and our hips were pressed to each other, my hard-on on full display as it pushed against her. She blushed and moved to hide her face in my neck. I continued to pet her hair, not wanting to push her. I didn't want to do anything that could be taken as me trying to get her to do something she didn't want to do. She was a good girl, a good girl that my best friend had painstakingly raised.

Shyly, she kissed my neck, and my body reacted. I pulled her into me by her waist, feeling the contours of her body against mine. I felt frozen in space and time, like my bed was a trap, like her body was a trap. I was next to a ticking time bomb. If I moved, I'd feel her move with me. I'd want her, and I wasn't strong enough to resist that desire.

I rolled over onto my back, trying to extricate myself from her, but all I succeeded in doing was pulling her even more on top of me. She was practically straddling me. A little moan escaped from her mouth, and I groaned in response. That was all it took.

My mouth was on hers hungrily, my hands on her hips, and she moved against me, teasing my cock through my pajama pants. I tore at her shirt, pulling it over her head to reveal her perfect, bouncy tits. She lifted her ass to let me push my pants down, and I watched the way her breasts hung when she did. Her nipples stood out, hard and perfectly pink, against her creamy skin. I groaned as I felt my length harden, betrayed by my body and my instincts.

I leaned up to kiss her nipples, one by one, using my tongue to make them hard and excited for me. I ran my hand around her waist and up her back. She stayed stiff and straight as a rod until I nipped at one of her pink buds. She yelped and bent her head down and, for just a moment, our eyes met. I could see us both thinking it

– this was wrong. She opened her mouth to say something. Something that started with, "Maybe we—" but I had already decided that right or wrong, I was going to give in. We both wanted it, and we could deal with the consequences later.

"Shhh," I told her, sucking her nipples again, flicking my tongue across the ridges. I gripped the back of her neck and pulled her in for a kiss, meeting her smile with my own.

She put her hands on my chest and lifted herself up, moving her hips and grinding against my cock. I felt frustrated. Torn between pleasing her and myself...and honoring a friendship with her father that existed before she was even born. I kept my eyes on her lips, her breasts, anywhere but her eyes. I didn't want her to see the battle warring inside me. And I didn't want to feel it. I didn't want to feel anything besides how wet she was through her thin PJ bottoms.

"I can feel how bad you want me," I groaned in her ear. I flipped her over. "Arch your back."

She listened immediately, her ass in the air for me. I peeled her pants down to her thighs and trailed a finger down her wet slit, enjoying the sensation of teasing her.

She groaned deliciously, and I commanded her, "Spread your legs apart."

Just then, my real life came crashing down on top of the fantasy that Madeline and I had created together. "Daaaad!" Kenzie shouted from what sounded like the top of the stairs. "Where are you?"

Madeline and I locked eyes and then she glanced at the bedroom door. It was unlocked. She gasped and flew off me, pulling her shirt on.

"Kenz doesn't just walk in," I said, to assuage her fears of being caught in a compromising position.

Madeline wrinkled her nose at me. "What is it that people say? There is a first time for everything. I'm going to head back to my room." Her eyes dropped down my body as I stood to my feet, my pants puddling on the floor, gravity taking them there after she'd pulled them partway down in bed. "Let's, um, revisit this later."

She smiled at me in a coy, sexy way, then left, the lingering scent of vanilla wafting in the air behind her. I picked up my pants and tossed them on the bed. My phone lit up and as soon as I saw Harry's name sending me a text, I went cold all over. What bad timing.

I took a look at it and instantly wished I hadn't. He was planning to come to Miami before the reunion. Both him coming and the reunion left a sour taste in my mouth.

I went to the shower and turned it on. Instead of using my hand to get a release, I just stood under the hot water, thinking. I had told myself I was going to stay away from Madeline for the sake of both of us and for Harry's sake, but instead, I had brought her into my house. I had moved her in...

I squeezed some shampoo into my hand and tried to push away the thoughts that no matter what I had told myself in the beginning, it was clear that I wasn't going to honor that promise. I had moved her in, knowing deep down how that would end.

***

Later that day, I was working in my home office on what started out as a quick phone call to Trevor, my PA. But soon, I found myself spending two hours reviewing documents that needed my approval before they could go out. To Madeline's credit, she didn't interrupt me, but knowing she was in the next room and we were alone in the house added pressure to my mind. She was there, my constant and beautiful temptation.

"Hi." Her voice was terse.

I startled a little in my seat at the sudden sound of her voice. I looked up at my office door, open just a crack, expecting to see her there.

But she wasn't standing in the doorway. I wondered what was wrong to make her sound so stern. I stood and stretched. Maybe one of my housekeeping staff was trying to clean the room where she was working. I opened my door all the way and stepped into the hallway. I could hear her voice, muffled but clear.

"No, Jon. I can't talk. Why are you calling me from an unknown number? This feels like stalking." I stepped toward the corner and saw her reflection in one of the wall paintings, the glass covering of it giving me a small glimpse into the living room.

Jon. This was her ex, the man I was supposed to be aware of and to keep her from doing anything wild to help herself get over him, according to Harry. In the stillness of the house, I could hear some of what Jon was saying.

"You blocked my number? Really, Madeline. That is so childish." Jon's voice was very loud through the phone as if he were angry.

"Yes. I did. But instead of respecting my space, you call me from an unknown number. That is childish." Madeline sighed. "I can't do this. I can't deal with you. I'm working. You cheated. You left me. You then somehow lost the woman you cheated on me with. Sounds like you're on a real winning streak there," she said sarcastically.

I fought back a smile. That's my girl. Spunky to the bitter end.

"I talked to my mother – also Joanna's mother, if you'll recall. Rumor has it that you moved in with Daddy's bestie. You're doing a home reno for the guy and what else? What other favors are you offering up these days?" Jon's voice was snide.

"I'm not doing this. I'm hanging up and, unfortunately, you have just mandated that I ignore all calls from unknown numbers because I don't want to run the risk of picking up a call and it being you on the other end of the line."

"We have things to discuss. I still have some of your stuff. And maybe, well, maybe I want to come clean."

Madeline stopped in her pacing. "Come clean?" Her tone changed and that surprised me. She was softer. "You mean, apologize?"

"Sure. Something like that." Jon continued talking but it was not loud or angry, so I couldn't hear it.

Madeline sighed again as I tiptoed back to my office. The last thing I heard from her was, "Sure, Jon. Sure. We can talk about anything you want after this project is over."

I very carefully and silently closed my office door. I quickly got Trevor and Linda on a video call, turning up the volume so that Madeline wouldn't know I just listened in to her conversation. I also wanted to sound very busy so that she wouldn't come in and talk to me.

I wasn't in the mood to talk. It had just become painfully obvious to me that she and her ex Jon were not completely over. She had just agreed to talk to him after my home design project was completed. From where I sat, that didn't sound like a woman who was completely over a man. That didn't sound like someone who had completely shut the door on the past, either.

119

For the first time since I saw Madeline in my Miami office, I regretted every look, every touch, every vain little dream of us being together. All of it was fake. She wasn't really into me. She was still keeping her options open.

Ultimately, this was a good thing. I didn't need the added stress of my guilty conscience in my organized life. I would back away from her and life would go back to how it was. She'd finish her design project with a glowing review from me so that her career would not be harmed. And that would be that. I'd never have to see her again.

I flicked the black stretchy band on my wrist as Linda and Trevor droned on in the video call about one of our projects. Part of me wished she'd come walking in through my office door. But the other part of me knew that would only make things worse.

Ten
Madeline

I stood there reeling after my call from Jon. I thought he was one of the suppliers I'd hired for fabrics since the number wasn't saved in my phone. I thought the number was a business call. I realized then that I should ask Justin for a work phone. All the senior designers had one. I should, too. For my own sanity and peace of mind.

He'd threatened to teach Hudson a lesson. He got nasty real fast. That was typical Jon. Immature, self-centered, and oh so charming when he wanted something from someone. By the time I realized he was a master manipulator, I was in deep with him. It became a question of sunk cost – should I stay with him because I'd already given him a year of my life?

Unfortunately, I decided that I would stay. That was, until the cheating and the disrespect. That was a bridge too far.

Why would he threaten Hudson? How did he know that Hudson and I had history? I thought back to his words: "If you don't move out of that old man's house, I will go there myself and teach him a lesson about taking advantage of women whose families have history!"

I didn't tell him. I wondered if Joanna let it slip to her mom who then told Jon? It was too jumbled to think straight about.

I needed to talk to Hudson. I didn't want to keep any secrets from him. We almost had sex this morning and our connection was growing. After all that he had been through, he deserved someone who would be honest and upfront with him. I knew from experience with my dad that he might not take too kindly to a perceived betrayal.

I tossed my phone on the couch and took a deep breath, looking around the living room. It was cavernous and minimalistic, making my own isolation feel even more pronounced. I made my way to Hudson's home office. His door was closed. I swear it had been left slightly ajar earlier. I raised my hand to knock but then I heard the sounds of voices coming from inside.

He was laughing and a female's voice was laughing, too. He clearly was on a call. But given the laughter, I started to wonder.

Yikes. Jealousy, already? I thought to myself.

It was more than jealousy. I stood there, not being able to hear any words but listening to the lilt of his voice as he spoke low enough to keep the conversation private.

My mind flashed back to Jon, the first time I had more than just a suspicion that he was cheating on me. I felt my stomach clench at the memory. My hands twisted in front of me as the fear and the pain of those weeks with Jon, knowing he was cheating but wanting to fix him, came back to me.

You can't fix cheaters was my conclusion to that experience with Jon. They are who they are. Joanna didn't agree with me, and not because Jon was the cheater in that case. They were not close then or before I dated Jon. Joanna thought all humans were redeemable. How lucky she was to have such hope, such promise for the future.

I listened to Hudson's voice another full minute and then I had to get away. The female's voice was taking over the conversation now, and I didn't want to think about him doing anything but working, just like he said he was.

I couldn't focus on any creative work. My feelings were too big and too strong for that. Instead, I went to the kitchen table and quietly got on my computer, doing the task of filling in a spreadsheet for J&W with line item costs for the plans I dreamed up. I'd been putting off this task for over a week. It felt good to use my brain and push Hudson away for a while.

When he did come out of his office, he was stoic toward me. He nodded politely as he went to the fridge in the open concept kitchen. I looked down at my computer. Everything felt great this morning. But now it all felt like it was falling apart.

"How is work going?" Hudson asked, suddenly, coming a step closer to me.

"Um, good. I'm just working on some forms for J&W." I glanced up at him, then attempted humor, "I'm not slacking or anything."

"I didn't mean to, but I heard you speaking with your ex. I know from your dad that your ex's name is Jon and that your father would prefer you to not reconnect with him."

He nodded then stood there as if waiting for me to say something. I was so caught up in my fear that he was just like Jon that I actually forgot that Jon had called me until Hudson mentioned it.

I glared at Hudson. "You've been talking about me with my father? All while we've been sleeping together? That's disgusting, Hudson!"

Instead of rushing to calm me down, he grew cold. "We have never had sex. Please don't overinflate any physical closeness we may have experienced."

I snapped my mouth shut after picking my jaw up off the floor. The nerve of this man. But I was used to Jon's manipulations. Maybe all men were this way.

I knew there was no winning with a narcissist or a manipulator. The best tactic for peace was to stay silent. So I did.

Hudson sighed, growing impatient. It gave me time to realize that, in this moment, I wasn't seeing him. I was seeing Jon. I was treating him as if he were Jon when I wasn't even sure that Hudson had done anything wrong.

I flushed bright red in shame. All this time, I thought I was the Good Samaritan helping out this sexy hunk of a man with his PTSD, but really, I had a huge issue myself, and it was staring me in the face right then: I no longer trust men.

"Your father and I spoke the day you came to my office. That's it. He asked that I make sure you were safe and that Jon didn't come snooping around."

I felt he was holding information back but I just nodded my acceptance at his words. "I see. I didn't gossip about you or anything related to you. I told my best friend that I would no longer be staying at the hotel. There's no crime in doing that. People need to know where I am for my own safety."

I thought back to the late night texts to Joanna and tried to remember what all I had told her about moving in with Hudson. At the time, I wasn't even sure I would have permission to move in with him. I shrugged.

"All I'm saying is that I need your word that you will not be gossiping about me." Hudson's tone was firm, but not as firm as it had been minutes before.

I looked up and met his eyes. "I wish you knew me better by now. That's not the type of person that I am, Hudson. It hurts me to think you believe I am that type of person."

I stood to my feet, closed my laptop, clutched it to my chest and quietly walked past him to my room. I didn't slam the door or throw a fit. I didn't even cry. I just sat at the desk overlooking the windows and stared out into his yard.

I felt empty inside. It was triggering for me to hear from Jon like that. It brought back all the pain of his cheating – his betrayal – and caused me to see Hudson in a way I didn't want to. Then, Hudson accused me of spreading gossip about him. It made it hard to not compare him to Jon, who was a liar.

I shook my head. I felt the walls of this spacious mansion closing in around me. I felt lost. And I felt like the best decision I ever made was to not sleep with Hudson Packard. I clearly had some healing of my own to do. And so did he.

Minutes later I heard the garage open and then a car leaving. I sighed. Good. I was alone. I went into the kitchen and made myself a small plate of food, intending to lock myself in my room and not come out until Hudson had left for the office tomorrow morning.

The last thing either of us needed was my distrust of men triggering his PTSD in some way. As hurt as I was, I would never intentionally cause him pain or anxiety.

Distance would be the only way to make everything workable between us for the remainder of this project.

Eleven

Hudson

"She has a headache or something like that," I said to Kenzie, for the third time. I brought back takeout and was sitting with Kenzie and her nanny at the same table Madeline was sitting at when I accidentally accused her of gossiping about me. I only realized after the fact that my words came out much harsher than I intended them to be.

Kenzie pouted. "Well, when I was sick, she stayed on the couch with me and we watched TV. Remember?"

I smiled and winked at her. "You mean you watched two seconds of TV and then fell asleep."

Kenzie pushed the lasagna around on her plate. "She gave me a hug and made me feel better."

Thankfully, the nanny redirected the conversation – again – and Kenzie moved on to a different topic. Her words made me think, though. Just because Madeline thought she wanted to be alone didn't mean she should be alone. That old tightness in my chest kicked up. I felt a combination of panic and sadness filling me.

I kissed the top of Kenzie's head and excused myself, claiming that I needed to do a little more work. My daughter was too busy negotiating a little extra time on her iPad with the nanny to notice my departure.

I walked down to my home office and stood by the windows. I stared at nothing while I practiced a tried and true method of calming down – box breathing. My threat perception had been skewed ever since my time in active duty service as a SEAL. It happened to a lot of us.

Some of us burned out completely and never felt anxious or excited or any big feelings ever again, a shutting down of that part of the nervous system, while others of us – including me – felt every little change in our environments as a big deal, a big threat to be handled.

I inhaled and held it, then exhaled and tried to let all my fear of the unknown go. I did it again and again until I felt lightheaded from all the deep breaths.

It helped. I stood by that window, lost in thought, lost in guilt, lost in sadness – just lost. Something had shifted between Madeline and me, and I didn't exactly understand it. But that phone call with her ex made the energy between us feel off. I didn't feel like we were on the same wavelength, maybe not even on the same team.

It grew dark outside before I finally tore myself away from my grumpy thoughts and decided to check in with her. I walked down the hallway of the quiet house toward her bedroom. Once there, I noticed only a soft light coming from under the door. It's either a night light and she's sleeping, or it's a bedside lamp and she's still awake.

I knocked twice. "Madeline? Can we talk?"

A calm, cool, and collected Madeline opened the bedroom door. "Hey," she said in a strong, crisp voice. "I've been working too hard lately. I'd like some privacy and alone time tonight. Anything you have to say can wait until some other time. Thank you for your understanding."

I knew it then – she was not okay. This façade of strength and cool detachment was one of several covers I myself had used over the years when I felt like my world was crumbling and panic was consuming me. I didn't think Madeline had panic attacks, but she was going through something right now.

"Okay. I can leave, and I will leave, if that's what you want," I said in a genuinely loving voice. I cared about her, no matter what. I felt it deep in my bones. No matter what she chose to do with us or her life or even with her ex, she had won my loyalty and my respect far beyond what she had before as Harry's daughter.

She nodded her thanks, eyes dropping to the floor.

"I wanted to thank you for being there for me during my panic attacks. If I can be there for you during anything you're going through, just say the word. I want to support you, too."

She opened the door wider, face going from tense to relaxed. She stepped away from the door and I took that as my invitation to come inside. I closed the door behind me.

"I'm sorry—" we both started to say at the same time.

Then, I was closing the distance between us. I took her in my arms, all my resolve to keep my distance gone.

"I assumed you were talking about me to your ex – that was ridiculous. I'm sorry."

She reached up to stroke the stubble on my cheek. "I was so triggered by your change in attitude toward me. It took me right back to Jon and how... well, that doesn't matter."

I kissed her cheek. "It matters to me."

She sighed and fidgeted with the sheets on her bed, her eyes glued to her fingers. "Jon used to cheat on me. All the time. There were so many women – a couple at the same time. But when they reached out to me to tell me, he'd deny it. Looking back, I don't even know why he wanted to be with me if he wanted other women so badly." She looked up to meet my eyes, and I could see tears swimming in hers.

I used my thumb to wipe away the wayward tear that had made its way down her cheek. "Some boys don't know what they want," I say, trying to comfort her. "You don't have to worry about that with me. I'm very sure about what it is that I want."

"And it's me?" she asked, her voice thin and quiet. Her chin wobbled as she held in a sob, and I pulled her into my chest.

"It's you, Madeline."

"Jon used to tell me all kinds of things to make me feel better, so that he could keep the game going for as long as possible. That's the only way I can make sense of it now. That it was a game for him about power and control. He wanted to manipulate me. He got some kind of enjoyment out of me believing him or forgiving him." A muffled sob spilled from her throat, and she clasped her hand over her mouth, trapping it.

I moved her hand down and linked our fingers. "It's okay to cry. Let it out. You're safe with me." Her forehead rolled around on my chest, and I stroked her hair.

It made me sick to know how she was treated. Despite the ways I felt our relationship had complicated things, some good and some not, I wanted the best for her. I knew she was an adult, but I still saw her as vulnerable, someone who needed protecting.

"I just feel like...he changed the way I love. I gave him everything. I didn't know there was a way to hold a part of yourself back in relationships. Now, that's all I see. I see all the cracks first. I want to run. I miss who I was before."

The way she was talking reminded me of myself in therapy. I knew our trauma was so different, but it was the same sentiment. Wanting to go back to the *before,* whatever it was. Wanting to be whole again, wanting to erase everything that had rewired my brain. "That's normal," I whispered, still stroking her hair. "And some of you *will* come back. And the parts that don't...you'll start to see the good in it, in who you are. One day, you'll look back and be in total awe of yourself for getting through it."

She sighed, the kind of sigh that releases bad energy after a good cry. She took my hand and squeezed it. "Thanks for listening. I'd heard about things like what I went through with Jon happening to other women, but it's not something you ever think will happen to you."

Standing to her feet with pure and honest eyes, she continued, "I know you don't want to disrespect my dad. It sounds like he asked you to look out for me. I hadn't realized how...difficult...this has been for you." She looked down at her hands then met my eyes, her gaze unwavering. "I won't be making it any more difficult than I have."

I looked up at her from my spot on her bed. I wanted her to make it difficult. Hearing her be so honest with me had made me want her even more. I couldn't stand it if she took it from me now. "I'm glad you shared all that.

I should tell you about what happened with Kenzie's mom."

She reached out and took my hands gently, whispering guiltily, "The nanny sort of took some liberties."

"What liberties?"

"Like, she told me all about it basically?"

I chuckled, a forced laugh that I didn't feel. I would rather have told Madeline myself. I felt the smallest amount of relief that I didn't have to, but I wanted her to have my perspective.

Despite her knowing so much already, she didn't seem scared off from wanting me. I'd come clean to her about her dad's instructions to me about looking out for her. She already knew about my old drinking habits and my PTSD. And now I knew how triggered she was by behavior shifts.

The air between us felt free and clean. I felt free and clean.

She smiled at me and rubbed the back of my hand with her thumb. "You feel it, too. I can see it in your eyes. I feel lighter."

I looked at our hands intertwined for a moment, then looked back up at her. Her gaze was so innocent and kind. I needed someone kind. I pulled her down to me and kissed her. It was spontaneous and I was prepared for her to pull away, but instead, she deepened the kiss.

"Madeline," I murmured. "I want you. I want all of you."

I felt her body grow warm as she pressed against me. I felt the rapid beating of her heart as I held her against me.

"I want all of you, too," she murmured, half on the bed and half off.

I felt every ounce of my masculinity come roaring forward at that. She was ready for me to finally cross a line with her, a line that we could never uncross afterward.

I slowly moved my tongue inside her mouth, slowly letting my body feel every sensation of the kiss. She melted into my touch, melted into my body. I could feel the energy of surrender rolling off her.

Her hands moved to undo my belt. Cold air hit my bare skin as she rid me of my clothes, then backed away, breaking the kiss. I took off her shirt and guided her hands to her breasts, and she obediently pinched her nipples, her eyes half closed with lust.

I pushed her leggings down, locking eyes with her, leaving her in a little thong as she pulled them down the rest of the way off her feet. I took one of her hands from her nipples and moved it down between her legs. "Show me how you touch yourself," I murmured, rubbing my palm up and down the back of her thigh. I leaned forward and kissed the crease where her thigh met her pelvis.

Shooting me a bashful look, she slid a finger inside her thong and stroked herself. A small moan escaped her lips, and she closed her eyes and shivered in front of me. I growled a little and stood up, taking a step toward her. That part of her body was all mine. I wanted to bring her pleasure.

"Don't cum, baby girl. Your body is mine. You only cum when I make you cum." My voice was heavy with need for her. She didn't seem to be listening, her movements getting faster, her breaths quicker, as she looked at my length.

I stroked myself as I watched her, but when her breaths got shallower, I abandoned my cock. I reached forward and took her wrists in my hands, pinning them behind her back. She let out a whimper, crossing her legs and biting her bottom lip.

I took her by her wrists and pushed her down onto her stomach on the bed. Her face went down into the mattress, and I took my other hand and pinned her legs down.

I reached out and stroked her cheek, feeling the blood spring to her face. She turned her head so that she could breathe, and I leaned down to look into her eyes to make sure she was okay. Her eyes had darkened, and she was still squirming, still ready for me.

Like a man released from a cell, I dropped to a knee and grasped her beautiful ass in my hands. I spanked one of her cheeks and watched it bounce as a handprint formed on her milky skin. She spread her legs and I kissed each cheek. "You are so fucking beautiful, Madeline."

"Taste me," she gasped. "Please."

I let my tongue slide between her ass, pleasuring her little pucker there. The guttural moan she let out was enough to make me explode right then. I used my tongue to move from between her cheeks down to her wetness, her precious center. I played with her lips before finally teasing her clit.

She arched her back so fully for me that I stayed there, flicking and licking until I could feel her arousal on me. I licked my way up to her ass and then back down. We did this dance time and again until she was demanding an orgasm, demanding a release. Now I knew she was ready.

I slid a finger into her wet center and then used my thumb to massage her sensitive nub. Her pucker was right there before me, begging for attention. I flicked my tongue across it, up and down.

I felt her body shift as her face went into the bedding, her cries breathy and begging me not to stop. When she orgasmed, it shattered my heart with how sexual it sounded. I knew she had wrecked me. No other woman would be able to compare to her, to this moment, to the sounds and tastes of Madeline.

I ran my hands up and down her legs as she gave in to her pleasure. I could catch a glimpse of her face as she turned it to the side, still flat on her stomach. Her cheek was flushed and her eyes were shiny. She looked at me and whispered, "I've never had an orgasm like that."

From the shaking of her legs, I believed her. It ignited something deep within me to know that only I had made her feel that way.

I flipped her over, and she was smiling dreamily and breathing heavily. Standing at the foot of the bed, I grabbed her ankles and pulled her toward me, earning myself a laugh and a shriek.

"Come to me, beautiful," I said, reaching down and pulling her into a sitting position.

My hands found their way to her ass and I lifted her up, feeling her legs wrap around me. I kissed her all the way to the wall next to the door. I knew exactly how I wanted her for the first time. I wanted to feel everything and I wanted it face to face.

Her arms rested on my shoulders as my rod brushed against her wet lips. I felt her forehead rest against mine as I looked deeply into her blue eyes. Then, I lowered her slightly, her back sliding silently down the wall. I felt myself enter her.

"My God, baby, you are so tight," I groaned.

She gasped, clutching me and moaning. I watched her eyes turn lustful. I watched as her face went from surprise at my size to pleasure as her tight walls relaxed around my cock. She bit her bottom lip.

"Deeper. I want to feel all of you!" she cried out, as she started moving her hips against me. I felt fireworks of pleasure explode through my core. I thrust into her, excited when I saw that she liked it. I thrust again and again, and she matched my pace, her hips moving and her breasts brushing against my chest.

I felt in that moment that we were one and the same. There was nothing between us, just pleasure and happiness.

We had mountains yet to climb, but for now, we were safe in our bubble of attraction. Safe enough to make love. At long last.

Twelve
Madeline

I felt like I was walking on cloud nine. Hudson and I had sex for the first time last night. It was so raw and passionate that I wasn't sure I would ever be able to get over him if things between us suddenly soured.

I shook my head as I attempted to eat some of my breakfast. I needed to let thoughts like that go. They are leftover fears from Jon, the idea that nothing lasts and that every cloud has a rainstorm hidden inside it.

Kenzie tapped my shoe with hers under the kitchen table and then giggled, playing a little game all her own. She was adorable. I winked at her.

"Oh, I think there is a dog or a cat in this house. Hmm, oh yes! There it is again! It's kicking me!" I teased her as she tapped my foot again.

She laughed and laughed, covering her mouth with a hand. Hudson walked in, then, and kissed Kenzie's forehead and then squeezed my shoulder as he walked past me. He sat at the table and drank his coffee. Kenzie must have kicked him, too, because suddenly he yelped, "Oh no, Madeline! I think the dog you were talking about has got me!" Kenzie laughed while trying to eat cereal. Cereal shot out of her mouth onto the counter and Hudson said, "Did it get you, too, Kenzie?"

I gulped down some orange juice and Hudson shot me a simmering look that stirred something between my legs. He was so damn handsome. I could barely even stand it. From those broad shoulders that I had held onto last night as he fucked me hard and fast, to his hands that had grabbed onto my ass and held me up against the wall. My heart fluttered in my chest. My gosh. That was amazing.

I watched his hazel eyes light up with happiness as he bantered with Kenzie about whether or not she really did all her homework or if she was just playing. I felt her little foot tap against mine as she giggled. Life was perfect.

Then, Hudson's phone rang. He was still laughing about Kenzie's homework when he took out his phone and looked at it. His smile went from carefree and genuine to worried and fake. He flashed the screen at me and I saw that my dad was calling him. He winked at his daughter and then stood up, walking a short distance away to take the call.

I felt a knot form in my stomach. Of all the mornings for Dad to call, it had to be the morning after Hudson and I had sex. I lost my appetite entirely as I heard Hudson talking to my dad on the phone. Kenzie's nanny appeared and ushered her off to school. I gave her a big hug and wished her a wonderful day.

Then, the house was quiet. Hudson was still on the phone with my dad. When the call ended, he sighed.

"Well, it appears that your father is making good on his plans to come visit you here in Miami before the big reunion."

I noticed that he was able to mention the reunion without getting that world weary look on his face, as if the reunion were becoming less of a big, scary unknown to him. I felt proud of him.

Now was not the time for that, though. "Oh. When?"

Hudson raised his eyebrows as if he couldn't believe what he was about to say. "Well. Now. He just landed and is getting a rideshare here. He wants to spend the day with you. And probably me, too."

"He's suspicious," I proclaimed. "He's checking up on us to make sure we're not—"

Hudson reached out and took my hand. It was a symbol of unity. Whatever my dad wanted, we were in this together, he and I. Everything would be okay.

I cleared my throat and let Hudson pull me in for a quick hug. I looked up at him. "So, I'm assuming we aren't going to come clean to my dad today, huh?" It was a joke, but it took Hudson aback for a moment, then he laughed, the tension of Dad's surprising news gone.

"I strongly advise against it." He kept his hands around my waist. He looked around the house. "I hope he thinks you have actually been working. Nothing has been started yet since we're still in the planning and ordering of materials phase."

I laughed then groaned. "Oh my God. That's a good point. We will just have to take him up to Kenzie's room and show him that first, since everything is done there now."

I wrinkled my nose up at him and then we both stepped away.

"I have so much to do before he gets here! The airport isn't that far away." I couldn't miss a whole day of work just because my dad was in town. I'd have to find a way to make his visit work into my schedule. I still had high accountability with Justin, who video called me every other day, it seemed, to check in.

"I'll take him to my office, introduce him around to everyone," Hudson offered after seeing me stressed out.

I rewarded him with a kiss, then I pulled back. "We can't get too used to that now that Dad is here."

It was meant as a joke, but the truth of it sobered both of us. We stood still, processing my words and the energy shifted between us. Hudson sighed a little and I felt anxiety rip through me.

"The timing of him coming could not be worse." I couldn't keep the stress out of my voice.

Hudson tried to lighten the mood. "Well, at least he didn't show up last night."

That got a laugh out of me. "You are impossible, my handsome lover."

"And you are beautiful, especially when you're stressed."

He made his way down to his home office and I went into the living room. Twenty minutes later my dad arrived. He was all smiles and big hugs. It put me at ease.

"The place is huge, I'll give you that," he said to Hudson, after being given a tour where I explained J&W's vision for the space. Really, it was my vision but I had to give credit to my company, I felt.

Hudson laughed and clapped his friend, my dad, on his back. "Is that your way of saying you don't like my sense of style?"

Dad laughed right back. "What style?"

The two of them headed out to Hudson's office, then, leaving me with my check in call with Justin. It went long as we went over the contractors we needed to bring in and the schedules we needed for each contracted team. We went over orders and their delivery dates. It was mentally exhausting, especially after a night like I'd had the night before with very little sleep and lots of excitement over what Hudson and I shared.

Finally, the call ended. I made coffee and settled in to enjoy a cup in the kitchen. It was not meant to be, however, as I heard the garage door open. My dad popped his head inside.

"Hey, Hudson lent me his car. Let's go grab lunch, Maddie. I bet you're starved!"

My dad was the jolly sort of man as long as things went his way. But he was broody when he was unhappy. The only good thing about that was it was painfully obvious when Dad was upset. Since he was still acting jolly, I'm sure he thinks life is peachy and Hudson and I are just friends. I felt nervous as I drove with my dad to an ocean-front restaurant. My guilty conscience must be kicking up into high gear.

We ordered our meals and he told me the latest and greatest about my mother and the upcoming reunion.

"Hudson's office space was top notch," he said, as he took a sip of his lemonade. "He really has done well for himself."

"Yeah. He really has, hasn't he?" This is the third time Dad has brought up Hudson already, but he doesn't know how awkward the topic is for me.

"How are the two of you getting along? You know what they say about guests in someone's house... they're like fish. They get rotten and need to be thrown out after a few days."

That got a laugh out of me. "Dad," I said as if I were a teenager and he was embarrassing me. "It's fine. I'm in a guest room near the living spaces so when I get up to start working or whatever, it's all right there. It's so much better than commuting from that hotel."

He nodded. "I don't know if he told you, but he has PTSD. Worse than mine ever was. That's the thing with war, Maddie, you never can predict how it will affect people. And the last I heard, he tried therapy but then quit." Dad shrugged. "I'm not saying he's a violent man..."

I gasped. "Dad, really. Don't say that, don't even hint at it. He has a daughter, for God's sake. He's not anything but kind and loving."

"I haven't seen him one-on-one in, oh, maybe six years? Back then, he was mad at the world." Dad's eyes studied me. "I came here as soon as I could to check on you. To make sure any anger he still felt toward the way the world works with wars and guns and such, and the anger he felt toward women, weren't going to hurt you."

Dad was always blunt. He sold his words with a friendly smile but his point was always felt deeply. I sat in stunned silence. Hudson, violent? I couldn't even fathom it. Not for a second.

Dad patted my hand. "I don't know Hudson the way I used to, Maddie, but I'm going to spend several days here to get reacquainted. I'm going to make sure he's okay. I see now that you're fine. But I also see that I let the ball drop on my friendship with him. The last time I saw him, he was drinking and playing women and full of rage at how his life turned out. I just need to make sure that part of him is cleaned up, put away, and is never going to come out again. It's the least I can do as his friend."

After Dad dropped that bombshell on me, he went back to eating his salmon dish as if he had just been talking about the weather or his golf handicap. But I was left reeling.

What the actual hell? Hudson used to be so angry that Dad was afraid he'd be violent? But Hudson had a daughter. And he had full custody of that daughter. He had to be a safe person. Right?

Thirteen
Hudson

Harry moved himself right into my home and announced he was planning to stay 'for a little while'. That meant he was here on a snooping mission.

I'd realized days ago that the last time he and I spent quality time together, I was a different man.

I was never like Harry. He was true blue, laid back most of the time, and didn't have much in the way of big feelings.

I carried my feelings deep inside me. When they erupted, good or bad, they were felt by all around me. I was constantly learning how to keep them at bay.

Having Kenzie, my sweet, darling little daughter, changed me forever. But the down side of twenty-six-year-long friendships was that you developed a past with that person. They saw you through some of life's darkest moments, and life's greatest moments.

Harry knew the old me, the me that was drowning in grief at Kenzie's mom leaving me and grief over our lost brothers-in-arms. That was the darkest season of my life. But it was clear to me that Harry still thought I was there, or worse, he thought that was who I was.

I watched Madeline roll her small suitcase into the front room. It was Friday morning and she had a flight to catch to NYC. Apparently, she had a bachelorette weekend to get to. One of her friends, Stacy, was getting married.

For obvious reasons, with Harry staying in my home in a guest room upstairs, Madeline and I had not had one moment alone together. He was either keeping her up late with talks about her career and family topics or me up late with talks about the reunion. I was flicking my black rubber band around my wrist a lot on those late nights, trying not to have vivid memories of war flash through my mind.

I longed to pull Madeline in for a hug, but I didn't. Kenzie was just heading out to school and Harry decided to top off his coffee. In that brief absence of his when he was in the kitchen and my daughter was scrambling for her backpack, I walked past Madeline and discreetly took her hand, hiding it with my body. I gave it a squeeze. It sent my heart soaring with happiness when she squeezed it back.

I stepped far away from her to avoid anything looking suspicious. "Have a safe and pleasant trip," I said cordially.

Of course, she and I had been texting nonstop every chance we had since private conversations didn't feel right or safe for either of us with Harry in the house. I knew all about her weekend plans but I feigned casual indifference in public.

"Thanks. I'm not staying for the whole thing. I'm not twenty-one anymore, so too much drinking and partying make me feel like death the next day," she said, with genuine excitement in her voice.

I suddenly felt a strong pang of jealousy come over me. I was looking at Madeline with her rosy cheeks flushed with anticipation of seeing her friends and going back to NYC, where she'd lived for a few years.

Even though she wasn't going to be gone long, I felt as if she were leaving me forever. I had enough common sense to know this was a trigger for me – Kenzie's mom left me, too, only she never came back.

This was just a little getaway and Madeline was definitely going to come back. I felt a strong urge to pull out my phone and text her, asking her not to go, but I had to trust her. I had to believe she wasn't going to abandon me or my daughter. Although, eventually, I needed to deal with her abandoning us when my house project ended.

I took deep breaths even as I forced a smile. In true Madeline fashion, she read me like an open book. She reached out for me and then caught herself, her hand falling to her side.

"It's all going to be fine," she said softly. I missed her touch. I missed the scent of her perfume. I missed the feeling and the taste of her. This pretend friendship game we were playing was killing me hard and fast in my heart. I had a wild urge to just come out with the truth, right then and there.

Then I saw her look at her phone and grin. "It's Stacy! She's at the hotel where the bachelorette girls are all staying! Oh my God – everyone is there, it looks like. I'm so excited that I'm going!"

I clenched my jaw and held my peace. I would not ruin this weekend for her. Nevertheless, I'd be a jealous man hiding away in this house all weekend until she was back, that much I knew.

Harry came into the room whistling. "Ready to go? I'll drive you."

Madeline shook her head. "Oh, no, Dad, that's not necessary. I decided to get a rideshare so that you and Hudson didn't have to bother with driving me."

In truth, she and I had debated if there was any way in this world I could steal away with her by myself, driving her to the airport. We knew Harry would, of course, tag along. She ended up landing on a rideshare for simplicity.

Harry looked at his watch. "That means that Hudson and I can get to the restaurant early today."

Madeline gave her dad a blank look, then she smiled. "Yes, that's the place you want me to renovate? Right? We'll have to set it up through J&W."

I remembered her dad knowing the owner of a trendy new bar and restaurant in Miami. Not on my side of the city, but down south nearer to the party district.

The thought of Madeline working near all those party happy – and usually very muscular and attractive – people wasn't my favorite thought to consider. But it was her career, and she had to build it, this is how I reasoned my way through my possessive urges on the topic.

"Of course. Today, Hudson and I will go check it out and see what the deal is. The owner left the decision up to his general manager, so it could be that the deal is a no go even before you present it to J&W." Harry looked very pleased with himself. It was clear he didn't know the owner well, but well enough to get the ball rolling for his daughter on the project.

I clapped him on the back, wanting to make him feel that I was excited about the opportunity to head down there with him. "We'll ask all the hard hitting questions so you don't have to." I winked at Madeline the same way I would wink at anyone, hoping it didn't look sexual or personal in Harry's eyes.

Madeline played along, pretending to be offended. "As if I can't ask my own questions, thank you very much." Then she laughed, hugged her dad and headed out the front door just as a rideshare pulled up.

I swore silently. The driver was a young guy with blonde hair. I clenched my jaw. Of course he was. I was suddenly becoming very aware of all the attractive and fit men in and around the city of Miami. Everywhere I went, I was noticing them and wondering if Madeline would find them attractive – more attractive than she found me. It was childish. But it was a leftover train of thought from Kenzie's mom leaving us for the glitz and glamor of modeling, a world full of hot bodies and attractive faces.

Harry and I watched as she safely got into the car and was on her way. Kenzie headed out to school and then Harry and I got into one of my cars and started driving.

"Our appointment is at nine, but we can get there early." Harry was on his phone texting the owner. He looked up at me. "When are we going to go to the hotel where the reunion is being held? Linda said everything is set, things are ordered, and out-of-towners have booked their rooms."

I'd been avoiding this topic. The reunion was right around the corner and I had yet to meet with the manager of the hotel and Linda to finalize anything. I'd given Linda carte blanche to handle everything.

I thought of Madeline on her way right now to a city full of bad memories with Jon, but she wasn't letting that stop her. She was intrepid.

I thought of my daughter not letting the lack of a mother stop her from her own happiness. And then I thought of myself and how far I'd come, pulling myself out of heavy drinking and into sobriety.

I knew the universe was nudging me to a new step toward freedom. I needed to face the reunion more fully. I needed to just let go and allow myself to enjoy it. Easier said than done.

I grinned at my longtime friend. "Let's talk with Linda and schedule a time."

"Good man," Harry said, with a nod.

Forty minutes later we pulled up to the restaurant, having hit morning commuter traffic. The place was trendy, bright, and fun on the outside. A little too bright for my taste. Harry pointed out some of the signage.

"My buddy Juan told me that this place used to be a high-end Mexican restaurant. But then he bought it and saw a gap in the market around here. No Cuban restaurants. So he changed the menu and most of the décor, but he did it quickly, you know? No planning."

I studied the signs and the colors. I started to see a mix of old and new. It made the colors look garish and gave the place a fun house look to it, probably not the vibe the guy was going for.

"Who are we meeting today?" I asked, as we got out of the car.

The place was right on the beach and I breathed in the hot, salty beach air. I loved Florida. Sure, we had bad weather this time of year and even now the skies looked overcast, but nothing beat a beautiful beach with an endless ocean stretching out for miles.

"Looks like the general manager's name is Matt." Harry waved at someone and I tore my eyes off the beautiful water.

"The guy over there in the tight t-shirt, tighter pants, and a bulge so obvious it would make a nun blush," I grumbled quietly.

Harry didn't hear me. He was too busy shaking hands with bodybuilder Matt and waving at me to catch up.

I had no idea I was such a jealous man until I had sex with Madeline. It awakened a beast in me that wanted to protect her and keep all the slimy guys of the world far away from her. I did not like the idea of her traipsing down here and working long hours with meathead Matt.

I didn't like that one little bit. As Harry and I walked through the restaurant with Matt, I hated the guy's guts. He had the audacity to not only be fit, but also be a former army guy who was even a super nice guy to boot! Everything a woman would love was in this guy. Then, I found out he was only twenty-nine and I almost full-on rolled my eyes.

Yeah, there was no way in hell I was letting my woman come down here alone with mighty Matt in his tight t-shirt, ready to charm her socks off and try to woo her away from me.

No fucking way!

Fourteen
Madeline

"We're over here!" Joanna and two other girls yelled out in baggage claim at the airport.

With Hudson being a billionaire, he had a private jet at his disposal that he tried to get me to use, but I wanted to return to my favorite city in the world like a normal person and be picked up at the airport by my friends, not driven in a limo as if I were a celebrity. Looking at their smiling faces now, I knew I made the right choice. The next twenty-four hours or so were going to be a blast with the girls.

I ran to meet them, my little carry-on bag trailing along behind me. Maybe I should have packed more and actually checked in a bag, but I wasn't planning on dolling myself up too much when we went out. My priorities were firmly landed on my work, and on Hudson and little Kenzie, of course.

"Stacy is at the hotel getting buzzed on mimosas!" Joanna said to me, as she pulled me in for a hug. She looked at my bag. "That's all you have? Girl, how did you fit all your shoes in that little thing?"

I hugged our other friends and let one of them grab my carry-on handle for me. I walked out arm in arm with my closest friend, which unfortunately meant that I would forever be tied to Jon in some way since this was his sister.

"I'm only here until Sunday morning. I might even fly back early. I bought a refundable ticket," I explained quickly, knowing she would protest. "I have so much work to do, Joanna. You know how it is."

She pouted. "I was hoping you'd realize how much you miss NYC and would come back to us! How is the on-site job going in Florida?"

I filled all the girls in as we took a taxi into the city. The hotel was in the tourist district and in walking distance to the best bars and clubs. I knew the area well.

New York was the type of place you could party in every night of your life and still not hit all the fun spots. I felt adrenaline course through me. The city was always alive with energy unlike anything I'd ever felt before.

We piled out of the taxi, claiming that we were going to be very financially responsible in our bar hopping and walk everywhere or take the subway.

Then, we were in the hotel and heading up to a huge suite that three of us were sharing. Of course, the other girls wouldn't spend much time in their room since we would all want to be with the bride-to-be, Stacy, staying up gossiping and looking at her wedding venue plans, catering plans and all of that.

One look at Stacy as we walked through the thick wooden door of the suite and I was appalled that I ever had a whisper of a thought that I should be anywhere but here this weekend. She looked radiant, and a little tipsy, in the cutest way. Her face smoothed out into a huge smile as she saw me.

"Madeline!" She pulled me in for a hug. "It is so good to see you that I can almost forgive you for missing all the bridesmaids' activities the girls and I have been doing here in the city." Her red hair fell in long curls down her back. She looked every bit the Irish beauty that she was, several generations removed from Ireland, of course.

"Oh, stuff and nonsense," Joanna said, pouring me a much too large flute of mimosa. "Madeline is a career woman. She can't be running back to the big city every chance she gets, you know."

We laughed and spent the morning eating snacks, drinking, and going through each other's clothes, planning what we would wear out tonight.

I stole away twice to check my phone and respond to a few work messages. It was Friday, so though Justin knew I was taking the day off, there were still contractors and suppliers to stay on top of.

I also heard from my dad and...from Hudson. Every text he sent made my heart flood with affection for him. I could tell he was trying to be respectful of my time with my friends, but there was a certain tone to his texts that let me know he was missing me and that he had so much more he wanted to say.

I slipped into my little black dress later that night, being the first to get ready since I kept my makeup natural and opted for a sleek ponytail for my hair. I snapped a selfie and sent it to Hudson. Before I could check for his response, the girls were asking me to help with a zipper here or a bobby pin there.

Of course, the star of the evening was our stunning bride-to-be, Stacy. She came out in a mini dress of pure white with white heels to match. She wore one of those cheesy little sashes that said, 'Bride to Be', and even put a small veil on. It suited her well.

"I guess I want all the guys to know to stay far away from me tonight!" she joked, twirling for us. "I'm basically a walking billboard for 'taken, do not approach'!"

We laughed as we made our way down to the lobby and out onto the street. People called out their congratulations to Stacy and wished her luck our entire walk to the first bar she had selected. She was eating it up and loving every minute of it.

It made me wonder how some people got so lucky. She and her fiancé had been engaged since they were fresh out of college. Sure, they'd had their ups and downs, but through it all they stayed together.

I felt a pang of jealousy wash through me that I quickly pushed away. Three bars later, I was the only sober one, having sipped my drink instead of chugging it at each bar.

"Come dance with meeee," Stacy cajoled me, her veil already lost somewhere on the dance floor and her sash crooked across her chest. I glanced at my phone. It was after midnight. Given that the girls were planning to stay through Sunday, I felt the pressure to be the Mother Hen and herd my wayward little chicks back to the nest.

I grabbed a bottle of water as the music thumped and the lights strobed. I danced my way to the center of the dance floor, where all the girls were dancing with Stacy. Stacy was right about one thing, the guys were mostly leaving us alone.

Hudson would be happy.

I felt homesick for him. I pushed the feeling away. Sex was one thing, but a real relationship? That was not even on the table. Too many obstacles – his age, my dad, his ex, and protecting Kenzie from any woman coming and going from her life.

"For me? Nah, I think that's a little too weak. I want gin!" Stacy said, trying to brush the bottle of water out of my hand.

I laughed. "Okay, young lady. That's enough partying for you for one night. I'm going to get us a rideshare –

I don't care how much it costs. You need to get back to the hotel room."

I looped an arm through hers and then looked over at Joanna. She was three sheets to the wind and I felt my pulse quicken when a man walked over to her.

"Hell, no," I muttered. "Not today, buddy."

I swung around with Stacy, letting out a "weeeee" as she whirled with me. I now faced Joanna, ready to give the guy a piece of my mind. But the face I came nose to nose with was no stranger – it was Joanna's brother! My cheating ex.

I fought the urge to run. The feeling of betrayal hit me in the face as if he had slapped me.

"Joanna," Jon said, his eyes on me. "Thanks for letting me know where you girls were tonight."

"Woohoo," Joanna slurred, a happy drunk but clearly a loose-lipped one.

"You told Jon we were here?" I asked in annoyance. The music suddenly felt too loud and the place too crowded. I tried so hard to move on from Jon, to let all of his hurtful behaviors go, but here he was in my face on a night that was not supposed to be about him.

"What? Are you afraid that your new boyfriend is going to be mad? Is he the jealous type, Madeline? The angry type?" Jon sneered, his attractive face contorting. Why did I ever date this guy again?

I herded my friends, luring them out of the club with promises of salty snacks and sugary treats. Jon tagged along.

Getting them into the rideshare was easy. Getting rid of Jon was not.

"In case you didn't notice, I don't have anything to say to you. Why are you still here? You weren't invited. I don't want to see you."

"You said we could talk," Jon said, feigning innocence.

I was just tired and frazzled enough to be honest. "I said that to get you to hang up the phone. I can't do this, Jon. I'm happy on my own—"

He snorted and leaned in, his minty breath a testament that the sinister look in his eye was just part of who he was, not alcohol induced. I'd never seen him look so angry. I stepped toward the open door of the rideshare, scared.

"I'll only say this once," he sniffed at me like he is some adonis and I'm a pauper. "Leave that old man. He's not good news. I've been looking into him, watching him. You need to leave. He's a loser." To his credit, he did look sincerely worried for a moment, but I knew him better than that. I knew he was a manipulator, pretending to care but really just trying to move people around like a puppeteer on his own comedy show.

"Thanks for the unsolicited advice," I retorted. "I'm done with this conversation."

"No, you're not," he said, with a grip on my arm.

I don't know what he had in mind, but I lost my cool then, jerking free, jumping into the rideshare, and slamming the door.

"Drive!" I cried out. "Just drive."

The driver looked lazily back at me, reminding me that what just happened was a common occurrence in this city. I felt unsafe until all the girls were in the suite with the door locked and the safety latch deployed.

I sat through the dramatic conclusion of the night – getting the girls out of their tight little dresses and high heels and into bed.

Joanna started crying, declaring that she forgot she had responded to Jon's asking her about the bachelorette party that night. I sighed and rubbed her back. I should have known that a man like him listens to every little thing.

It was almost three in the morning when my phone lit up as I lay in bed while my friends slept in that restless sleep from a night out. I looked at the screen and smiled. It was Hudson, wishing me a safe night out and asking if I was back yet. Somehow, me replying to him led to me changing my flight and leaving at noon that day.

I might have stayed longer, but Jon's presence put a damper on any fun I might have had. If he popped up once during the weekend, he'd pop up again.

***

"How did you manage it?" I asked Hudson, as I walked out of the airport and straight into his arms Saturday afternoon.

He looked pleased with himself. "Linda. She's got your dad working full-time today with the reunion stuff. Thankfully, I had an honest excuse to work from home – a big project coming up that I need to rework the budgets for. It needed my full focus."

He smiled at me, that strong jawline softening with that look. His hazel eyes were alive with emotion. It took my breath away. It also brought a pang of hurt to me to remember that he had to 'sneak' away from my dad to be here. It felt wrong, and the words of Jon haunted me: "He's a loser."

If my expression changed, Hudson didn't comment on it. "How was NY?" he asked, taking my bag and putting it into the trunk of his Bentley.

I quirked an eyebrow at the glam car that looked every inch 'old money'.

"Really? Nothing subtle today, huh?" I said, as I noticed everyone either staring at the luxury vehicle or taking photos of it.

"Only the best for you," he said, with a wink.

I settled into the spacious vehicle, wondering if I should bring up Jon to him.

"Tell me everything you girls got up to," he said casually, but I could feel his protective energy filling the space around us.

I glanced at his muscular body, on full display under his shirt. I smiled to myself – yes, he certainly could protect me if I needed it. Those biceps and strong arms weren't just sexy to look at. He was strong and tough.

"You like what you see?" he asked, with a deep heat in his voice, his first question forgotten.

I bit my bottom lip, sneaking a glance up at him. "I might need a closer inspection...it's been a while." My fingers reached out to rub up and down that sexy arm of his.

He picked up my hand and kissed it. "Hmm, we could get a hotel. My place is too risky." He quirked an eyebrow at me. "Or is it?"

I glanced at the large backseat of his car. "I mean, we almost have a cot built into this car..."

The truth was, I was feeling really turned on. I was horny. I felt intimidated by my ex. And I felt a deep need to remember what it felt like to have Hudson make love to my body. The more I was with him, the faster I wanted to rip his clothes off and make love to him.

His voice was a low rumble. "I know exactly where we can go."

I loved how in charge he was as his strong hand gripped the luxurious steering wheel while his other hand caressed my thigh.

"Something is wrong. I can see it in your eyes." He gripped my thigh reassuringly. "I'm here if you want to talk. Remember? We support each other."

I let it out then. "Jon showed up last night. That's why I left early." My voice was monotone. "He manipulated his sister, I'm sure, into telling him where we were." I sighed. "I don't know what he meant when he said some things," I told him, relaying what I remembered Jon saying.

Hudson's grip strengthened around my thigh. "I'm glad you left. He sounds like a desperate man and desperate men are dangerous men."

He turned off the highway to a cozy looking Bed-and-Breakfast. "One of my personal properties. I bought it from the owner, an older woman, a widow, who was too old to run it alone or so she said. It doesn't make a lot of income for me, but it's mine. We can park outside the back guest house. It's under renovation, so it'll be abandoned."

I sat quietly, both of us thinking about Jon, no doubt.

"I don't think Jon would be brazen enough to come to my house, but it is obvious that he has put his nose into more things than he has a right to. So, I'll up the security at my work and at home. If he shows up with ill intent, we'll have it on camera."

I shivered. It felt good to know Hudson was ready for whatever may come with Jon and his pathetic little threats. But was he ready for whatever may come for me... for us?

Fifteen
Hudson

The Bed-and-Breakfast had a shady backyard with weeping willows and oak trees. That was why I loved the place – it had a quaint charm to it that many other parts of Florida did not. I tried to hide my Bentley from prying eyes by parking it behind one of the separate guest houses away from the main house.

"Kiss me," Madeline urged me, leaning over the middle console to capture my lips like a woman starved. Her breath was soft on my skin, my mouth craving hers with a passion. My thumb moved along her soft cheek, pushing a strand of her hair out of the way behind her ear.

Everything about her was appealing to me. From her looks to her personality to her unquenchable lust for me. Soon, my little touches on her breasts and up her dress weren't enough. Her hand rubbing my crotch over my pants didn't help either.

"Meet me in the back," I said in a raspy voice. I opened my car door, the weight of it an indication of the quality of the vehicle. I had a stray thought that I hoped it was going to be soundproof. The way I felt for Madeline right now meant that I would be releasing into her hard and fast. I felt my breathing shorten as the anticipation of being intimate with her again consumed my mind.

Madeline flew out of the car and into the back seat. I slid in, my fingers finding the soft core between her legs. She whined breathily, her legs so shapely and lean, opening for me just enough to grant me access. She leaned over to me, fondling me. Her lips were soft and warm as she kissed me.

"You are fucking perfect," I groaned. I needed a release badly.

She leaned up, her breasts in my face, my length pushing painfully against my pants. With that little space she gave me, I jerked off my belt and then shoved my pants down, loving the feel of her pussy as it slid back down my stomach and toward my member. I was bottomless but she was still in her thong. I could see by the look in her eyes that she loved this feeling of power, where I was wanton for her, swollen painfully hard for her while she resisted me.

I growled a little and let her play with me, her soft thong brushing up and down my rod, focusing on swirling in little circles over my tip. She was so free in this beautiful moment, so relentlessly sensual that it took my breath away.

I pushed her away from me and spun her so that she was on all fours, her hands against the car door. Seeing her ass pointed at me awakened something in me. My hands found the zipper of her dress and I unveiled her inch by inch, the view of her back coming into focus.

I pushed up the bottom of her dress even more, bunching it around her stomach, revealing her lips spilled out around her thong. I could already see how wet it was, soaked through. I pulled it aside and pushed two fingers into her. She gasped and threw her hair to the side to look back at me.

I mounted her, pressing my member between her legs, and thrust it inside her, bucking into the wet, tight spot that I had been yearning for so badly. Her scream bounced around the back of the car as she threw her head back in ecstasy. I gripped her hair and tugged her head back so that I could kiss her mouth with all the longing that I'd been holding in. I felt it in her, too, as her mouth searched for me hungrily, and I continued to buck into her, gripping her around her stomach.

I used her body the way I'd been dreaming of, feeling the way her walls constricted when I plunged deep inside her and relaxed as I pulled back out. We had a rhythm of our own, and her grunts matched mine as our mouths pressed against each other, not kissing anymore, fused together in the moment.

I slipped my lips down to her shoulders and her back, kissing everything I could see as the tip of my penis felt the deepest parts of her body, the parts that only a select few had had.

Rage filled me as I realized that others had had her, too. The all-consuming jealousy of Jon having been with her intimately, having felt her the way I was filling her, fueled me. I slammed against her as hard as I could, and she pressed her face against the door of the car, bracing with one hand on the back of the driver's seat. Her moans were muffled by the door, and I continued to fuck the experiences out of her. I wanted her brain empty of anyone and anything but me. All of our energy colliding to make her feel like an extension of me and me like an extension of her.

She orgasmed loudly, and she stopped moving with me for a moment as she went limp, and I used that moment to thrust into her as wildly as I could. I sat up higher, pressing one hand down on her lower back, my other hand bracing against the seat where hers had been earlier. I fucked her hard and fast like the animal she made me feel like.

When I finally felt myself cumming in her, I leaned back over and bit her shoulder, pleased by the red mark it left. She was mine. We both knew it. And one day, the whole world would know it. The jealous anger that had risen so suddenly subsided as she twitched on my cock, milking it .

I slid back out of her, thinking how perfect we were together. Doing everything I could to not think about how many bridges we still had to cross.

***

"It's been a pleasure hosting you," I said honestly to Harry. We were walking out of the hotel venue where the reunion was going to be held. I finally got through a planning meeting with Linda and Harry, my PA popping in to have me sign a few documents, giving me cover to check out intellectually and let Linda handle everything.

"Ah, I can't tell you how great it's been catching up, old friend," Harry's voice boomed out. "You've come a long way. I'm proud to call you my friend, brother."

I chuckled. That was Harry. Always honest and never filtered. "Well, I'm glad I've come a long way. It wasn't easy, and the work isn't done."

He shook my hand as his rideshare pulled up into the parking lot. I'd offered to drive him to the airport, but of course, he'd declined, preferring to make his own way out of town.

"That's the way it goes," he agreed. "Madeline looks happy."

His sudden switch to the topic of his daughter caught me off guard. "Well, good."

"Yeah, I think the work suits her. I'm glad she left that New York frat boy far behind her. Now, all she has to worry about is her career. I don't think she should settle down anytime soon. I've spoken to her about just taking a break from dating. Her mother and I got married young, as you know, and it luckily worked out. But nowadays, it usually doesn't."

He patted me on the shoulder. I was at a loss for what to say.

"I'm glad you're taking good care of her. She needs strong men in her life who remind her that not everyone out there is a scumbag like that Jon fellow."

Harry got into the car, tossing his duffel bag into the back seat. "See you at the reunion, Hudson."

I waved as he drove off. Well, this was not a pleasant way to end his visit. Now, not only was I supposed to be watching out for Madeline, but I was also supposed to be an example to her of what a knight in shining armor was!

The guilt I have been working hard to keep at bay rears its ugly head, and I just stand there in the shadow of my own hotel, staring out at the ocean and feeling guiltier than ever.

Sixteen
Madeline

"I know how to use an app, Hudson," I said, with a playful shove against his shoulder.

Dad had been gone for two days now and he was just starting to relax around me. I know Dad talked to him about watching out for me or something again, which pushed Hudson away for a while.

"If what Jon said carries any weight at all, you'll need to be logged in and be able to access the cameras." Hudson put his arms around me and hugged me.

We were enjoying a rare moment after work, home alone, while the nanny went to pick up Kenzie from band practice.

I shivered at the thought of Jon, of that strange glint in his eyes that I saw at the club in NYC. It took three phone calls with Joanna to convince her I hadn't left early because I was mad at her for drunkenly texting Jon where we were that night. It's not her fault her brother is who he is. And I won't let him get in the way of my relationship with her.

I dutifully opened the app on my phone and let Hudson walk me through how to use it. He was very detailed and punctuated each detail with a kiss on my neck. The hickey had healed but the act of trying to hide it for a few days had given me a secret thrill.

Once he was sure I was adept at using the app, turning on and off the security alarm and looking at all the camera angles from the updated camera system he had installed around his house after Jon's threats, he turned me around to face him.

"This is nice," he said, glancing around us. "It's just the two of us here in my home."

I wriggled my way closer and closer to him, leaning my head against his shoulder. It hurt a little that this is 'his' home, but of course, it's his house and not 'our' house. The hint of a smile that was on my face dropped slightly. It reminded me that I had my own home, my own life, and my own career that certainly was not in the state of Florida nor was it in Miami where Hudson's life was.

I squeezed Hudson and then released him. As if sensing a change in me, he said, "Stay with me tonight."

I raised an eyebrow. "Oh, to keep the ghosts away?"

He laughed ruefully. "If you mean your ex, no. If you mean my nightmares, well, yes."

I leaned into him. "I'm sorry, I didn't mean—"

He kissed my cheek. "I know. Whether to keep your ex or my PTSD away, or both, just say yes."

I hesitated. It felt like a big step forward. We had been so well-behaved since my dad had come for a visit. And since he left, we had given each other a little space, each dealing with our feelings about the situation, I'm sure.

I was saved in that moment by Kenzie coming home. I felt weird deep inside my heart. Wasn't this exactly what I wanted? I wanted Hudson to want me, right? I wanted him to be with me – to be mine. But with the shadow of my dad looming over us, it felt wrong. It felt very wrong and I was struggling to say yes.

Hudson looked at me with hurt eyes before he turned and greeted his daughter.

"Dad, Dad! Can we go to the beach? Please! Just for an hour."

The nanny apologized, "Some of her friends mentioned going to the beach today so she sort of felt left out."

Kenzie threw her arms around Hudson. "Please, Dad!"

Hudson looked so gently down at his daughter. It melted my heart. Whatever Dad thought he knew about Hudson once upon a time being out of control or an angry person surely was wrong. I regretted not following up with Dad about it. By the time I came back from my little NYC trip, Dad was fully invested emotionally into planning the reunion. So, the topic never came up.

"Well," Hudson pretended to hesitate, but I knew him well enough by now to know a beach evening was in our future. I swallowed hard. I had a deep fear of the water. During a game of mermaid when I was a kid, I almost drowned in a swimming pool. I'd be okay as long as I didn't get too deep into the ocean water.

"Yay! That means yes." Kenzie whirled around and ran up the stairs. "Maddie! You're coming, too! We'll build a sandcastle! We'll make sand angels! We'll find seashells!"

I indulgently smiled up at her. "We'll do all the things that you want to do." But inside, I was nervous. What if Kenzie wanted to swim in the shallow water by the shore? I wasn't sure I could handle that.

"If you have work to do," Hudson started to say to me.

I smiled at him. "It's four o'clock, so I'm sure I can end work a little early today. It's already over eighty degrees outside, though, so you better have a huge umbrella ready to go so we have some shade," I teased him, before turning to walk to my room on the opposite end of the house from his.

With the nanny and Kenzie upstairs, I heard Hudson take advantage of our privacy and follow me to the room, spanking my rear end as we walked. I laughed and jumped a little.

I heard him close the door behind me and instantly I was turned on.

"I wish we had time for a quickie," he mumbled, as I pulled out a bathing suit and started to take my clothes off.

I bounced my breasts as I pulled my shirt off and he groaned, his cock growing hard in his pants. I wrinkled my nose at him as I smiled. "Later, right?" I said, that ever present push-pull between off-limits and lust throwing us into each other and then away from each other.

He closed the distance between us, leaning down to capture my nipple in his mouth, pinching one and sucking the other.

"Oh, Hudson," I moaned. "I can't—this is going to make me too horny for a family day at the beach!"

His hazel eyes twinkled up at me. "Family, I like the sound of that."

I brought his lips to mine in a kiss. But then the sounds of a very excited Kenzie running toward the stairs separated Hudson and me, the longing clear between us.

"Hudson, um, about the water, the beach..." I felt embarrassed to admit my fear, to admit that I hadn't really been swimming since the mermaid incident. "Well, I don't think I'll go in. Okay?"

He cocked his head at me curiously. "Whatever makes you comfortable. I'll go in with Kenz." He grinned and then hurried out of the room toward the hallway.

"I hate this sneaking around," I mumbled. "I hate lying to Dad." I thought of Hudson and how good he was to me and how attentive he was to his daughter. "But Hudson is worth it. This guilt I feel is worth it."

With renewed determination, I emerged from my room with my swimsuit coverup on, sunscreen in hand, big sunglasses, and a hat.

We arrived at the beach, just the three of us, since the nanny wanted to get a few chores done at the house. Kenzie held onto my hand and Hudson's hand, skipping between us.

I could tell by the way Hudson was looking at me that he was feeling the same 'this is meant to be' vibes that I was. But the moment I looked at the ocean and saw the steadily moving waves, I felt a surge of unease rush through me.

"Hey, Kenzie," I said, with a smile. "I think today I'm going to just stay on the sand and play with you there. But your dad said he'd go in the water with you!" I kept my voice light but I felt enough fear to announce right away that I was not planning to go into any water, no matter how shallow.

Her sweet little face fell for a moment and she opened her mouth to protest, but Hudson was ten steps ahead of me.

"That means more time for me to chase you in the waves!" he said, and then they both dropped their towels and a bag onto the sand and ran to the shoreline where lots of other families and kids were playing.

I felt silly then. Everyone was having fun in the shallow water. Why couldn't I?

I took my time setting up the umbrella that I rented from the nearby stand, along with a lounge chair. Once everything was laid out for Kenzie, I started to get antsy. I was all alone on the sand while Hudson and Kenzie were splashing and running in the shallow water.

A dark cloud passing overhead hid the sun long enough for me to feel the chill of the late afternoon air.

I glanced up. Just one cloud, nothing too crazy. It hid the heat so thoroughly that it cooled down the temperature by at least ten degrees, it seemed. The sounds of Kenzie laughing and playing pulled my heartstrings toward the water. I went a bit to the right of them so as not to be called into the water by a very determined Kenzie.

They didn't seem to notice me so I wrapped my arms around me and put a toe into the water. It was shockingly cold. But it wasn't as scary as I thought. I slipped off my coverup and tossed it into the dry sand a few feet away. This was it. I was going in.

I slowly walked into the water until it was to my knees. It was thrilling! I kicked a foot up and laughed as the water splashed. I let myself stand there, feeling the push of the waves around me until I felt confident enough to move toward Hudson. Kenzie and Hudson were busy digging their feet into the wet sand in the shallow water, Kenzie giggling every time the water washed away the sand around her feet.

All of a sudden, I hit a shelf in the sand, the point where the sand dropped off a few feet. I'd heard about things like this happening. The constant push of the water can erode parts of the shore until the tide turns. Suddenly, I was in up to my waist. So, this was why parents were in the water with their kids all around me – this was dangerous!

I gasped as water suddenly crashed over me. The cold, tangy salt water filled my mouth and some went into my lungs. In just a moment, I went from thinking I was okay to feeling just like I did as a little girl when I was sinking in the pool, unable to get to the surface, unable to get air.

I tried to kick my feet, instincts taking over. But the sand was like sludge, like quicksand. I panicked, then. I flailed around, my lungs burning. My feet were kicking up murky sand the color of mud. My eyes opened desperately only to sting. I snapped them shut. I used my arms to try to force myself to the surface of the water. But, no matter what I did, it was useless.

I didn't want to die that day. I wanted to live. I wanted Hudson! I needed him now more than ever.

Seventeen

Hudson

I knew something was terribly wrong the minute Kenzie's little face went from smiling and laughing to horrified. Mute, she pointed.

I whipped around, ready to face a shark or something equally sinister. But what I saw made a clawed hand squeeze my heart, talons piercing into it. I froze.

On the shore was that bright yellow bikini coverup Madeline was wearing. In the water was a human struggling. It had to be her. My mind focused, my SEAL training kicking in.

First, secure the scene. "Kenzie! Get to the umbrella. Talk to no one. Stay there." I didn't want any bad guys taking advantage of this moment to try to lure my daughter away.

I saw an older couple running toward Madeline. In the wrong hands, a drowning person could die if the rescuer doesn't know what they are doing. I held up a hand to them, trying to halt them even as I ran toward Madeline and kept an eye on Kenzie. I saw her pick up a phone and felt proud of her. She was a smart girl. She'd call 911 if needed, or she'd call the nanny if someone tried to approach her.

"I've got it! I've got her!" A sudden gust of cool air hit me from the ocean. "Shit." Sudden weather changes were common in Florida. It could be sunny and sweltering hot one minute, and cool with a thunderstorm the next.

I glanced at the sky as my toes hit the water, running at top speed. The sky didn't look too ominous, but further south I could see dark clouds gathering. That was where the wind was coming from. I had to act fast. Wind speeds were notoriously dangerous and fast around here.

I was up to my knees when the shelf dropped off, plunging my whole body into the water. I cut through the water as the waves increased. I saw Madeline's hands above the water and her head appeared before a wave knocked her around.

I reached her and in typical victim fashion, she flailed about, thinking that her kicking and writhing were going to save her.

I grabbed her small waist and hoisted her up so that her face and shoulders were out of the water. That typically calmed people down enough for me to talk to them. Madeline gasped, sputtered, coughed, and then stared at me with wild eyes.

"My foot – it was stuck in the mud! It's free now. Get me out, Hudson! Get me out!" The panic in her voice broke my heart.

Another wave chose just then to crash over her, plunging her down into the water despite my attempts to hoist her up. She was freaking out now, wildly thrashing around. There would be no convincing her to lay on her back and let me pull us those few feet onto the shallow part of the shelf and up to shore.

Instead, I pulled her into a vice grip, her head cradled in my elbow. She fought and fought while I pulled us to shore, breathing in water and coughing it up.

"Relax, baby. Relax. Please." I kept my voice calm. It took me longer to get her to safety with all the fighting she was doing. But I had to keep going. I couldn't wait for her to calm down. She was choking on too much water.

Finally, I pulled her onto the shore. She sat up, turned around, and threw up nothing but water. Self-doubt and anger gripped my chest. I should have noticed her fear of the water. I should have asked her more about it. She would have told me she couldn't swim if I had only asked. I could have kept her safe. I rubbed her back and looked at my daughter. Kenzie waved wildly at me, looking worried.

My girls were safe. My heart relaxed slightly. A crowd had gathered as the wind picked up. I was sure Madeline didn't want a bunch of people staring at her so I waved them away, stating I was a SEAL and this was my girlfriend.

That seemed to appease everyone. I was amazed at how easily the term slipped off of my tongue. If Madeline noticed it, she didn't say anything. My girlfriend.

I patted her back and reached over for her coverup, still reeling from almost losing her. As she sputtered, my mind swam with what almost was. I held her close to me, my terror subsiding as her coughing calmed.

"Dad! Is she okay?" Kenzie said, over my shoulder. I froze. *Did she hear me call Madeline my girlfriend? Does she know what that means?*

"I'm okay," Madeline croaked out. She reached up for Kenzie, who gave her both hands to help her stand up. "I'm sorry. I don't swim very well and I only wanted to go in the shallow water..."

Kenzie hugged her and I stood to my feet, wrapping an arm around Madeline.

"It's called a shelf. We've gotta watch those," my little girl said, taking Madeline's hand. "And rip currents, right Dad?"

I nodded, watching Madeline with concern. She looked a little pale and her nipples were hard as pebbles under her swimsuit.

The sun was hiding behind a cloud and the temps had dropped. My SEAL training reminded me that shock like that from almost drowning would make a person feel abnormally cold and once they started shivering it would be hard to warm them up.

"Kenz, please pack up the toys and put them in the bag. I think we need to get Madeline into our car and turn the heat on." I tried not to show too much concern so as not to scare my daughter.

My daughter looked at me funnily while I grabbed a bottle of juice the nanny had packed in the cooler for Kenzie. I gave it to Madeline and then wrapped a towel around her. "Drink this," I murmured. "You need the sugar."

"But Dad, why would we put the heat on in the car when it's not cold out!" She threw her toys in the bag in a rush, like a child who doesn't want to do a chore so they do it sloppily. Normally, I wouldn't let this slide, but today my concern was for Madeline.

"I'll explain it all once we are in the car. Please get your towel," my voice was measured and calm as I rubbed Madeline's arms vigorously. She looked shaken, but the color was returning to her cheeks.

Kenzie didn't miss a thing. Her eyes studied Madeline. "She's not feeling good; is she, Dad?"

"She'll be okay soon. Ready to go?" I had to be strong for both of my girls. Kenzie and I marched to the beat of the song she decided to belt out at the top of her lungs while Madeline walked in a daze between us.

The juice took a minute to do its work on her blood sugar levels, but once the sugar hit her system, the symptoms of shock and hypothermia went away. By the time we reached the Jeep that we drove there, Madeline was looking normal. That vacant look of trauma victims was gone.

"That was scary," she said to me quietly, after I loaded up Kenzie and the bags into the car. She was standing in the sun that had come out from behind the clouds. Her face was tilted up to the heat and she had let the towel slide off of her shoulders. "Thank you for saving me."

Her back was to my daughter, so I stole a quick kiss, my heart still clenched in my chest. I felt like I could have lost her today, and that feeling awakened a mountain of fear within me.

Madeline's eyes fluttered open, their blue depths clear and strong. "I'm okay, Hudson. I'm sorry I gave everyone a scare."

Another cloud danced across the sky, hiding the sun. She shivered again.

"Let's get you home." I stroked her cheek and then opened the car door for her.

"Did you almost drown?" Kenzie shouted unnecessarily loudly from the back seat.

I jumped in. "No, princess, she was just surprised by the deep water. Remember last summer when you jumped into the swimming pool at the country club and you didn't realize how deep it was going to be?"

She laughed, distracted from the topic of Madeline for the moment. "Yeah. The water was taller than you, Dad! I got scared."

"That's right. The deep end was really, really deep. What did you do?"

She shrugged. "I cried. Then I swam."

"But you didn't drown and you were okay, weren't you?"

Kenzie nodded. Madeline reached for my arm and squeezed it. The look of horror completely gone from her face.

"Thank you," she said.

Whether she was thanking me for saving her or thanking me for diverting my curious daughter away from the topic, I wasn't sure. But the look of peace that gradually came back to her face warmed my heart through and through.

The nanny was more than ready to help Kenzie get a bubble bath to wash off all the salt and sand. I barely let the two of them disappear upstairs before I scooped up my beautiful Madeline into my arms and whisked her away to the master bedroom.

She laughed. "What is this – my pirate saved me from the ocean and now I must do as he says?"

I carried her, bridal style, into my room, closing and locking the door behind us. "Think you're ready to ride the plank?" I teased her.

She giggled in my arms and widened her eyes. "No, please, I have a family!" she joked back, grinning at me.

I put her down in the bathroom and turned on the shower. "Finally, I can ask you how you really are. Madeline, I didn't know that you couldn't swim!" I put my hands on her shoulders as she slipped out of the bikini, her body looking cold and small again.

She avoided my gaze. "I was going to tell you, but I got kind of embarrassed. I didn't want to ruin Kenzie's time, and I guess I just...pushed myself too far. I can swim, but I almost drowned in a pool as a kid, so I kind of...panic around water."

I pulled her naked body to me. "You poor thing. I'm so sorry. You could never ruin Kenzie's time being yourself. I could have held you the whole time. We could have made a game of it."

I kissed her sun kissed hair and then released her. Her ass jiggled as she hopped into the shower, stepping into the hot water with a satisfied moan. That moan of hers got me hard instantly, like an on switch. I tried to will my penis to mind its manners. I couldn't be getting hard after Madeline's traumatizing experience. I needed to be there for her, not there inside her.

She crooked her finger at me, beckoning me to her as she posed for me in the shower, her curves rounding out in all the right places.

I followed her into the shower hesitantly. She started kissing me deeply as the water ran over our bodies. I pulled away and shook my head at her. "I don't want to push you– you just went through a near drowning," I reminded her.

She looked at me for a moment before kissing me again. Her kiss was full of need, the energy that I was afraid of. It felt manic and fearful. Gripping her by the forearms, I held her away from me and looked into her eyes.

"Madeline ..." I trailed off as she leaned back against the tile, closing her eyes and lifting her chin to feel the water on her face. "I want you, but I want you when you feel good."

"I do feel good, Hudson. I feel alive. You saved my life." Her eyes opened and she smiled. "Please just kiss me." She stared at me from the wall, a foot between us, twenty years between us, an experience between us. I didn't know sometimes how to bridge all the gaps we had. I wanted to be right with her in life, but I kept falling behind.

"You scared me today," I whispered, stepping forward to wrap my arms around her. I pressed her cheek against my chest, feeling the warmth of the water and her warmth merge. "I thought I might lose you. I would never forgive myself if that had happened."

"But you didn't lose me. You have me right here. What are you going to do with me?" Her breasts were pushing against me, and I could feel how hard her nipples were despite the serious conversation. Something about being so close to death made people horny. It was an undeniable fact.

"Fuck," I groaned, disappointed in myself. I knew I was going to take her in the shower, whether I thought it was the right choice or not. I couldn't deny her body on mine. I couldn't deny her submissive eyes. She took my hands and placed them on her ass, and I gave in instantly, letting one slide between her cheeks.

I moved my other hand between her legs so that I was holding her by both her pussy and ass with my fingers. She gasped and leaned her head back. Water spilled down over her face and slapped her breasts, bouncing off her nipples and soaking into her skin. She wiggled against my fingers, but I didn't move, enjoying holding her there. I looked down at her and told her, "You stay just like this. I like feeling the inside of you from both ends."

"Please, I want more. Faster," she whined, and I smirked at her begging. I waited, watching her sweet face contort with desire. When she seemed like she couldn't take my stillness anymore, I picked up the pace. I moved my wrist hard and fast, shaking my fingers inside her until she was quivering before me, undone in her orgasm. Her first orgasm, if I had anything to say about it.

Then, I lifted Madeline up as she'd asked me to, the movement taking me back to that first time we'd had sex. She wrapped her strong, wet thighs around me and looked me in the eyes, her mouth open and gasping. Holding her ass, I adjusted her so that her slick entrance rested against the tip of my cock. All I had to do was thrust, and I'd be inside her, feeling her walls tighten around me.

She must have had the same realization because she bounced a little when she felt me pressing into her, swallowing me deeper inside her. As she sunk lower on me, my cock plunged into her, and her mouth stretched wider with her pussy. "You feel so good," Madeline breathed, as her nails dug into my shoulder blades.

I could barely think, let alone respond, and I pressed her against the cold tile, thrusting in a slow and purposeful rhythm. I could feel her hard nipples dragging against my chest, and the water hit my back as I continued to take her slowly, methodically. Madeline's arms cradled my head as her breathing turned ragged. My cock started to pulse inside her, and she screamed out as her pussy did the same, responding to my body with hers.

There had been a moment that I almost told her I loved her, seeing her blue eyes rolled up toward the water and her pink mouth calling out to God as I fucked her brains out. But I came to my senses as I came inside her, realizing that if this was all she wanted from me, that was fine. I could spend my days saving her and feeling her from the inside. I could do it until I died and die a happy man.

She had been consuming me since the day I saw her all grown up. By now, she had consumed me completely.

She was mine, but what was worse, was that I was hers.

Eighteen
Madeline

Life took a fast turn after I almost drowned. Justin was calling me nonstop – the furniture was being delivered for the rooms that did not need any structural changes and the painters and contractors were coming and going in the rooms that needed a column removed here or an entryway widened there.

The house was well on its way to increasing in value and looking every bit the modern, elegant mansion that I was hoping it would be. It felt like ten years ago that Hudson was resisting me at every turn. He still resisted me, but not as often when it came to color choices and toning down the excessive use of his favorite dark cherry wood cabinets and desk.

"I know. They're here now," I yelled into the phone to Justin, plugging one of my ears with my finger to try to hear better as the hubbub around me grew louder. Yet another contractor banged a hammer against some surface. The noise indicated change and excitement for me, but I noticed that Hudson was struggling with the noises. Or maybe it was the changes.

I had moved a few of my overnight belongings into his room and bathroom. It happened bit by bit, without me even thinking about it, but my nightly tiptoeing down to his room had become normal somehow. Whatever guilt we felt, we never talked about. Life was busy. I figured we'd have to have 'the talk' one of these days.

I felt my phone buzzing. I looked at it and saw Joanna calling me. "Look, I've got it under control. I promise you." I said a few niceties and then hung up the call with Justin. But by the time I tried to take Joanna's call, she had already ended the call.

"Damn," I swore. Then I heard the most unexpected sound of the day coming from the open front door.

"Holy cow! This is a madhouse, Madeline!"

I jumped and gasped, a hand going over my heart. "Oh my God, Joanna! I didn't know you were here already! You sneaky thing, you. Wait a minute – you've got a hotel room, you said, how did you even know where I was?"

I pulled my best friend in for a hug and squeezed her tight. Seeing her here made my heart feel much lighter. All the work and noise was terribly exciting, but it was also terribly chaotic. Joanna brought some sense of peace into my world.

A guilty look crossed her face. "Ugh. You'll be so mad. But I told Jon I was meeting you for drinks tonight at the hotel where I'm staying. He suggested I surprise you instead and gave me the address."

I started to speak, but she held up a hand to stop me. "I know. You're mad. But Jon has been putting some effort into building a brother-sister friendship with me. He's actually being nice, Maddie! Imagine that. I still can't stand him, but I think he's sad that he lost you and I think he's sad about how things ended."

She looked so hopeful at her own words that I didn't have the heart to remind her that this was her extreme narcissist brother we were talking about – the one who lied to me so many times that I lost all faith he had the capacity for truth in him at all.

I was terrified that Jon knew where I was. "Well, you certainly surprised me," I told her, my voice shaky.

"Are you mad?" she prodded.

She looked so guilty that I decided to drop it for the night. I knew that Joanna didn't mean any harm. I made a mental note that I should tell Hudson. Sighing, I told her, "No, of course not." I drew her in for a hug. "I'm always happy to see you."

The topic was dropped and Joanna proved very helpful, seeming to love bossing the delivery men around and then making two sweet lemonades.

The noise died down around six, but Hudson and Kenzie were still not home. This wasn't unusual. Hudson didn't like the chaos, and he didn't want Kenzie to have to deal with it, either. But it had been making me feel like we were less than a 'family' and more like an employer and employee.

Joanna looked around the living room. The old furniture had been donated except for the pieces that still worked with the new design and the walls had fresh, bright paint on them.

"Wow, this place looks amazing. I'd love to live here. Where's your room?" she asked. All afternoon, in between the lemonade and the bossing around, she had poked her nose in every room. It was cute.

I pointed. "Down the hallway."

She laughed at me. "You expect me to believe you stay all the way down there when I saw the master suite was at the other end of the house." She winked.

I just gave her a look, but she grabbed my arm and pulled me to the room. She made a big deal about being exhausted, falling back onto the bed. "How do you even survive such hard work! I'd rather be an attorney any day. All I do is sit on my butt behind a desk and use my big ol' brain to solve other people's problems." She laughed.

"Well, most of what I do is also just use my big ol' brain, silly you." I laughed and fell onto the bed next to her.

"Oh my God, that reminds me. After you left NY and the rest of us stayed with Stacy, I ran into a lady I used to work for before she retired. She's got this huge estate in Park City, Utah. I totally bragged all about you and how great you were and that she absolutely had to hire you to redo her place. She bought it as an investment, she said, so it hasn't been updated in a while."

I sighed. "So much work to do."

She nudged me. "Oh, shush. How do we make this happen? I love Park City. I'll come visit you. And this is what we'll always do – you get the fun jobs out of state and I'll just come out for a weekend to distract you with good times!" she laughed.

I rolled over to look at her. "You're the best, you know that. I'd love the opportunity. I'll run it by Justin. If the lady wants to hire me through J&W and they want the portfolio project for me, I'm in."

She groaned. "So much red tape. You should just open your own design firm."

I shook my head. "Yeah? And it's just that easy, huh?" I snapped my fingers.

"We should go out. Dinner and drinks. My treat. Let me get cleaned up – where is my suitcase?" She spotted it in the corner. "Then we'll go to dinner and then you can drop me off at my hotel. It'll be fun to go out with you!"

I considered it, then an idea came to mind. "Oh, let's go to the restaurant I'm working on. My dad set it up and J&W jumped at the chance. It's a real hot spot in South Miami. The manager, Matt, is a cutie – just your type, I think. All muscle and big smiles." I did my best rendition of a cheesy grin.

She threw a pillow at me. "I'm too busy for a man. Let's just go have fun!"

When we left an hour later, Hudson still hadn't come back. I knew Kenzie was at an afterschool event so she wouldn't be home till later, but the fact that he hadn't returned bothered me. He knew Joanna was coming into town tonight. I would have hoped he'd have tried to make it home before I was scheduled to go out to meet her. I did my best to hide my disappointment as I drove Joanna and I to the restaurant and bar.

I chattered all the way about the house plans and the budget, more to keep my mind off of Hudson's silence than anything else.

Finally, I couldn't take what felt like him ghosting me. After I parked the car, I sent him a quick text letting him know that I was on my way to the restaurant with Joanna and for him to join us if he wanted to.

Ten minutes later, his text came back. We were just being shown to our table, Matt nowhere in sight. I stared at my phone.

He was griping about the changes in his home – changes he had signed off on! Then he asked me why I chose that place of all the places to take my friend.

"Everything okay?" Joanna asked me, after she ordered us drinks.

I fixed my face, painting on a smile. I wouldn't let Hudson ruin my evening. He'd become a little standoffish during the daytime, only letting me in emotionally at night. I knew he had PTSD, but I also knew that he had agreed to his house being turned upside down. I was feeling resentful that he was seemingly taking out his feelings on me like this.

I flipped my phone over after putting it on DND. I wasn't going to let him control my emotions. Joanna had paid for her flight and hotel here and I was going to show her a good time.

"Here are the pics that I got from Gloria just now – I hope you don't mind that I literally texted her as soon as you showed interest. You know me, if I don't do something right away, I'll just forget to do it completely."

I reached over and squeezed Joanna's hand. She was the total opposite of Jon. I often couldn't even believe that they were siblings. She was sunshine while he was a dark shadow looking for ways to use people and get ahead.

"Are you sure you're okay? You have that look on your face you got after my brother screwed you over." She frowned. "Which I will always be sorry about, by the way, no matter how nice he is to me to make up for all the shitty things he's said to me since we were kids."

I knew the look she was talking about. My dad described it as a haunted look, as if the rug had been pulled out from under my feet and I had been left in a perpetual free fall. I hated the feeling of being lost that Jon's betrayal had given me.

I squared my shoulders. Hudson was nothing like Jon. He was just going through some pretty big triggers right now. I should remember that and keep it all in perspective. Still, I could feel the weight of resentment creeping in on me, weighing down my shoulders even as I tried to sit upright and feel good.

I focused on the photos Gloria had sent to Joanna, oohing and aahing over the beautiful home and its even more perfect backyard.

Then, a muscled man made his way to our table, his eyes fixed on Joanna. I smirked. This was Matt. I'd only met him twice – the first time was when my dad and I had stopped by so I could get the lay of the land, so to speak, before the project started. The second time was when my dad, Hudson and I had come by.

Hudson had made it extremely clear that he did not like Matt. He was so jealous every time I spoke to the guy, let alone even looked at him. It was cute, sort of.

"Well, hello, you gorgeous ladies. Anything you order tonight is on the house. So, enjoy." He grinned at each of us. He really was a handsome guy, objectively speaking, but totally not my type.

He looked at me. "You ready for the project? You're starting any day now, right?"

I started to answer him and then noticed him looking around. "Where's that old guy who was in here with you and Harry? Is he your bodyguard or something?"

I saw it all clearly then – that's how people perceived me being with Hudson? They just thought that it was me with that "old guy"? I wasn't sure if I should feel offended or thankful to know how Hudson and I came across when we were out in public. *Was our age gap really that obvious to everyone but the two of us? And more than that, should I even care?*

I suddenly felt like my dad was right all along in insisting that I take a nice, long break after Jon cheated on me. He'd tried to drill it into my head that I needed to heal, that I was vulnerable after such an intense breakup.

I had a sinking feeling deep in my bones that maybe Dad was right. I'd jumped into another emotional attachment with another man – a way too off-limits man twice my age – way too fast. But for now, I was also certain that I needed Hudson to protect me. In the back of my mind, I hadn't stopped thinking about what Joanna said about Jon knowing my address.

Whether I'd jumped into things too fast or not, I was glad I had a former Navy SEAL on my side.

Nineteen
Hudson

"Still here?" Linda asked me, looking tired but happy. She was what one might call a good soldier. Patient, loyal, and fiery to the very end. I'd never known her to quit on a project or leave work early since she started working for me.

I glanced at the clock on the wall of my office. It was after nine o'clock. I fought back a scowl. I bet Madeline and her friend were still having a jolly good time without me down at the bar where Matt worked.

I was being unreasonable, the logical part of my brain kept telling me. But I couldn't keep the images of her laughing and smiling up at the muscled gym-bro out of my mind. I hated the thought of that guy getting any thoughts in his head about Madeline.

But she wasn't my girlfriend. My opinions and worries on the topic seemed over the top, even to me, in my rational moments. I would have felt like a total douchebag if I'd gone to her and sat her down like a little child, insisting she not talk to, or grin up at, that guy. I raked a hand through my hair.

It came down to whether or not I trusted her. I trusted Kenzie's mom once, and look where that got me.

"Sir?" Linda said, in her efficient way.

I looked up at her, eyebrow raised. "Yeah, I'm just finishing up that new project. If we develop the condo community, that will max out our portfolio in commercial real estate, correct?"

She suddenly looked a little tired. "Honestly, I have been so deep in the weeds with the reunion, that I haven't been on top of much else."

I felt a wave of guilt rush through me. Linda has been cheerfully burdening the responsibilities of my Navy SEALs boot camp graduation reunion along with her regular duties. And why? Because I was taking forever to heal and work through my triggers, work through the grisly images stuck in my mind from my days in active war zones.

"I want you to know you will be receiving a generous bonus for your hard work." It was poor compensation, indeed, for all the time and good energy she'd put into the project.

She smiled tiredly. "That is very kind of you. Honestly, I'd love to come to your event, if I may. Harry tells me they planned a slideshow to honor each graduate who died. It's going to be such a touching way to memorialize each fallen soldier."

I perked up at that. "Really? As you know, I've been out of the loop." I waited for the familiar rush of panic to come through me. Photos of each man we lost would normally send me snapping the black band around my wrist to focus on anything but my racing thoughts. But today, I only felt Linda's sincerity, and I saw her admiration for my lost brothers-in-arms. It gave me strength.

"Oh, yes. It's going to be accompanied by a short testimonial from each of their family members who want to speak. I cried when I saw the first draft of it – I can't imagine how heartwarming it will be once it is finished. Each man was so brave, Hudson. You were lucky to have gone through boot camp with so many good souls." She nodded reflectively. "I would hope to be as brave as each of them one day, if the need arose. I can't imagine being so noble as to rush into the face of danger for the safety of us all back home."

We remained in respectful silence as the truth of her words went into my mind like a warm balm, calming my fears and reminding me of the other side of my grief – there was also pride. There was also admiration. And there was also inspiration from their courage. I looked up at Linda.

"Thank you. I needed to hear that."

She just looked at me blankly, not knowing my struggles, not knowing why I had nothing to do with the planning of this reunion.

She didn't need to know. She was just a faithful and loyal employee with a good heart. But Madeline needed to know. My heart sank again. If only she wasn't out on the town tonight with that Matt guy.

"Here are the final invoices for the reunion." She placed a file on my desk. "And here are the initial reports your PA wanted you to take a look at. I guess we are looking at that old shopping mall near Boca Raton?" She laughed dryly. "If you can save that old place, well, my hat goes off to you. It's a dying area and malls are a dying form of shopping."

She smiled politely and bid me a good night. After she left, I eyed the shopping mall file, picking it up and looking through it.

She's right. Shopping malls are losing popularity. But it was in such a nice area and the building was so well made, I just really wanted to save it if I could. I pondered my options as I looked through the layout, the HVAC system, the security, and every other detail.

An idea formed in my mind. I wanted to run it by Madeline. Why? I didn't know. It wasn't in her wheelhouse of design, but somehow I knew she would be able to trust her instincts and tell me if it was a good idea or not.

"You've got to get over this damn jealousy," I told myself out loud. I knew I was avoiding going home. I didn't want to be sitting at home waiting for her when she got back late tonight.

But if I hurried now, I might make it back in time to read Kenzie a bedtime story – she didn't always let me do that now that she was a big girl.

I'm being dumb, playing these games.

I stood to my feet, picked up the files, put them in my briefcase and then locked up the building, door by door, as I left.

The security company I hired had assigned one guy to my office space, and I didn't see him on my way out, which wasn't that unusual. I approved the patrol routes the guys would take, whoever was on duty just following the patrol of the building rather than doing much in the way of critical thinking.

I thought about Jon and his little threat to Madeline. Maybe I should have increased security here at the office, too. If Jon was bad enough of a human to destroy Madeline emotionally – which she has recovered from most admiringly – then he would likely not think twice about messing with me at home... or at work.

I whistled as I walked to my car, the Miami heat a welcome reminder of the ever-present feeling of summer that Florida provided.

But then I stopped. Something felt off. I couldn't explain it. I never could explain it in the SEALs when I was the first one to know danger was approaching. Some called it a spidey sense. I called it good training.

I continued to whistle, knowing that if I stopped, I would tip off whoever was staring at me from somewhere in the shadows that I was onto them.

I took my time walking, casually looking up as if to check for rain but really I was scanning that part of the parking lot. All clear.

I pretended to fumble with my briefcase for a moment, affording me a look over another part of the parking lot. All clear.

My car was the only one parked. I cursed myself for being so relaxed. My car wasn't even under a streetlight. It was near the front door.

I didn't even remember when I started choosing convenience over safety. Always parking under the streetlights— that's the most basic rule of personal safety when out in public. Cameras could spot you with clearer images and people were less likely to attack you if you were under a light.

I studied the vehicle as I approached it. I didn't see evidence of tampering with my tires. I did a quick scan of the interior. All clear.

Maybe I was being paranoid. It happened. I'd been triggered quite a bit lately. This could just be an overflow from that. I casually opened the backseat, out of my norm, and put the briefcase there. I could now say without a doubt that no one was lying in wait for me in my car.

Interesting. Not a sound to be heard other than the noises I was making. And not a soul in sight, but I knew I was being watched.

I got in my car and started the engine, idling just long enough to pretend to check my phone, but really I was scanning the area around me.

Nothing moved. No sounds. I tried to ignore the bad feeling that I had as I slowly pulled out of my spot.

"There you are, you little spy, you," I muttered, as a nondescript Honda pulled out of an adjacent parking lot. Any untrained person would not have noticed it, but I was trained to notice everything.

I might be a little rusty after years of living a civilian life, but I knew I had a tail on my car when I saw it.

I did a few low stakes maneuvers down side streets and doubled back once just to check, and sure enough the car was still behind me. He kept between three and five cars between us, which told me this is no amateur. It was hard to do a tail from that distance... unless there was a tracker on my car.

I decided that there likely was a tracker on my car or he'd hacked into my phone, depending on the type of adversary I was now dealing with.

In either case, there was no point in dilly dallying. This guy knew who I was and where I lived already; of that, I could be sure.

Once I was home, I noticed that Madeline was still out and my daughter was asleep.

I felt unsettled by the tail that dropped off only a block from my house. I was starting to think that he wanted me to see him. He wanted to toy with me. And he did.

I walked around my home, checking every window and every door.

Then I logged in to my home security. He was smart enough to evade the cameras with his car.

I called the security company's twenty-four-hour hotline for my office. They told me that no suspicious persons or activity had taken place in the past two weeks on my office property.

Then I went through the difficult process of checking on each of my active investment properties. But at the end of it all, there was nothing.

That was bad news for me. That confirmed to me again that this guy was not some random person trying to get to me. This guy had skills. And I had to figure out how to get him to stop before my daughter noticed anything was wrong. Or Madeline.

Twenty
Madeline

Joanna had returned home, and I'd turned over the reins of the home renovation project to contractors to finish up the interior of Hudson's home.

Life should be going back to normal. At least, that's what I told myself after the second night I got home late after working in the restaurant.

I could tell Hudson was being strange, and I knew he hadn't liked how much I'd been around Matt, but he wasn't a child, like Jon. That woman I'd heard him on the phone with could have been anyone, even a coworker. He wasn't the type to be vengeful.

The budget for the restaurant renovation was a bit smaller than what J&W had initially been told when we took on the project, so that design update would mostly consist of new furniture and lots of new décor and paint. It would help the place look classy, but it wouldn't be the vision of change and modern elements that I had hoped for.

It was early morning and I was ready to go to the restaurant to capture some images before the place opened. I needed to spend a good amount of time documenting paperwork today and updating my design portfolio. J&W sent out a company portfolio as well as an individual portfolio when pitching their services or when attempting to close a deal.

Keeping my projects up to date was crucial for me to show that I was more than just a new designer. I wanted everyone to be impressed enough to believe that I could take their project from ground zero all the way to something special.

I tiptoed over to Hudson's office door to knock but I could hear him on the phone with someone in his office. I had wanted to touch base and make sure we were okay, sit with him and drink coffee. But now I'd have to drive through someplace and get coffee. Or just swipe some at the restaurant. I just talked to him, with a bit of a louder voice, through the door, "I'm going to the restaurant!" I didn't hear a response.

I backed out and started down the street, almost hitting a gray Honda. The guy behind the wheel had a hoodie on and big sunglasses.

I chuckled sarcastically. "Nothing says 'I'm hungover' quite like that look you've got going on there, buddy."

Instead of being mad that we almost collided, the guy —overdressed for Miami heat in a dark hoodie and sunglasses— just paused and waited for me to pass. Then he pulled into the driveway, backed out and drove off the way he came. It struck me as odd. But the world was full of odd people.

I received a welcome phone call on my drive. "Joanna!" I said. "I miss you, girl. How is the law treating you?"

"Uh oh," she replied. "This is the exact type of fake happy you had in your voice whenever you and Jon were having issues, which was basically all the time."

I sighed. She knew me too well. "I'm overworked, underslept, and just tired. Kenzie started swimming lessons, so she has practice after school most days. I rarely see her. It sucks. But she'll only get busier the older she gets." I hoped my diversion tactic worked on my friend.

"I'm sorry. Hopefully, you're not too worn out for that Utah project, though." Her tone was bright and chipper. I needed this today. I was so glad she called.

"Really? What's new?" I sat up a little straighter in my seat. "I could use some good news today."

"Well, Gloria was approached by an architectural magazine. I guess by your boss, Justin, right?"

"Right."

"Well, Justin is your new best friend because he was at a networking event and connected with the editor for the magazine. Catch this – Gloria agreed to let her home be featured in the magazine with a before and after photo spread. Can you imagine it? Your work in a huge magazine!"

I almost pulled over, I was so excited to hear this. "I hadn't heard a word about it! When did she tell you?"

Joanna laughed. "Like five minutes ago. She talked with the magazine people this morning, so I doubt even Justin knows that she said yes."

"Wait." My mind raced, putting together the pieces of what she was saying. It was all coming so fast. "This is insane."

"Yeah, girl, get excited. He just opened up a whole new career world for you by putting that house forward. This could be career changing for you. You know that, right?" She was gushing, her voice, now, stern and excited. She wanted me to appreciate the moment.

But I was worried, my thoughts snapping to how she had worded it. He put forward the *house*, not me. "What if they take the project from me and give it to a more senior person?"

She laughed dismissively. "Oh, honey, don't you worry about that. The way I talked you up, Gloria has insisted she work with you on the project directly. She looked at your portfolio, and she is certain she wants you. This will be your project! No one else's."

I let out a sigh, relieved and afraid all at once. A huge step forward for me...and so much responsibility.

I chirped, "I cannot thank you enough for giving me this connection. I owe you something big, Joanna. I mean it, like a trip to the Maldives or something crazy awesome!"

Inside, a storm of insecurity was brewing, but I couldn't show it.

She laughed again, delighted with me. "Yeah. You do." I could hear the teasing in her voice. "Look, I've got to get to work. Just wanted to give you a heads-up! The next few years are going to be great for you! This opportunity is just one. I bet there will be more."

I ended the call, beaming in spite of my anxieties. This was good news. I might be afraid to fail, but that only meant that I had been given a chance to succeed.

Then, as if on cue, my phone rang again and this time it was Justin.

"Hi, I just heard that you networked with Architectural Digest Magazine! Justin, that is so awesome!"

He laughed in a way that didn't quite sound genuine. I felt anxious right away. Did he want to take the Park City gig but then was surprised when Gloria wouldn't let him?

"Yeah. What a surprise that you were tight with the home's owner. You do know this is a twelve-bedroom mansion with ten bathrooms, a pool, a tennis court, and an entire outdoor terrace to entertain wealthy guests? It is a huge undertaking." His tone was cordial, but I felt he was more than hinting that it was too much for me to take on.

"Yes, I remember that from an earlier conversation about the project."

An awkward silence sat between us. This one was, I think, from a sense of jealousy, or maybe he thought it was unfair that I'd be in the magazine and not him, as he is my senior.

I pulled up to the restaurant, my good mood quelled. "Is there anything you need?" I ask him, politely. I needed coffee and five minutes of peace before I started my work day.

He sounded unsure, but he told me quietly, "No. If you think you can handle it, you think you can handle it."

I was getting tired of all the men in my life underestimating me; Jon calling me to tell me to break up with Hudson, Hudson's seemingly jealous disgust over Matt, and then my dad.

I blurted out, "I can handle it! Thanks," and, without waiting for his response, hung up, readying myself to go in and finally –finally– get a cup of coffee.

I wish I had just seen Hudson this morning to nip whatever awkwardness was festering in the bud. I wish I could read his mind and figure out what he was thinking.

Part of me felt like maybe I was imagining it. Maybe we had just missed each other for a couple of days. I had been working late nights at the restaurant, and he usually went to sleep early so he could see Kenzie off to school in the morning.

Maybe we were just exiting the fantasy part of the relationship –or whatever you could call this– and this is what it would really be like to be together.

I steeled my nerves and called him. The phone rang for a couple of rings, and then he answered, his voice clipped. "Madeline, where are you? I didn't see you this morning."

"I called for you. I let you know where I was going."

"And where did you go?" he repeated, his voice gruff. He sounded angry with me. *But why?*

"The restaurant."

"Matt's restaurant," he corrected me.

Is this what his mood is about?

I rolled my eyes as I got out of the car and slammed the door, just to make myself feel better.

"Mhm, Matt's restaurant, which I have been assigned to, just like I've been assigned to your place!" I instantly felt my stomach drop. That wasn't the right thing to say.

"*Just* like you've been assigned to my place?" he repeated.

"I didn't mean it like that." I walked into the restaurant and into the kitchen to help myself to some of their awful, bitter coffee.

Matt grinned and greeted me, "Well, hello! Look who's here early!" His eyes roved up and down my body, and I flinched. Maybe Hudson was right to have some of his jealousy. Matt wasn't exactly an angel.

Hudson must have heard Matt because he snapped, "Sure seems like it. I haven't seen you in days. You've been so busy with *Matt*." He spit Matt's name out like an insult.

"Look, I *did* try to talk to you this morning. *I* called *you*. I was trying to check in on you *because* I haven't seen you in days. You have got to learn how to start trusting me, Hudson. I've got to go." I hung up quickly, wincing as I did. Hudson had gone through so much with his ex, but that didn't make it fair to take it out on me.

"Trouble in paradise?" Matt asked me, pouring me a cup of coffee.

I sighed and looked at the mug instead of him. I didn't know what to say about it anymore. Whatever little slice of paradise we'd carved out together when I first arrived was gone.

"It's just the project," I lied. "He wants it to be done faster. He thinks I'm spending too much time on your project." I looked up and met his eyes. I could tell by his smirk that he knew it was a lie.

"Sure. Well, look, if you ever need someone to...talk to...I'm here." I blushed, uncomfortable with all the male attention I'd been getting lately.

If I was uncomfortable, I could only imagine how Hudson was feeling.

Twenty-One
Hudson

"I am ready, Harry." I still had not left for work yet. I might as well have just worked from home today.

I kept waiting for the typical chaos of the contractors to show up, but the house was blessedly quiet. A cleaning crew was there, but that wasn't unusual; I had cleaners come every week.

"Good. Let me know of any last minute things that come up. I saw you took over some of the email communications with our vendors – is everything okay with Linda?" he asked.

"All good. I just decided to put her back on her regular tasks. I'm taking over to give her a break."

The absolute truth was that after my late night conversation with her, I had a change of heart and a burst of courage. I was facing my demons and it felt great.

Of course, the three times I've seen that same Honda with expired plates since that night outside my office had left me paranoid.

It was crazy how one part of life could fall into focus, like with the reunion, and I could feel so good about it, only to see another part of my life crumble, like my paranoia about being followed.

I told myself if I saw that Honda once more, I'd hire a PI. I was still struggling to decide if it was coincidence or intentional.

My gut told me the latter, but if that were true then that would open up a whole mess of problems that would take me back to watching my every step the way I did after the SEALs. I thought I'd left that sort of life behind me. We were trained to always watch our backs. It took a lot of effort to actually deprogram myself from that.

"How's my daughter, Hudson?" Harry asked, casually.

"She's at the restaurant right now," I said evasively. "She seems to be doing great work there, too. Have you talked to that Matt guy recently? I haven't had time to stop by so he would know better than me how she's getting along out there." I forced a friendly edge to my voice.

"You trust him?" Harry asked. He didn't say it, but what he meant was do I trust him to be alone with Madeline.

Little did Harry know, it was me he had to worry about when it came to Madeline's heart. I felt my loyalty waver – who was I actually loyal to in this mess of emotions between Madeline and me? Harry? Or her? And why did I have to choose?

"I think he doesn't want to lose his job, Harry," I said cajolingly. "He won't try anything with her. I'm pretty sure about that." And I meant it. Guys like Matt would push the line but they wouldn't be likely to cross it unless it was safe to do so.

"I'd like it if you just stopped by. If you can. Unannounced. I don't trust that kid with my daughter. I saw the way he looked at her that day I went over there with her. He was better behaved when you were there."

I gulped. *Did Matt pick up on the connection between Madeline and me and that was why he kept his distance when I was in the building?*

"Sure thing, Harry. I wouldn't mind taking a trip down there."

"Good, that would set my mind at ease, brother. Thanks."

I chewed my bottom lip and then I asked a question I'd been holding onto for several days.

"Hey, so, I heard from Linda about that slideshow or a video of some sort about the guys we lost?" I was surprised that I could talk about this topic without feeling a rush of survivor's guilt. It felt good.

Harry sighed. "Look, I know you don't think I see it. But I do. I know how hard it is to survive when we lost so many. I didn't want to tell you because I didn't want to trigger you."

I felt like I was blindsided by a semi-truck.

"How did you know?" I paused. "Doesn't it hit you hard, too, to see their faces, to remember how strong and alive they were before we lost them?"

"Sure, of course, it does. But we can't let it stop us from living. They wouldn't want that for us, Hudson. You know this. I was going to tell you a few minutes before the ceremony started. I figured you would walk out for some fresh air and then come on back in once it was done. Was I wrong?"

I hesitated. "No. You were operating with what you knew. But I've been working on myself. Like we talked about – it never stops, right? And I think I'm looking forward to this year's reunion. Honestly, I think it's going to be a really good experience. And thank you. Thank you for putting that video together. It'll mean a lot to their families."

Harry paused. "You really have come a long way. I'm proud of you, brother. I look forward to coming back with the missus to Miami and seeing you and my little girl at the reunion."

I hadn't thought about that – since Madeline was still here working on a new project, I guessed she would attend this year. Typically, she hadn't been coming the last several years.

"Sounds good, Harry."

"Keep up the good work," he said, and then we ended the call.

Talking to Harry was a good reminder of what a good person he had raised. He was a good man with a good heart and a good daughter who only wanted the best for me.

And I had snapped at her out of my own fears. It wasn't fair to her, but even her dad seemed to see that Matt guy for what he was. And we all knew what kind of guy Jon was.

I knew I had pushed her patience, but I was hopeful that we could talk things through, no matter where we landed afterward.

Unfortunately, all the shiny feelings I had had about her after my conversation with her dad went out the window as the hours ticked by. Madeline stayed at the restaurant much longer than I had anticipated and I grew impatient waiting for her. I pushed off the kitchen island and walked to the front door, hearing the door to the garage open up into the house. Kenzie was home. I could hear her cheerful banter right away.

Whatever conversation Madeline and I needed to have would have to wait.

"Kenz, let's get your homework done so we can do something fun," I called out to my daughter.

"Where's Madeline?" she asked instantly, the pout on her face evident. It had been days since she'd seen her, and she was perceptive. She could pick up on the change.

I could forgive Madeline for whatever was going on between her and Matt, but I couldn't forgive her for hurting my daughter in the process.

Kenzie had grown to expect her around. That was at least partially my fault, I knew. I should have put up more boundaries, made the lines clearer before letting Kenzie get attached.

I knelt down. "She's at work, honey. You know she's our interior designer, right, Kenz? She's not Daddy's girlfriend." I looked away when I said it. I had called her my girlfriend so easily at the beach. Now, suddenly, I wanted to make it clear to my daughter that she wasn't. I had dropped the ball.

"I know…" she looked down at the ground as she dropped her backpack by her feet. "So she's not coming back?"

"She'll come back. It's just we can't expect her to be around forever. Okay?"

"Okay." She looked crushed, and I felt a stab to my heart. This was the result of my betrayal of Harry. I had hurt Kenzie, and now I had to hurt, too.

"Hey, let's have a pizza party by the pool!" I grabbed her forearms and rustled her a little.

"Okay!" she yipped. Kids are resilient, at least. She would bounce back if this thing with Madeline went sour, which it was looking like it might.

The night was not at all fun for me. Kenzie seemed to enjoy the pizza making party and the time out back by the pool, but I kept checking my phone for a message from Madeline. My ears pricked at every noise, thinking it might be Madeline coming in through the door.

I kept thinking she was down at that bar with Matt, giggling and cooing up at him. Part of me wanted to get in my car and drive down there and confront them both.

As darkness fell and it grew closer to eight o'clock, I had played around with the idea long enough. I asked the nanny to put Kenzie to bed for me, apologizing to her that I would be there to tuck her in the next day, and I got in one of my cars and turned on the engine.

I drummed my fingers on the steering wheel. I felt jealous rage fill me. How dare that Matt guy put a finger on Madeline! I'd all but decided that that was exactly what was going on.

I pulled out of the garage and started the drive down to the bar where Madeline was renovating it. I grumbled at her dad for setting this whole thing up for her.

I was losing all rational thought at that point. My paranoia was so strong that even flicking my bracelet was no help at all. I was convinced she and Matt were an item. And that was that. I was a fool to trust her.

When I stepped inside, I glared around me. The music was muted compared to the last time I was here.

A pretty young lady looked over at me as I walked in. "Hi, how many in your party?" She looked behind me.

"Oh, I was just here... I was just looking for the interior designer."

Matt appeared out of nowhere, eyeing me curiously. "What's good, my man?" he said in his too-friendly tone. "Looking for V?"

I gaped at him. *Since when did he call Madeline by a nickname?*

"I'm looking for *Madeline*," I growled out. This guy was obnoxious in every way.

He smirked at me. "What's your problem, big guy?" he asked, up in my face like a jock with too much testosterone.

I took a breath. "Don't get cozy with contractors. That's a lesson you should know by now," I said, trying not to look personally interested in his life choices.

"Right. A lesson I'm sure you've learned, right?" Matt asked, with a wink and a smirk. I wanted to punch that smirk off his tan face.

Madeline popped out from the back, looking flustered. "Hudson, what are you doing here?"

"I'm looking for you," I grumbled at her, grabbing her hand. I put the car keys into her palm. "Go to the car and wait for me."

She looked at me like I had grown another head. "I'm not –" She tried to give me back the keys. "I'm at work.

You need to leave." She looked desperately between me and Matt, and I almost felt bad for a second.

Matt turned to her. "V, you need to get out more," he said. "Meet new people. Hanging around an old man like that will kill your spirit, you know?"

"Don't call me V," Madeline said quickly, holding an arm out to me like she might be able to hold me back.

Matt kept going, turning to me. "You're a friend of her old man's, right? You like a second father to her or what?"

"Doesn't really matter. Either way, I'm about to fuck you up," I told him, losing myself.

Matt took a step back from me, seeing the fire in my eyes, but it was too late for him to back out of the fight now.

"I'm not into your girl, dude, if that's what this is about. You can chill. She's not really my type. I'm more into models."

In a way, it was what I wanted to hear. I didn't want Matt to be into Madeline. But the way he so casually tossed the idea that he was with her aside, acting like there was someone more beautiful than her, enraged me further.

I lost all sense of composure. It was like I watched myself as my fist connected with his eye, my knuckles pushing into the soft tissue as he flung his hands up too late. When he covered his face, I came in with an elbow to his chin next, and he crumpled then, cowering into a ball in the corner.

He looked at me like I was an idiot or a monster, both of which I maybe was. His hand had blood on it, and he looked over at Madeline with shock. "Your dude just fuckin hit me!"

Madeline's eyes flew in my direction. "Yeah. He did," she said plainly, unsure of what to do.

I took her hand and pulled her out of the restaurant, leaving Matt on the floor, tending to his wounds.

"You can bill me for your doctor's visit," I told him as I left.

Twenty-Two
Madeline

I had managed to calm Hudson down enough to convince him to let me take my rental car back to the house instead of abandoning it. We'd gone to our separate areas, taking a much-needed break from each other.

Now at the house, I heard his steps approach the room where I was staying. I held my breath. He lingered outside the door for a moment.

"We should talk," his deep voice said from the other side of the door.

"Come in." I turned from the door, looking out the wide wall of windows that spilled out over the backyard. It was lit up, as it was every night, with gentle lighting, the new security cameras and floodlights ready to flick on at any moment. Hudson's once-careful protection of me to install the cameras made me sadder still.

"Madeline," he said. He stood just inside the door, his reflection in the window almost as sexy as the real thing.

"You came over and started a fight. You could have cost me my job. Who knows, maybe you did. How dare you? What I do is my business, not yours," I spat out, ready to fight already.

"It *is* my business," he insisted angrily, running a hand through his hair. "You are my business. Are you mine or not?"

"No, Hudson, I'm not! I'm my own person!" I was getting frustrated. I liked it when he called me his, but this was too far. He couldn't literally mean that I was his. I stared at him. His narrowed eyes burned holes into mine.

The room was quiet, save for the soft hum of the designer fan overhead. A fan I picked out and installed.

I was in a room that belonged to my father's best friend. And now, we were fighting after weeks of blissful sneaking around and making love.

I turned to the window, unable to look at Hudson. I rigidly stood by the window, my arms crossed tightly over my chest in an attempt at a self-hug. I stared out at the backyard lights.

I felt him watching me from across the room. I heard him sigh, his heart heavy. Matt's words about Hudson being old came back to my mind, unbidden.

What had I been thinking? This was wrong. I shouldn't have let myself fall for Hudson. The years between us had always been a point of private questioning, but tonight it felt like a chasm that had opened up.

I could see the tension of my own posture in the window's reflection, the way my shoulders were drawn up tight, as if I were bracing myself against the world… against him.

He cleared his throat, the fog seemingly lifting from his eyes. He sighed and ran a hand through his hair.

"Okay, I'm sorry. I know what I did was wrong. I lashed out at you, and at Matt, and you're right, I could have cost you your job. I'll fix that. But Madeline, you hurt Kenzie in trying to hurt me. You have more than just me to think about if you want to be…in this."

In this? Is that how he's referring to our relationship?

The thought of hurting Kenzie sat with me for a moment. I hadn't thought about her.

The anger deflated from me a little as I realized what I'd been doing. I'd been so caught up in work that I hadn't seen her. And tonight, when I'd considered if I wanted to be 'in this' at all and stayed at the restaurant...well, I'd been immature.

I dropped my crossed arms. "I didn't mean to."

"Madeline," he began, his voice rough, raw. I didn't turn around, but I saw the slight twitch of his hand, a sign that he was itching to be close to me. And against the odds, I wanted that right now. I shouldn't have. But I d id.

He took a step closer, cautious and careful. I felt my breath catch in my throat. "I'm sorry," he said, the words thick in his throat.

"I never wanted to hurt you. I should have talked to you. I was feeling..." He paused. Talking about feelings was hard for men like Hudson. "...insecure." He met my eyes. "I saw Matt, and I saw everything I wasn't, everything I thought maybe you deserved."

He was being so nice. He didn't have to explain anything about his past. I knew this rationally, but emotionally I was still upset. Relationships were hard!

I squeezed my eyes shut, fighting back sudden tears. I had promised myself I wouldn't cry over a man again. But his voice, the genuine regret in it, and the deep desire to make amends made my resolve waver. I felt my heart flicker between running and staying.

Slowly, I turned to face him, my eyes meeting his. "I know," I whispered, my voice barely audible. "But that was...scary. I'd never seen you like that."

The anger that seemed to have fueled me, and started the fight, was gone now, replaced by a deep ache that settled in my chest.

Hudson took another step towards me, and then another, until he was standing before me. Slowly he took my arms in his hands.

"I have a past, Madeline," he said softly, reaching down to gently take my hand in his. "The longer you're with me, the more of that you'll find out. I'm working on myself, but it's going to rear its ugly head occasionally. I used to drink a lot, fight, and had my fair share of women. I wasn't the man that you know now. I was so broken after Kenzie's mom left, and I drowned those sorrows in alcohol and women."

He raked a hand through his hair and continued, "Today, I let my fears get the better of me. I hadn't seen you in a couple of days, and it felt like you were spending a lot of time with Matt. I'm just... I'm afraid of losing you. You're otherworldly to me... the way you understand me and my trauma. But I feel as if I could blink and you'd just be... gone."

I looked up at him, surprised by the vulnerability in his voice. He was so strong. I couldn't believe he was harboring that fear. I could see the lines of worry etched into his face, lines that told stories of a life lived longer than mine, of experiences I hadn't yet had... and maybe never would.

I studied him. I had always admired his strength, the way he seemed to have everything figured out. But now, seeing him so exposed, I realized just how much he needed me, too.

"I don't plan to run away," I said, squeezing his hand. "I don't plan to finish this project and then just disappear.

But we have to talk to each other, really talk. I can't guess what you're thinking about us... or Matt."

He snorted at that.

I continued, "Or Kenzie's mom or anything else. Can we do better at talking?"

Hudson nodded and pulled me closer, wrapping his arms around me. There was nothing sexual in his touch. It was comforting, like a promise that we could learn to trust each other to be there, to listen.

I let him hold me, resting my head against his chest. We stood there in the quiet, holding onto each other as if we were the only two people in the world.

"I don't want to fight anymore," I murmured against his shirt, the fabric soft and familiar under my cheek. "I just want to go back to us against the world. I want to be okay."

"We will be," he promised, kissing the top of my head. "We'll figure this out together."

I felt his heart beating steadily beneath my ear, a comforting rhythm that grounded me.

I tilted my head up to look at him, my eyes searching his. "I believe you," I whispered, my voice full of emotion.

Hudson leaned down, capturing my lips in a kiss that was tender and full of promise. I felt myself melting into the kiss, my arms wrapping around his neck as I pulled him closer.

The fight, the anger, it all faded away, leaving only the connection we shared.

When we finally pulled apart, breathless and flushed, Hudson rested his forehead against mine. "I'll fix it with Matt, I promise. I'm sorry I did that."

"I'll be more sensitive about...Kenzie's mom. About how you feel afterward and about how she feels. I would never want to hurt that little girl. I messed up. I'll make it up to her. But you have to know I'm in this with you," I managed to say, the heat between my legs building.

He kissed me again and then pulled away. "Let's slow-walk this, okay?"

I knew he had a good point. It would be foolish to rush back into sex after a few big misunderstandings had stacked up between us that quickly. I nodded.

"Your reunion is coming up," I said. "My parents will be there so we can't really be close. And I have to go to Utah to get started on that project..." I sighed. I couldn't really see a future with him, and that hurt. He was here and I was going to be traveling all over the country for J&W.

"I know," is all he said. He gave me a small smile and then walked to the door. "I won't lock my door. But please don't feel obligated to be with me. I want you to take time to think about what you want, about your future."

I opened my mouth to aggressively protest his words, but he had gone. I knew he was trying to be the better person here. I knew he was trying to help me think with my head and not with my heart. I plopped onto the bed. My phone dinged with a new email.

Great, a distraction.

I didn't want to sit in this room all by myself right now. I opened the email I'd been waiting for for over a month.

I was shortlisted in the top twenty list of up and coming interior designers! I had submitted a piece for consideration in a house and home magazine at Justin's insistence. He had made the list himself seven years prior and he thought I should try, too.

"Oh my God! I made it!" I couldn't believe it. And there was only one person I wanted to tell right now. Hudson.

I read the email three times before jumping off the bed and scurrying down the hallway. I almost shrieked when I saw a car pull into the driveway.

Who the heck could it be at this hour?

I stared at the person dressed all in black. They didn't do much. Just got out of the car, turned on a flashlight and waved it around at the windows along the front of the house. I was frozen in place.

What the hell!

I clasped my phone to my chest. Why weren't the alarms going off? Why weren't the floodlights turning on?

The flashlight moved slower along the windows, coming to a stop right on me.

Twenty-Three
Hudson

"Stay put. I saw it, too!" I said to Madeline. What I didn't tell her was that I also saw a Honda in the driveway. The flashlight had flashed right into my bedroom windows.

This was not the work of someone trying to be discreet. This was the action of someone who wanted to send yet another message – they were watching me.

I dashed down the hallway and to the front door. Of course, by the time I got there, the car was gone. Madeline's hushed whisper sounded from behind me, she was hiding in the hallway.

"Who was that? Are they gone?"

I was on my phone, pulling up the security footage, but the cameras had not been triggered to turn on. I'd been hacked, despite the expensive system I had installed.

I took her hand in mine and together we walked every room of the house, except for the rooms where my daughter and the nanny were sleeping.

Madeline's footsteps were light as a feather as she clutched my arm and walked beside me. She didn't say anything, but her eyes were wide and alert. I felt terrible for offering her a place to stay only to have my gated home invaded in this way. I needed to keep her safe. To keep my daughter safe.

Once we were downstairs, I finally opened up. I admitted to seeing the Honda before and that I hired the best PI that money could buy to find out whose car it was and who would be interested in trying to scare me.

"It's probably just someone from the past when I was in the military," I said dismissively, not wanting to alarm her. "Things like this happen."

"Did you talk to my dad? Is someone also stalking him?"

I shook my head. "He hasn't said anything to me about it." I pulled her to me. "Stay here tonight. I don't think we should rush back together, but stay."

"I have so many questions," she protested the idea of sleeping. Then, her expression changed. She smiled shakily. "I guess I should tell you my good news."

She reached for her phone and opened the lock screen. She told me about this shortlist she was on, her cheeks pink with excitement.

I smiled at her. She was so young and she had so many things to look forward to. What was I thinking by stealing her heart? She deserved better than me.

As we drifted off to sleep, close but not entwined as we usually were, I felt my heart shattering. There was something about being called old and hitting Matt, that anger that was supposed to be a remnant of my past, all in one day that made me know I needed to pull back from Madeline romantically. I could still be there for her and support her... I rolled over. But who was I kidding? I couldn't pull back.

I felt so conflicted. I had no idea how to move forward.

***

I left Madeline sleeping soundly in my bed this morning. The reunion was this weekend and Linda had been blowing up my phone since eight o'clock reminding me of the last walk through today. The venue was set up for the event – my hotel. Who would have thought I'd ever be healed enough to be here?

As I walked into the lobby of the hotel and saw the welcome banner already erected and the two tables outside the ballroom with table top signage on them, a wave of nostalgia hit me. I kept my head down and went down the hallway to see the ballroom.

It had been a year since I last saw my old Navy SEAL buddies, and the thought of gathering with them again this weekend brought more than a little bit of apprehension. I'd been tasked by Linda with checking on the venue before the big reunion event, making sure everything was just right. I owed her a lot. She had put in hours with Harry for the event.

I paused to look at the large sign with all of our faces from bootcamp on it. I smirked. We looked so young. I wonder whose idea this image was? Probably Linda's. I chuckled. Somehow, I beat her here today. But I didn't mind. I needed the time to settle into the big feelings that were inevitable with an event like this for me.

The hotel – indeed, every part of my expensive life - was a far cry from the field tents we were used to back in the day during the rigorous parts of boot camp. Marble floors gleamed under the soft lighting, and the air was filled with the faint scent of expensive freshener and polished wood.

I adjusted the collar of my shirt, feeling a bit out of place in such a refined setting. But I reminded myself that this was a celebration, a time to reconnect with the men I had shared some of the toughest—and ultimately the most rewarding - experiences of my life.

Except for Kenzie. I smiled at that thought. Nothing could compare to fatherhood. Nothing.

I turned around and approached the front desk, where a young woman in a crisp uniform greeted me with a professional smile. "Good afternoon, sir. How can I assist you?" Then her eyes widened. "Oh! You're the owner. I'm sorry..."

"Hudson," Linda's voice sounded behind me. I turned from the young front desk attendant who must have seen me here before in executive meetings or the like.

"I'm here," I announced to Linda, forcing a smile. "Ready to check on the venue for the Navy SEAL reunion?"

"I'm surprised you are early," she replied, quickly scanning her tablet in her organized way. She breezed right by the front desk girl and together we walked back down the hallway where I just was. "Everything is in order. Would you like to see the ballroom or pop into a smaller meeting room and discuss the catering changes we had to make?"

Catering changes? That was a bit too much in the details for me. "Just the ballroom is fine, Linda."

She nodded and gestured for me to follow her. As we walked through the luxurious hallway, I took note of the opulence around me—crystal chandeliers, richly patterned carpets, and walls adorned with tasteful artwork.

It was a far cry from the brutally difficult environments we'd trained in, yet it felt right. We had earned this, all of us. After years of service and sacrifice, a night of comfort and camaraderie was well-deserved.

As to how I would get through the memorial of our fallen brothers... that was something I was still working on.

When we reached the ballroom, I opened the doors and stepped aside, allowing Linda to enter first. I followed suit, noticing every detail in the space.

"Wow!" I said, appreciatively. "You put your magic touch all over this, didn't you?" I praised her. The room was in the colors of the SEALs and many US flags and other Navy memorabilia were tactfully placed around the room.

She looked at me. "What better way to honor those who served?" She smiled sincerely.

The room was as expansive as I remembered it when I bought the place, but much fuller than it was the last time I was here. It had high ceilings and floor-to-ceiling windows that offered a breathtaking view of the city skyline. Round tables draped in white linen were set with gleaming silverware and crystal glasses, and in the center of the room was a long table, where I imagined the reunion speeches would be made.

I walked further into the room, my footsteps echoing slightly in the vast space. Linda gave a satisfied nod as she watched me. She knew she did well. Even though I'd scaled back her involvement to take over myself, the work she'd done before that was visible in everything.

"You deserve a raise," I teased her.

She nodded. "I won't say no to that!"

The evening was going to far surpass any of our other reunions from years gone by. I could almost see it now—my fellow grads, my fellow SEALs, older but still carrying that unmistakable air of brotherhood, gathered around these tables, laughing, reminiscing, maybe even shedding a tear or two.

Linda did a walk-through of her own and then returned, waiting by the door, giving me space to take it all in. I appreciated that. I needed this moment to absorb everything, to prepare myself for what was coming. This reunion was more than just our annual event; it had become something else for me since Madeline's arrival in my life. I saw it as a chance to reconnect with a part of myself that I had run away from, buried under the years of pain and loss that had come after my time in the SEALs.

I approached the dance floor and turned to survey the room. A wave of memories washed over me—missions, both successful and tragic, faces of brothers lost, and the bond that held firm among us over the decades. I reached one hand over for my bracelet, flicking it as big feelings coursed through me.

As I stood there, lost in thought, I realized how much my mind had shifted, how much I'd grown. This year was a defining year for me. More than I had realized prior to now.

And there was one shining light that had been the impetus for so much of it: Madeline.

I thanked Linda as we made our way back to the lobby. We went over the paperwork that was outstanding and confirmed any last minute details that she had questions about.

But under it all, I was seeing Madeline in my mind. Now was not the time to back away. Now was not the time to retreat. I needed to fight for her, for us.

Twenty-Four
Madeline

I knew Hudson had a big last minute meeting today with Linda at the hotel, but it was still disappointing to wake up alone. I was horny for him and not ashamed to admit that to myself.

"Ugh!" I said to myself as I drove to the restaurant. The kitchen in the restaurant had some sort of big issue, according to the restaurant owner. He had called me three times already this morning– not Matt, but the actual owner – that morning.

The kitchen had been redone, minimally but effectively, even though we were still working through the redo of the dining area and the back area.

"I'm hungry, thirsty, in need of coffee... and Hudson's..." I didn't say 'cock' out loud, even though that's what I was thinking. It had been days and days. After our little argument last night, I was hoping he'd wake me up to make up for it. But no, he ran off to his meeting. I chewed my bottom lip.

I pulled up to the restaurant. It looked empty. I knew from the owner's messages that he saw the issue on the cameras. Something about a flood or water? All I knew was that it was way too early for this. I knew that Matt was on his way, not that he'd be much help. If there was a leak, then we'd need a contractor out here.

My phone chirped with a text. "Just finished – where are you?" It was from Hudson with a smiley face. *Good*. I hoped he would work on his communication. I texted him back that Juan told me of an issue at the restaurant and that I was there.

I stepped out of the rental car, concern bubbling in my stomach as I approached the restaurant. Was Juan, the owner, exaggerating? Because everything looked normal.

I almost turned around and left but then, I gasped. The door was open.

What the hell?

I strode toward it then stopped. Was someone inside?

I fumbled for my phone only to see that I left it in the rental car. My eyes dropped to the ground around the restaurant. Dry as a bone outside. What was the water issue? Juan must have gotten it wrong.

But I did not sign up to walk into a burglary. The front door was ominously opened. I took a step forward. Juan had cameras inside, right? I would be fine. He wouldn't send me here to check on things if he'd seen an intruder.

Besides, this project had been both a joy and a pain – because of Hudson's barely hidden jealousy about Matt - for the past few months. Every detail, every design idea was mine. Sure, Justin had his own inputs, but the bones of the design were mine.

I got closer, stepping into the doorframe, half in and half out. I was no Nancy Drew, but something felt off. The air inside was heavy with a dampness that shouldn't have been there. The humidity was what you expect outside. Was it just from the open door? Why wasn't the AC kicking on?

I hesitated at the entrance, my hand on the door. A feeling of unease flooded me, but I shook it off. I was just tired, I told myself. The argument with Hudson last night messed with my good judgment. I was fine. He was fine. This place was fine. Everything was... fine, right?

I pushed the door open further and when I looked into the big room two steps down, my heart stopped.

"Shit."

Water. The pungent scent of old, rancid salt water. It was everywhere.

The polished wooden floors were submerged at least three inches under water, chairs and tables were lifted just slightly off the floor, and menus floated aimlessly in the water that gently massaged against the walls.

The custom lighting fixtures I had painstakingly chosen reflected off the surface of the water, creating an eerie feeling that chilled me through and through.

The pops of colorful wallpaper, the expensive brand I'd spent weeks finding, were curling and peeling, sodden and ruined at the bottom.

I reached for my phone again. "Damn it." I needed to take photos. I looked for the cameras. They were twisted, pointing to the ceilings. That turned my blood cold.

This was sinister. Somehow, someone had done this – on purpose!

I stepped into the kitchen, the sticky water coated with old grease sitting on the tiles soaked into my shoes. The impact of it, the shock of it, gave way to fear. My mind raced, trying to make sense of it. *How had this happened?*

I tilted my head. Was that heavy breathing I could hear? I froze. I wasn't alone. I heard another sound – water running. I noticed ripples in the water that started strongest in a corner under the metal sinks.

I sloshed over to it. I'd try to turn off the running water and then go get my phone. I'd call the police – I'd call Hudson! Fear gripped me. The memory of the beach with Hudson and Kenzie flashed through my head, and my body turned cold.

I stood for a moment, watching the water rise. It was three feet high already. How high would it get if I did nothing and waited for someone to come save me? I knew I couldn't let things get any worse.

I took a deep breath and stepped in. The water was freezing cold, not like the water at the beach, more like the water at the pool when I almost drowned as a kid.

My mind swam, going fuzzy, and I continued to breathe deeply, trying to steady my heart and still my vision.

I approached the industrial metal sinks. There! I could see the source—a water valve in the corner, wide open, water spilling out. It smelled like the ocean.

Someone had turned off the blocker that kept the untreated water from entering the restaurant. Miami was an old city and the pipes were old, outdated systems no longer used.

This was bad. Ocean water mixed with untreated water was filling the room.

I rushed over, slipping on the slick surface, and managed to shut it off, but it was too late. The damage was done. It would take weeks to get the smell out, long after the water was removed.

Juan thought this was my fault – but that can't possibly be true. It was the employees' fault at best and Matt's at worst for not checking that the plumbing was correct.

I stood there, chest heaving, as I took in the destruction. Everything I'd worked so hard for—every late night, every careful choice—ruined. My dream had turned into a nightmare, and I felt a sickening sense of failure welling up inside me. I'd let everyone down. The clients, the staff, my dad...

Oh, God, what would my dad think? I had failed him after he was so proud to help me – really, J&W landed this job. I didn't think they would blame me. But maybe they would, too. Maybe this would impact my awards coming up or my chance to lead the Utah project. My mind was in full panic mode then.

I swallowed hard, trying to push back the tears. I couldn't afford to break down, not now. But the fear had already crept in, consuming my thoughts. This wasn't an accident; someone had done this on purpose. The open valve, the deliberate sabotage—it was clear as day.

My eyes snapped open wide. And they were still here – I'd heard their breathing!

I stayed very still, then turned around toward the lobby of the restaurant, planning to walk as quietly as possible back outside. I needed to get to that rental car and check my phone. All was quiet over the pounding of my own heart. I felt absolute terror.

Suddenly, a noise off to the left of me broke through my panic, and I whipped my head around. My breath caught in my throat.

A man stood at the other end of the kitchen, dressed in dark clothes, his face hidden behind a mask. My heart pounded in my chest, each beat louder than the last.

For a split second, we seemed to just stare at each other, though I couldn't see his face behind the ski mask. Then, instinct took over. This guy had just ruined all my work! He had to be caught!

I lunged at him, almost falling, and then I ran, my feet splashing through the water as I dashed toward the lobby. But the man was faster. He darted away from me. I lost sight of him in the lobby until I arrived. I barely had time to scream before he grabbed me, his gloved hand clamping over my mouth.

I had a fearful thought that I might die today. I shivered uncontrollably, adrenaline and fear taking over me.

Panic surged through my mind, confusing my thoughts, its clutches cold and paralyzing. My mind was racing but going nowhere, every thought a jumbled mess of fear and disbelief. How could this be happening?

This was supposed to be another milestone moment in my career, and now I was here, alone, in a flooded restaurant with a stranger who wanted to hurt me. Except, he wasn't hurting me, exactly.

In fact, he was squeezing my neck from behind just enough to cause panicked breathing but not enough to kill me.

I struggled, encouraged by the lightness of his hold compared to how tightly he could be pressing on my neck.

The man tightened his grip then, and I tried to elbow him, but it was no use. He was too strong. I lost my thoughts of escaping him because now I really couldn't breathe, couldn't think. All I could do was hope that someone—anyone—would find me before it was too late.

As the darkness of my brain shutting down from lack of blood flow closed in around me, I realized that this moment could be the end of everything. My life. My career I'd worked so hard to build. The end of me being a daughter to my parents. The end of... Hudson and me. Of Kenzie.

I desperately tried to get in air, but it was no use. I slackened against the man's body, giving him one last jab of my elbow. He grunted and flinched. Encouraged, I did it again.

Then, in that brief moment when he loosened his grip and the ringing in my ears subsided, I heard the door to the restaurant slam open. My heart leaped, a surge of hope coming alive... I was coming alive. I'd never give up on this chance to live! The man holding me froze, his grip tightening again for a moment before loosening long enough for me to gasp for air.

A surge of anger propelled me to kick him in the groin. He doubled over, squashing me. I gasped and gasped – air had never been so precious to me before.

"Madeline!" Hudson's voice cut through the haze, deep and commanding.

The man yanked me backward, using me as a shield as he turned toward Hudson. My eyes locked on Hudson, who stood in the doorway, fists clenched. His eyes were blazing with a rage I had never seen before.

He took in the scene in an instant—me, the water, the intruder—and his expression hardened. He looked every inch a SEAL. He looked every inch the warrior. My throat burned. I felt tears streaming down my cheeks. I felt sick. But he was here. And he was going to save me.

"Let her go," Hudson growled, his voice low and dangerous. He took a step forward, holding out a fist and a hand – the fist for the masked man, the hand for me.

The man hesitated, his grip on me faltering. In his uncertainty, I violently writhed around again, trying to break free.

Hudson moved in a blur, crossing the room with a speed that showcased his strong physique – a body of pure muscle. He lunged at the intruder, grabbing him by the arm and twisting. The guy yelled out, something about this being way more than he signed up for.

The pain of Hudson's move seemed to force the guy to release me.

I stumbled back, hand on my sore throat as Hudson wrestled with the man. The intruder tried to fight back, but Hudson was relentless, driven by a fury that seemed to give him the strength of ten SEALs. With a swift, brutal motion, Hudson tore off the man's ski mask, revealing a face twisted in anger and covered in sweat.

But before I could register any details, the man with wild eyes shoved Hudson hard, sending him stumbling backward.

The man bolted for the door, disappearing outside before either of us could stop him. I stumbled, lightheaded, to the door just in time to see a Honda pull out from behind the neighboring building.

Oh my God! That car!

I tried to call out for Hudson but my throat burned. I heard the screech of tires as a car sped away.

Hudson was by my side in an instant, eyes following the car, his hands on my shoulders. His eyes tore from the Honda and he scanned me for any sign of injury. "Are you okay? Did he hurt you?"

I shook my head, still trying to catch my breath. "I'm okay," I managed to croak out, though my voice trembled. "I'm okay, thanks to you."

Hudson pulled me into his arms, holding me close. The fear that had gripped me moments ago began to ebb away, replaced by an overwhelming sense of relief. I was safe now. Hudson had found me, just in time.

But even as I clung to him, a new fear crept in—someone had sent that guy here to wreck this place. That meant that Hudson was not the only target. In fact, maybe I was the target all along!

Hudson pulled back slightly, cupping my face in his hands as he looked into my eyes. "We need to call the police. We've seen the guy's face now. That makes him even more dangerous."

Hudson's words cut me to my core – never had I felt such fear before.

Twenty-Five
Hudson

I tailed Madeline's rental car closely all the way home that afternoon. Most of the time we'd been gone had been spent cleaning up the best we could and checking if Juan had cameras up.

The statements we gave the police had been thorough, but we didn't have much in the way of answers.

I did my best to describe the guy in the Honda, his scowl permanently imprinted on my mind, and I had the plates from the PI firm I had hired.

All we knew was that the plates were stolen. And, of course, that this guy wasn't Jon, after all. That complicated things.

With Madeline's only real "enemy" being her ex, Jon, it made everything difficult. When we'd thought I was the target of the Honda guy, we'd come up with a long list of potential people out to hurt me. As a former SEAL, the list was almost endless. With Jon being the only person who'd ever want to hurt her, it made no sense. He wasn't the guy in the Honda, so who was he? Why would he want to hurt her? The attack at the restaurant broadened everything past my little bubble. I needed to think bigger. Madeline was under attack, too.

Never had I been so grateful that Kenzie was at school, safe and away from all of this. It was hard enough worrying about Madeline. If this guy was after me, he might come after my baby girl, too.

The situation had me on edge, and I needed answers fast. But when I came back to the living room, I saw Madeline sitting on the couch, her face pale and her phone clutched tightly in her hand. Something was wrong.

"Madeline?" I asked, concern lacing my voice as I walked over to her. "What's going on?"

She looked up at me, and the fear in her eyes sent a cold spike of anger through me. "It was him," she whispered, her voice trembling. "My ex. He just called."

That was all it took to light a fire inside me. I'd never met the guy, but I knew enough from what Madeline had told me. He was controlling, manipulative, and clearly still trying to worm his way into her life. I sat down next to her, trying to keep my anger in check for her sake.

She looked at me. "I blocked his number. But he just went out and got a new one. He set his Caller ID to one of my friends' names, one of the girls at the bachelorette weekend."

I frowned. How twisted this guy was. Poor Madeline, to answer the phone expecting a friend only to hear the slimy voice of her ex.

"What did he say?" I asked, keeping my voice as calm as I could manage.

She took a shaky breath, looking down at the phone like it might bite her. "He said... he knows about the restaurant, about what happened today. One of his friends saw the local news – remember, the news camera was there trying to get us to make a statement to the media? Then, he offered his dad's legal help, but it wasn't an offer, Hudson. It was a threat. He was gloating, like he was happy this happened. And then he said... he said it would be a shame if more accidents happened."

Her words hit me like a punch to the gut. The thought of that bastard threatening her, after everything she'd already been through today, made me see red. But I couldn't let her see how angry I was—she needed reassurance, not more fear.

I took her hand, feeling how cold it was, and squeezed it gently. "Madeline, listen to me. He's just trying to scare you, trying to make you feel like you're alone in this. But you're not. I'm here, and we'll deal with this together, alright?"

She nodded, but I could see the doubt in her eyes. She was still shaken, still under the weight of the fear he'd planted in her. I wanted to make him pay for that, to make him understand that he wasn't going to get away with threatening her.

"If Jon really is behind all of this, I will make sure he's held accountable," I told her, pulling her into me. "Don't let him get to you. He doesn't have power over you anymore."

"He does, though. He's scaring me," she cried out, and I held her tightly.

"He shouldn't scare you. I would kill anyone that tried to hurt you," I said simply, stroking her hair.

Madeline looked up at me then, really looked at me, and I saw some of the fear start to fade.

"I just don't understand why he'd call me like that. It's weird," she murmured. "It's been over for a long time. Why can't he just leave me alone?" Then she sighed. "I should call my dad."

I wished I had an answer for her about Jon, but I didn't. Some men just couldn't let go, especially the ones who thrived on control.

"It sounds like he's a coward," I said simply. "He knows he's lost you, and this is his way of trying to keep you under his control."

If her ex thought he could scare her into submission, he was in for a rude awakening. I wasn't about to let him hurt Madeline, not physically, not emotionally, not in any way.

I pulled her into my arms, feeling her relax slightly against me. "Let's call your dad tomorrow. By then, Juan will have talked to him and you won't have to rehash every little detail."

I was wrong, though. Her dad video called her shortly after and together, Madeline and I had to walk through everything.

The end result was her father coming into town for the reunion two days early. When we ended the call, there was only one thing Madeline and I both wanted: to feel loved, together, united.

I held my hand out to her and led her to the guest room where she was staying, thinking she would want to be in what she considered her own private space.

But she didn't. I was grateful that she didn't. She kissed me deeply, putting all her passion into the kiss. I felt the energy of need vibrating through her. I felt the energy of desire match my own. It was a heady combination that left me wanton for her.

I closed the door behind us, pulling off her clothes and then mine.

I craved the taste of her kiss, the feel of her slick lips surrounding my cock. Everything about her was perfect. Everything about her was what I needed. And today, when I'd walked into that restaurant and saw her with that masked man threatening her life... I shuddered, pulling her to me.

I lifted her in my arms, cupping her soft ass and carrying her to the chaise lounge by the large back windows that overlooked the yard. The semi darkness of the room set a romantic mood for the moment. I set her on the cushioned armrest of the lounge, kissing down her cheek, licking and nipping at the soft skin around her collarbones.

Madeline arched her back, letting her shapely legs wrap around my waist. She pulled me into her, my cock grazing against her wet heat. But I wasn't ready to enter her yet.

I took my time, kissing her soft skin down to her breasts, sucking on each nipple as she played with my hair. The moment felt peaceful, a stark contrast to the day we'd had.

I could feel the tension slowly easing out of her body in the way she draped her legs, the way she placed a hand on my shoulder while her other hand moved to trace a finger down my jaw as I worshiped her breasts. I was in tune with her every sound, her every move.

She'd been through so much today, and the fear had still lingered in her eyes moments ago in the living room. I was not going to stop my gentle lovemaking until every bit of her fear was chased away. I wanted nothing more than to make her feel safe, loved, and cherished.

I pulled back as she whispered my name. Her eyes shone at me from her cushioned perch on the love seat. I gently tilted her chin up so no part of her face was hidden from me.

There was so much in her gaze—relief, pleasure, and trust. It thrilled me to have her surrender after all she'd been through.

When I looked deeper into those eyes, I saw the connection between us that we've had for weeks, only now it was stronger.

"Madeline," I said softly, brushing a strand of hair away from her face. "I'll never let anything bad happen to you. I couldn't stand it if..."

She gave me a kiss, shushing me, but I could see the weight of the day still hanging on her. I wanted to take that burden from her, to make her feel loved and comforted. Leaning in, I pressed a soft kiss to her forehead, then another to her cheek, letting my lips linger there.

"I want you," she whispered.

"I want you, too. I want to lick every inch of you, beautiful." I kissed her cheek and whispered back to her.

She moaned. "Yes. We deserve to feel so good."

I loved her use of "we."

"I want to make your body feel alive. I'm going to lick your nipples," I said, as I dipped my head down and captured the rosy buds in my mouth one by one. "Then I am going to lick your belly button and then I will kiss all the way down to your pussy."

"Promise," she purred at me, quietly.

I jolted at that. "Have you been my good girl?"

She pushed my head down her body, nodding. "I need your tongue on me. And your cock inside me."

I felt the pressure of her hand on my head but I moved slowly. My lips trailed down to her belly button, planting gentle kisses along the way.

I felt her breath catch, her body responding to my touch, and it made my heart swell with affection. This moment wasn't for me, although I was enjoying it. It was for her, to show her how much I cared, how deeply I wanted her to feel loved... and protected.

I pulled her thighs apart as I got on my knee, her glistening core beckoning to me. I let one hand slide up her stomach and then around her back, my fingers gently tracing the curve of her hips and her spine, while the other hand teased at her soft lips below. I was kissing her inner thighs now as her legs hung off the lounge.

"Here, baby girl," I said, gesturing to my shoulders. She draped her legs, one on each shoulder. I kissed and nipped at the skin by my face. My thumb brushed over her wet clit in a soothing motion.

"Oh my God," she moaned, her face smoothing out into an expression of bliss. I kissed toward her center. I could feel her relax even more, her tension giving way to something warmer, much more intimate.

"Hudson..." she whispered.

I could feel her body responding to me, the wetness and the warmth. I loved the way her breath hitched and her muscles tensed as my thumb moved. My tongue flicked out to taste her skin, moving up her slit and then back down.

"You feel so good," she murmured, her voice breathless. I could hear the desire in it, and a vulnerability that made me want to be even more gentle with her.

"I love the way you taste," I said, against her pussy, my breath hot on her skin, my voice low and filled with an emotion that was so strong it scared me.

But as I felt her respond, as I felt the tension in her body finally slip away completely, I knew that I had succeeded. Madeline knew she was safe in my arms, both now and... forever.

I focused my tongue on her clit, that smooth line of skin above her perfect lips. I flicked and massaged her with my tongue until I felt her shudder, arousal flowing from her in her orgasm. It was quieter than before but intense. Her breathing was ragged as her breasts bounced when she sat upright.

"That was so good," she moaned. "I felt it all through my body."

"That's what I wanted," I said.

"Fuck me, Hudson. Fuck me like today never happened. Fuck me like you want me." Her eyes were bright and wild.

I knew that look. It was the desperation of someone who saw their life flash before their eyes. And I knew that she did today when she was being choked.

I leaned over her and kissed her deeply. "I will always protect you," I said, in a ragged voice full of feeling.

She told me the best words she could in this moment, "I believe you. I trust you."

I felt her hand grasping onto my length, lining me up to her and letting me slide into her. She was warm and tight, squeezing around me like we belonged together.

I thrust into her fast, holding onto her waist with my arms while she held onto my biceps. We locked eyes and didn't break eye contact once until I came inside her, the moment so intimate and raw it took my breath away.

"I need you close to me," I murmured, lifting her up while I was still inside her and carrying her to the bed.

We fell asleep wrapped up in each other, closer than just our bodies.

Our hearts were close, too.

Twenty-Six
Madeline

The day of the Navy SEALs reunion had finally arrived.

Dad had been so caught up in meeting up with fellow SEALs and dragging Mom with him to luncheons and coffees that he hadn't been hanging around Hudson or me the past two days.

I was glad for the respite. I needed a little time to process the disaster at the restaurant – of which I was fully cleared as having no part in, of course – and prepare to pretend to not be sleeping with Hudson.

I was in a tight dress and Hudson was in his suit. He looked more handsome than ever. I was proud to be on his arm as we entered. I was proud of him in general, too. He had shown me photos of each of the fallen men, both to talk about them with me but also, I think, to prepare himself for the difficult few minutes of the reunion where a video would play to honor their lives.

Hudson and I were closer than ever. What we shared felt real and, dare I hope, lasting.

We decided to not try to hide from anyone that we'd been living together. As long as they knew it was in separate rooms while I completed work for him, then who cared?

"You ready?" I asked him, as we joined the throngs of people arriving. He didn't want to be too early. I didn't want to be too late, so we compromised.

He squeezed my arm affectionately. "I'd be a lot better if I could kiss you."

"Behave," I admonished him, with a smile. "We're just old family friends tonight."

"No, we're just old family friends this evening," he said, and then leaned close to growl into my arm, "But tonight, you're mine," he added. I grinned, too happy to hide it.

"Or maybe right now," Hudson murmured, and I looked up at him, into his smoldering hazel eyes. Without another word, Hudson held his arm out to me. I glanced toward my parents, but they weren't watching me. Nor were any of their friends. I held onto his bicep and ducked my head, sneaking out of the ballroom with him.

I couldn't believe my own audacity.

I was slipping away gracefully from just a few feet away from my father's seat to have – what I knew would be – one heck of a mind-blowing orgasm in a room just a few feet away.

As much as I tried at that moment, knowing what my man's skillful hands and chiseled body would do to me, I couldn't resist a minute longer.

As we were sneaking out of the big reception hall, I saw familiar faces, my father's friends, in the crowd. Music was playing softly from the live band on the stage. Dozens of military men and their families were there to commemorate their fallen brothers.

I tried not to meet my father's eyes – I was carrying too big a secret to face him. I was falling in love...*love?* Yes, I was falling in love with the most off-limits man in the whole world... my father's best friend, and I couldn't help myself.

We'd been eye-fucking each other the whole drive over, as we put on nametags, and as we walked down the hallway. My eyes were exhausted after the past hour. My pussy needed to take over for them. My heart was racing in my chest, and my breasts moved freely in my sexy dress as I rushed to keep up with him.

We didn't go far. This was his hotel, so he knew exactly where to take me. Inside the smaller event room down the hallway, he locked the door. He kissed me, the taste of him as familiar as my own name, but I pushed away. We didn't have much time. Our absence would be noticed.

I pulled up my dress and took his hand, placing it on my naked thigh. He needed no prompting. I gasped as his finger slipped inside my thong. My hand moved to his cock – that massive, girthy cock that I knew would pleasure my pussy with each thrust. I moaned, leaning back into his kiss, grasping his length over his pants and stroking it.

"Cum for me, baby," he whispered, his finger flicking gently across my clit.

"We don't have time—" I started to say, but he silenced me by biting on my lower lip, quick and sure, just like everything he did. I closed my eyes, giving in to the bliss building in my body.

The thrill of so many people nearby, of being so easily caught, turned me on so much that I came moments later on his hand, riding it as my muffled cries filled the empty room.

I felt him kiss me, then his free hand was on my bare back, finding the zipper to my dress and pulling it down. Cool air caressed my skin as my dress slowly fell away from my body, my naked breasts revealed to Hudson's hazel eyes.

I undid his suit pants and eagerly reached for his length. I wanted this. I needed this.

His lips captured my pink nipples as I stroked his hard cock, naked and huge in my hand. I panted, and then whined, as his finger started playing with my clit again. He was always a generous lover.

He lifted me onto one of the small tables in the room. Then, his finger was back on my clit. I closed my eyes to relish every sensation. I felt his strong hands on my thighs, opening my legs for him.

And then, oh glorious bliss, I felt his cock as it slid into me. My eyes flew open as he kissed me again. I could feel that familiar connection between us. Each thrust felt deeper. Each moan felt less controlled.

"Yes, take me please..." I lost myself in the feeling of this god of a silver fox pushing his rod into me.

"That's my good girl," he said, in that dangerously deep voice.

The room was filled with the sounds of my quiet moans and his guttural groans as he thrust into me hard and fast.

"Cum inside me. I need it!" I was ready. I threw my head back and felt his warm seed as it filled me.

Minutes later, we were dressed and ready to return to the event before we were missed. Hudson stole one more forbidden kiss, nipping at my lip before pulling back to study me with his intelligent hazel eyes. He was unlike any other man I'd ever dated. My heart swelled with emotion.

"You are perfect." I saw he meant it by the look in his eyes.

He pulled open the door, and we stepped into the hallway. The sounds of music and voices were distant. All was quiet in the hallway. He stiffened a bit when we walked down the hallway to the ballroom. I could feel the tension in the air the moment we stepped into the grand ballroom of the hotel, coming face-to-face with a large screen that showed images of days gone by when Hudson and each of these men here were SEALs in active service.

Hudson had been quieter than usual all morning, his brow furrowed in thought when he didn't know I was watching him. Even the event room sex hadn't seemed to calm his thoughts down.

I knew him well enough now to know he was mentally preparing himself for what lay ahead.

I stayed close to his side as we walked through the crowded room, the noise of laughter and conversation filling the space. Men in their old dress uniforms and others in casual attire were scattered around, some already sharing stories and others catching up after a year apart.

I used to attend these reunions when I was younger with my dad, as strange as that seemed now, but it had been a while. There was a sense of camaraderie that was not to be dimmed by time, but beneath it all, I could feel the undercurrent of bittersweet nostalgia that each man carried.

Hudson squeezed my hand discreetly as we moved through the crowd, and I squeezed back, letting him know I was there for him. I glanced up at him, catching the way his jaw was set as if he were steeling himself for what was to come. "Are you okay?" I asked, softly, trying not to draw too much attention. I knew this was hard for him, and I wished I could do more to help.

Hudson nodded, but his eyes were distant, scanning the room as if he were searching for something—or someone. "I'm fine," he said, his voice steady but lacking its usual warmth. "Just... a lot of memories all at once. I will be fine, though. I just need to remember the good times, right?"

"You're doing great." I stepped away from Hudson's side when I spotted my dad across the room, talking to a group of men. He was laughing, his shoulders shaking with enthusiasm, but as he turned and saw us, his expression shifted. Had he seen us standing too close together?

I looked around for my mother and spotted her at the appetizer table, talking with a few ladies. I stepped even further from Hudson and instantly felt the absence of his closeness. I felt my heart skip a beat, realizing Hudson and I had become way too comfortable around each other. We could not act like lovers tonight. When we came clean to my dad, it would need to be private, not here.

"Dad," I called out, trying to keep my voice light as we approached him.

But I shouldn't have worried. Dad was in his element. He whisked Hudson away jovially, and the men began sharing jokes, Hudson joining in. I slowly drifted away, happy for his moment of connection. I found my mom and gave her a hug.

"That looks delicious!" I said about her plate of appetizers. As I glanced up, looking for a table for us to sit around, I blinked in surprise as I saw a familiar face.

I gasped.

Was that Jon? What the fuck?

My blood ran cold at the sight of my ex-boyfriend, Jonathan fucking Wright, but when I looked back, I didn't see him anymore.

I followed Mom to a table and, as she settled in with some friends, I strode to one of the doors that led to the hallway, looking for Jon.

I must have been mistaken. Some other guy in a suit just looked like Jon. I didn't see him anywhere. *You're going insane, Maddie.*

I shook my head, realizing how paranoid I must be after the bachelorette party that Jon crashed and the way he had seemingly taken credit for the restaurant sabotage.

Still on edge, but determined that I was being crazy, I returned to the table to see that Hudson and Dad had arrived in anticipation of the slideshow.

The whole program was timed to perfection and, as we inched closer to the slideshow, I felt Hudson's eyes on me more. I tried to smile encouragingly at him, but his eyes had something in them beyond anxiety over the slideshow.

He was eyeing me with a ferocity I didn't quite understand. I knew I couldn't understand. He'd had experiences I never had and never would have.

Pride swelled in my chest as I realized once more how much he had gone through to be a functioning adult after all that pain. My dad, too.

I reached out and squeezed my dad's hand, suddenly full of love for the both of them, and he tossed a smile my way, his eyes flicking back quickly into place to stare at the projector screen.

As the conversation around us shifted and then quieted down, the video began to play.

I was seated at the round table with my dad to my left and Hudson to my right. There was very little chance I could touch Hudson under the table without Dad noticing, so instead I used my foot to gently rub his leg.

He smiled, keeping his eyes on the screen. In that moment, I felt connected to him. I felt alive. Then, it happened.

I felt a pit in my stomach open up and yawn, and my heart quicken to a pace that felt like it might explode out of my chest. The silence in the room was palpable, like something thick, real and observable. I looked over at Hudson, and he seemed frozen in place.

There, on the screen, was a picture of me, then a picture of Hudson, then a picture of Hudson's hand on my ass out in front of his house, then a picture of Hudson and me at his bed-and-breakfast property, through the window.

That was pretty damning. My hands clutched around his back, my head thrown back in ecstasy. I remembered the moment well. My legs were wrapped around Hudson's waist, and he was moving inside me as slowly as he could, making my toes shake as I felt my pussy swallow every single inch.

That was the one that woke me up, or rather made me realize I wouldn't wake up from this nightmare, that this was really happening.

I stood up, my chair scraping crassly across the floor and clattering backward.

"Linda!" Hudson boomed in a commanding voice, and a small woman squeaked into the same awareness we had, jolting a little from a chair and running up to the stage and behind the curtain.

My dad looked at me first, and I saw a brokenness inside him as we made eye contact before he looked back at the screen to see a picture of Hudson and I that very morning.

It was unmistakable. I was in the dress I was wearing at this very moment, and Hudson was in his uniform. I was wearing his eight-point cap, something that deeply shamed me now, looking around at all the servicemen commemorating their brothers who had died for the honor to wear it. Hudson was between my legs, his face between my thighs, and I was holding his hair like I was holding a horse's reins, my feet propped up on his shoulders. I couldn't look at my dad, but from my peripheral, I could see him drop his head into his hands.

I hazarded a look at my mom, and her eyes were gentle, her forehead on my dad's temple as she rubbed his back and whispered into his ear.

My legs were shaking, and I thought I might pass out as I got more and more lightheaded with the sheer effort of not meeting anyone in the room's eyes.

Hudson was at my elbow, taking my arm, trying to pull me away, and suddenly my dad was standing up and removing me, like I was a piece of furniture in the way of where he wanted to go.

His eyes were narrowed as he stared into Hudson's.

Twenty-Seven

Hudson

I met Madeline's panicked look with one of my own. This was not how either of us wanted this private information to come out to Harry.

I put my hands up like I was fending a wild bull off, and Harry slapped my hands down. "You know what, actually? Put them back up."

He took off his eight-point cap, the one he had just seen his daughter donning as I ate her out, and cracked his knuckles.

Fuck.

"I'm not going to hit you, Harry. If you want to hit me, fine, but I won't defend myself," I said, making my stance wide and holding my wrist behind my back, jutting out my chin for him.

If I thought that would hold him back, I was sorely mistaken and not at all prepared for him to sling his fist at me. I took the punch in the jaw without making a sound.

It wasn't his full strength. I knew him well enough to know he could have broken a few of my teeth if he'd had a mind to. However, I had a feeling that he was only holding back because of the other SEALs watching the show.

"Dad!" Madeline shouted at the same time that Harry's wife, Julie, screamed, "Harry!"

"What the hell, Hudson?" Madeline's father spat out. He took a step toward me, and I could see the fury in his eyes, intermingled with the betrayal. "You promised me you'd look out for her, not take her to your room at night for your daughter and God knows who else to see! Actually, I know who else! This entire fucking room!"

I was angry, too. Angry that I'd been forced to hide this and angry that it had come out this way. Angry that this moment had been stolen from us and angry that I was being admonished in front of my peers this way.

And finally, I was angry that I had done this, that I had gotten involved with my best friend's daughter, that I had no discipline when it came to her. Angry that I could be so small and pathetic. I had a daughter myself. I knew how Harry felt, and I was angry for him.

My jaw was throbbing, but I ignored it, taking care not to rub it and show weakness in front of Harry.

"I didn't mean to break that promise," I said, my voice steady. "I...I *didn't* break that promise. I *did* take care of her."

He laughed angrily, his fists clenched at his sides. "Say you took care of my daughter again, Hudson. I want to hear you say it again."

"Dad, stop!" Madeline shrieked, her tone disproportionate against Harry's quiet tone but appropriate for the screaming I knew he was doing in his head.

He ignored her, his focus entirely on me. "You should have told me the moment you realized what was happening between you and my daughter. You should have had a man-to-man talk with me." He almost spat at me.

"You took advantage of her. She's young, Hudson. I told you she was liable to act out. And you smiled in my face and said she wouldn't, like a fucking snake," he continued.

I swallowed hard. Hearing him say it like that, I felt dirty and low. I *was* a snake, indeed.

I took a moment to look around the room and wallow in my shame as a group of my peers looked at me with what I can only describe as disgust.

That's exactly what it was. Everyone in the room was disgusted by me. And I was disgusted by myself. I had nothing to say to defend myself. He was right.

"I didn't take advantage of her, Harry, I swear on everything we have shared and everything we've lost. I would never." I looked over at Julie for a lifeline, but she didn't meet my eyes. Her jaw was clenched, one of her hands tight on Madeline's hand as Madeline stood near her dad. She was holding her there, keeping her from disrupting.

"You would never? Except you did, Hudson, you did. You may act like you're different, like your choices are enlightened, but you still think with your dick like you always did."

He held his hands up in a gesture to the room. "You put all this together, for what? To pronounce some brotherhood, some allegiance to all of us? If this is your allegiance, I'd rather have your betrayal."

He looked over at the men seated at their tables, their wives silent and embarrassed, and screamed, "You'd all better watch out for this guy! He'll gladly fuck your daughters, too, I'm sure!"

"Dad, that's enough!" Madeline screamed, wrenching free of her mom's grip and grabbing at him.

It was a mistake because it only fueled Harry's fury even more. He punched me again, this time crushing my nose with his knuckles, and I stood and took it again.

He looked me square in the eyes and muttered in a quiet voice that somehow scared me more than his yells, "You're nothing. You should never call yourself a man. You think I will ever allow you anywhere near my daughter? You think you can declare it an accident, and I'll hand her over? Never. She will stay far away from you as long as I live, and I intend on living a lot longer than you, however that has to happen." He punctuated his statement with a jab at my chest with his finger, somehow sharper than a stab.

I stared at him, willing myself to stay calm. I looked down at my chest where his finger had been, my anger welling inside me. I narrowed my eyes but forced myself to remain quiet.

"I trusted you, Hudson," he continued, his voice rising again. "I trusted you with my life back in the SEALs, and I trusted you with my daughter. But since she came here, all she's endured is chaos. That's you, though, isn't it? You claim to be different, but I know better. Well, enough! She's coming home where she belongs. I can't trust you. So, I will protect her my damn self."

Just when he was reaching for his wife and for Madeline, the fire alarm went off, blaring and flashing lights.

Twenty-Eight
Madeline

Sprinklers sprayed water over everyone, and the speakers hissed and cracked as they shorted out. Hudson reached for me, finding my dad's hand on my arm next to his. The two of them made eye contact, and Hudson said, "Get them out of here."

Before I could protest, my dad nodded, pulling me and my mom out the doors where people were spilling out, trying desperately to leave the ballroom.

I watched Hudson's eyes follow the smoke that was now streaming out of the ballroom as he assessed the situation.

His SEAL instincts kicked in as he pushed through the crowd, searching for people who needed help evacuating.

Panic was spreading, people looking around with growing alarm. But at least the embarrassing fiasco from a moment ago was forgotten for now.

I pulled out of my dad's grasp and followed Hudson. The smell of smoke was getting stronger, and then I saw it—a small fire licking up the drapes in the corner, rapidly spreading across the fabric and up the wall.

"Move!" a former SEAL shouted, breaking out the fire extinguisher from its plastic case on the wall.

People were scrambling. The heat was intense, and the smoke was so thick, making it hard to see. I could hear someone screaming. Hudson began herding those who could walk out. Some people had fainted from the smoke and fear.

An older woman fainted, and I dropped to my knees at her side, crying out, "HUDSON!" His eyes landed on me from feet away. Even with the chaos of screams and being separated by the smoke, he instantly found me by my voice.

My dad appeared at my side, trying to convince me to get up, tugging at my arm. I elbowed him away from me, waiting for Hudson.

"Madeline, get out of here!" Hudson shouted at me, pulling me to my feet.

"No, Hudson, I'm staying with you!" I shouted back, but he shook his head at me. "I can help!" I insisted. I *needed* to help. I couldn't imagine leaving him here.

"Madeline," my dad said to me, now calm and collected, the heat of the conflict earlier set aside for the emergency. I wondered if it was like this in the old days, if they always set aside their problems when an emergency arose. "Hudson will be okay. He's trained to do this," he said, to my surprise.

When I didn't move, Hudson sighed and picked me up by my waist, slinging me over his shoulder. "Hey!" I screamed, punching his back, but he just walked out the door and out the building as I kicked and squirmed, my dad walking in front of me, helping others that needed it, until we reached the front.

He dumped me onto my feet on the sidewalk and looked at my dad. They shared a silent look of resolve, then a nod, and Hudson pushed a lock of my hair out of my face. My dad looked away as he did.

Hudson murmured, "There are more people inside – some are older. We can't wait for the firefighters to get here."

"But—"

"Madeline. I can do this. You can't. That's all there is to it. You and your mom need to stay with Harry. He'll keep you both safe."

And then he turned around and went back into the building as smoke and people poured out the doors.

Fear clawed at me as I watched Hudson disappear back into the building, every cell screaming at me to follow him, but I knew he was right. I was coughing and shaking like a leaf in the wind. I was just as terrified as everyone around me. I was not trained for this, not like he was.

I walked backward, bumping into my dad, who caught me by the ribs and held me upright.

I watched in horror as Hudson turned, ran toward the dense smoke, and disappeared into it. I heard the wail of sirens in the distance.

"Oh, thank God!" I shouted.

"I'm going to go stand near the entryway to see what I can do to help," my dad told me, and then added, "You two stay here." He kissed my mom on the cheek, and she nodded at him, hugging him tightly for just a second before letting him go toward the doors.

I knew we were safe, but I felt helpless. The firefighters were on their way, but I wasn't sure if they'd make it in time. The flames were spreading too fast, and Hudson was still in there, risking his life to save people.

I saw an older couple shuffling out, he with his cane and her with her hand on his arm. I rushed to them, guiding them to the waiting arms of a few SEALs' wives who were calling out to anyone who could hear them that they were nurses, ready to help until ambulances arrived.

My head whipped around on a swivel, unsure of where I could help or what I could do.

Hudson emerged from the smoke, coughing and covered in soot. He was supporting two men, both of them barely able to walk, and behind him, another woman was stumbling out and her face streaked with tears.

He relieved himself of the couple and handed them off to my father, who quickly sat them down on the ground for the EMTs to give them oxygen.

I ran toward Hudson and wrapped him in a hug, not caring about the soot that sat freshly in a thin coat over his clothes or about the looks that a few of the people there still managed to give us despite the havoc that was going on.

He pulled me in tightly with one arm, his fingers gripping my waist. I felt a rush of energy run through me. The firefighters ran in, taking over the search and rescue.

"Hudson!" I heard the voice of my dad behind me. I stepped away, but Hudson held me still, not moving away from me.

"You're mine," he said simply. "I'm tired of hiding."

Dad's eyes registered Hudson's arm around me but he simply said, "Take your mother home. Hudson and I will handle this. I want you out of this area and safe."

I wasn't sure where 'home' was supposed to be, but I didn't hesitate. I stole a look over my shoulder at Hudson. My heart melted at the love I saw in his eyes.

'You're mine,' he had said.

I hope he meant it forever, but I didn't have long to sit in the blissful feeling.

As I piled into the rental car my parents had gotten, my mom nearly mute with all the stress of the night, I noticed over the crowd of people scrambling into their own cars, that same face I had seen before.

Only this time I knew I wasn't imagining it. I saw Jon standing near the building, still as a statue, with a huge grin plastered across his face. He was wearing a baseball cap, and he tipped it at me before letting the darkness of the night swallow him up as he ran off.

Still, I had more on my mind than Jon and his mysterious attendance at the Navy SEALs reunion. More than that, my heart pounded as I put the car into drive and left the scene of what I was sure was Jon's crime.

I felt sick watching people scream, seeing smoke billowing, knowing that the man I was falling for and my dad were in that building.

If anything happened to either of them, I would never forgive myself. I would never be able to move on.

I looked over at my mom, the worry etched on her face, too. She hadn't spoken a word since she saw the slideshow, the turn of events sucking all the energy out of the moment.

"I loved an older man once, too, you know," she said suddenly, surprising me. Her face was resting against the car window, bouncing as I hit potholes.

"Really?" I asked, trying to still my heart, willing my breathing to even out.

"Mhm, he was so romantic, and I felt like I could trust that he knew what to do." She looked up at me for a brief second before relaxing back against the window. "But then I met your father, and everything else seemed to fade away."

That is how I felt. I felt like I didn't have to think so hard about what was next with Hudson at my side. I could relax and trust him. And everything else seemed to fade away. I had the best of all the loves she'd had.

She smiled against the glass, her breath leaving a circle of fog on the window in front of her mouth. "And you can't beat a Navy SEAL, as far as men go. Just be careful. They're a lot of work."

"But so am I," I pointed out, my fingers tightening around the steering wheel.

I couldn't believe she was saying this. She didn't sound angry at all. She sounded like she...understood.

"But so are you," she agreed, a small chuckle escaping her and crashing against the window with her breaths.

For a moment, it felt good to be with my mom alone, to know that we both were once girls. Just two girls in love.

Both of the men we loved were in a building on fire, our hearts intertwined in the danger.

Twenty-Nine
Madeline

The snow-capped peaks of the Utah mountains stretched endlessly outside the plane window, a stark, cold beauty that made me feel smaller than I already did.

Park City would be the serene escape that I needed, and Joanna would be the welcome comfort that I needed. But no matter how far I flew from Miami, I couldn't escape the feelings built up from that terrible event.

It all seemed to mount at once –the damning slideshow, the fire, and the fight between Hudson and my dad.

Guilt gnawed at me, overwhelming me with an ache in my chest. I shifted in my seat, smoothing my fingers over the armrest as if the texture of the leather could ground me.

Hudson had offered to fly me in his private jet, but I just couldn't bring myself to take advantage of his good will and money, knowing that I had destroyed his friendship with my father.

He still insisted on buying me and Joanna both a first-class ticket, swapping them out over the phone while I slept soundly next to him. Our last night together, possibly ever.

My mind was busy replaying the last conversation with my dad. His words rang in my ears like a broken record, each one sharper than the last. "*Come home*" followed by "*I'll never forgive him, Madeline.*"

My stomach churned.

How did we get here? How did I become the wedge that tore apart a twenty-five-year friendship? How did I ruin everything by falling for the one man who was off-limits to me?

Hudson's name blinked on my phone screen, the unread text taunting me. I couldn't open it. I knew what it would say—something reassuring, something that would probably make me smile.

But the guilt was suffocating, and I wasn't ready to confront any more emotions than I was already battling.

"Are you good?" Joanna's voice snapped me back to reality. She was sitting across from me, her laptop open and her fingers dancing across the keyboard. She hadn't pried into my mess, thank God. But she knew—she always knew when I wasn't okay.

"Yeah, just tired," I lied, offering a tight smile.

Joanna gave me a look, one of those *I-don't-buy-your-bullshit* looks, but she didn't push it. "We'll be landing soon. I'll have the car service ready to take us straight to the estate."

"Perfect," I replied, my voice hollow. This project was supposed to be a huge milestone for my career, and yet, it felt like a backdrop to the chaos that was my life.

I turned my phone over, face down, and leaned back in my seat. Park City was supposed to be totally independent of the mess of my life, a chance to clear my head and prove my worth, but all I could think about was Hudson. And my dad. And how I'd been the catalyst for this disaster.

The cabin lights dimmed as the plane prepared for descent. My stomach tightened at the thought of stepping off the plane into a place that was so far away from Hudson—and yet, somehow, he was still everywhere.

***

When we stepped out of the car and onto the estate grounds, I forced myself to focus. This wasn't the time to wallow. This was my chance to prove, to myself and everyone else, that I was capable of pulling off something incredible.

Joanna was already on her phone, making arrangements with the contractors as I took in the sprawling mansion.

I stood in the grass, right next to a sign telling me not to, and craned my neck back.

The building was huge and beautiful, with its wood beams and massive glass windows that looked out onto the snow-covered landscape. It screamed *success,* the kind of success I'd worked so hard to achieve. But the victory felt hollow.

"Madeline." Joanna nudged me as we walked through the foyer. "We need to talk about the award situation."

I nodded, even though my mind was elsewhere. The false accusations about me bribing the judges to win that award had been a nightmare. I hadn't even had time to fully process it with everything going on with Hudson, but now that we were here, it was impossible to ignore.

"I'll get to the bottom of it," she continued, her voice firm. "I'll send inquiries to the committee tomorrow and start digging into who might have made these accusations. You won that award fair and square."

I glanced at her, grateful for her support. I was a little worried about the possibility of what she might find if she started digging. Seeing Jon as I drove away from Hudson's hotel, the building ablaze, had scared me. And it had made me more certain than ever before who was behind all of this mess. There was no denying it was her brother.

"Thanks, Joanna. I just... I didn't think it would come to this. I've worked my ass off to get here. Being submitted for that award was a dream come true...Now it's like everything is unraveling."

"It's not," she said, with conviction. "I admit, you've had a hard go of it lately. But you're going to get through this, and we'll clear your name. You're too good for this to bring you down."

"Yeah," I said, though my voice trembled. "And when you say you're going to do some digging...you mean as my attorney, right?"

Joanna smiled a small, flat smile and tilted her head. "Is that what you want? Are you worried you need an attorney?"

I swallowed. "Yes."

There was a brief pause before Joanna answered, her voice bright. She shrugged, "Then of course. I'm here for you, Maddie. I'll start making calls first thing tomorrow. Don't worry—we'll figure this out."

I smiled, but it didn't reach my eyes. "I hope you're right." I knew she was. Logically, I knew I hadn't done anything wrong so, of course, we'd figure it out. But it was hard to stay logical when everything felt so personal—when Hudson, my dad, and my career were all hanging by threads that I didn't know how to hold onto anymore.

Later that evening, I sat on the balcony of my hotel suite, the cool Utah air brushing against my skin. The lights of Park City twinkled below me peacefully. Everything here felt so far removed from Miami and the mess I'd left behind. This place was so...simple.

Joanna had gone back to her room to catch up on some work, leaving me alone with my thoughts—and that was dangerous. I missed Hudson. God, I missed him so much it hurt.

My father had forgiven me, but that didn't stop the guilt from eating me alive. His words about Hudson still cut deep. He would never forgive him, and I didn't know how to make peace with that.

How could I? I was the reason their friendship had fallen apart. And Hudson... I didn't even know what we were anymore. *Lovers? Partners? Something more? Something less?*

I hated the uncertainty. I hated not knowing where we stood, not knowing if we could ever really make this work with my father's disapproval hanging over our heads. *What if Hudson resented me forever because of all this?*

I stared at my phone again, the screen still dark. I wanted to call him. To hear his voice. To tell him that I missed him, that I couldn't stop thinking about him, that I didn't know how to fix this.

Another piece of me wanted to call him and hear his sultry, nighttime voice. I wanted to tease him and touch myself while I thought of him. But I couldn't even bring myself to text him back, let alone initiate phone sex. Not yet.

I stared at the phone for what felt like forever before finally, hesitantly, dialing a number. The phone rang once, then twice. And when the voice on the other end answered, I let out a breath I hadn't realized I was holding.

"Hey... can we talk?"

Thirty

Hudson

Every day without Madeline felt like trying to breathe with a weight on my chest. I sat at my desk, staring at the papers spread out in front of me, but none of them stuck. Real estate deals, contracts, numbers... none of it mattered. Not without her here.

The house was too quiet, too big. It felt cold again, the way it did before she came into my life, before she filled every corner with warmth.

I missed her laughter echoing through the halls, the way she'd challenge me with her sass and her smile. I missed... everything about her. So did Kenzie. She'd been asking a lot of questions, questions I didn't know how to answer.

I'd told her that Madeline was on vacation with her friend. I wasn't sure yet if I'd have to tell her that Madeline was just here for work and had to leave permanently. I didn't know how Kenzie would take it.

I glanced at my phone, the one sitting there as lifeless as I felt. She hadn't called. I hadn't either. We both needed space, but the more days passed, the more I realized how much I needed her in my life.

I thought I had control of my life—six years of sobriety, six years of facing the nightmares head-on—but the emptiness she left behind was something new. Well, not totally new, but something I hadn't experienced since my ex. I had worked hard to never have to feel it again, and here it was, rearing its ugly head. It was something I didn't know how to handle.

I sighed, running my hand through my hair, trying to shake off the tension building in my shoulders. I had to focus.

Work had always been my escape, my way of staying grounded. But lately, even that wasn't helping. There were a few deals I should've been excited about—prime beachfront properties in Miami—but it all felt hollow without Madeline.

Well, that and I still had so much to deal with regarding the fire in the hotel. Insurance would, of course, cover it, but the police had said it was arson, and they wouldn't let insurance come in until they were done with an investigation. That also meant no one could be in it until it was given a pass, structurally. It was all a mess.

Just as I was about to force myself to dive back into the contracts, I heard voices outside my office. They were raised, sharp, cutting through the quiet. Not what I needed today. I'd specifically asked not to be disturbed.

I stood up, irritated, and walked to the door, already planning to tell whoever it was to leave me alone. But when I opened it, my breath caught in my throat.

It was Harry.

Linda, my office manager, looked at me nervously. She had been there for the fiasco. She knew how Harry felt about me, and she knew that last time, those feelings had given way to physical violence. "Mr. Packard, I tried to tell him you were busy—"

"It's fine," I said, cutting her off, keeping my eyes on Harry in case he decided to lunge.

"Do you want me to call the police?" she whispered.

I looked at her with surprise. I would never call the police on a brother.

"I'll handle it," I told her, my voice tense but steady.

Linda gave me a worried glance before retreating, leaving me and Harry standing there in the hall, staring at each other with narrowed eyes. The tension was thick enough to cut with a knife.

"Come on in," I muttered, gesturing toward my office. I didn't want to have this conversation in front of anyone.

Harry didn't say a word as he followed me in, but I could feel the weight of his anger like a physical thing. As soon as I shut the door behind us, he turned to face me, his eyes sharp and full of fire.

"You really think you can avoid me forever, Hudson?" His voice was cold, hard.

I clenched my jaw. "I wasn't avoiding you. I had a lot going on."

He laughed, a raw laugh with no positive emotion in it. "Yeah. And you're about to have a lot more."

"So we're doing this?" I asked, sitting down at my desk, sensing his manic energy and hoping to calm it down.

"Yeah, we're doing this," he growled, still standing tall, towering over me after I sat down. "You've been out

337

here, playing house with my daughter, and you think we don't need to talk?"

I felt my fists tighten at my sides. The last thing I wanted was a confrontation with Harry. But there was no avoiding it now. "I wasn't playing house with her. I care about her, Harry. More than you know."

Harry's eyes narrowed, and I could see the anger building even more.

"You *care* about her? If you *cared* about her, the way a man your age should, you would have nipped anything like this in the bud. I *told* you she was going through a lot."

"I'm not going to apologize for how I feel," I said, planting my hands on my desk and shaking my head.

He stepped closer, his voice rising. "This isn't just about how you feel, Hudson. It's about Madeline. It's about what kind of life she deserves. She's a real person beyond your *feelings*." He said 'feelings' like a dirty word. "You really think you can give her the life she deserves?"

I felt the familiar stir of frustration in my chest, the old anger I'd worked so hard to keep in check. But I wasn't the man I used to be. I wasn't going to explode, no matter how much Harry tried to push me.

"I know what she deserves," I said quietly, but firmly. "And I'm doing everything I can to be that for her."

Harry scoffed, pacing the room now. "Your PTSD, your alcoholism, your violent tendencies—you think that's just going to go away? You think Madeline can handle that? You think you can handle a relationship *and* all that? You're a runner, Hudson. You always have been."

I clenched my fists tighter. "I've been sober for six years, Harry. I've been through therapy. I've done the work. I'm not the man you once knew, and you've got to stop thinking that I am. I've changed, whether you believe that that's possible or not."

Harry leaned back into his heels, not on the offensive anymore, surprise visible on his familiar face. "You're sober?"

I nodded, and he continued, "And what happens when the pressure gets too much? When the nightmares come back?" He stopped pacing and looked at me, his eyes full of accusation. "You think Madeline's going to be able to save you from that?"

"I don't expect her to save me," I said, my voice low, my anger barely held in check. "I've saved myself already. I don't expect anything from her."

Harry shook his head, his frustration boiling over. "I've known you a long time, Hudson. I've seen you at your worst. And I know how bad things can get."

"I'm not running from it!" I exploded, pushing my chair back and standing. "Not anymore. I'm not that man, Harry. I'm not the man who drowns himself in alcohol or hides from his demons. I've faced them. I'm still facing them. Every damn day."

Harry stared at me, his jaw clenched, his hands balled into fists at his sides. I could see the war going on inside him—the part of him that still saw me as the man I used to be, and the part of him that was trying to see the man I was now.

"And you think that's enough?" he asked, his voice quieter now, but still hard. "You think that's enough for Madeline?"

"I love her, Harry," I said, the words coming out before I could stop them. "I love her more than anything, and I'm not going to let her go. Not because of you, not because of anyone. You deserve love, don't you? Even with your PTSD? So why don't I?" I sat back down, concerned that I had escalated things. "You know, maybe I was naïve, but part of me had hoped that you'd...I don't know, be glad Madeline had a man like me, someone who you once trusted with your life. You could trust me on a rescue mission but not with your daughter? Now, that doesn't make a whole lot of sense, does it?"

Harry looked away for a moment, his hands still clenched into fists. When he turned back, there was something softer in his eyes, something that wasn't quite approval, but wasn't pure anger either. "Things changed since we were in foxholes and jumping from helicopters. You have to admit that."

"Yeah, we're adults now. We have to take our baggage and be better than it. You did it. You carved out a little life for yourself. I want one, too. And I'm sorry, but I want one with your daughter."

"You've really been sober that long?" he asked, his voice quieter now.

I nodded. "Six years now. Every single day."

He let out a long breath, rubbing his hand over his face. "I don't know, Hudson. I just... I don't know if you're the right person for her."

"I'm not asking you to decide that for her," I said, my voice steady. "That's up to Madeline. But I am asking you to let her decide for herself. She doesn't want to disappoint you, Harry. You deciding you hate me will end us before we even start."

Harry stared at me for a long moment, the silence between us thick and heavy. I could see the doubt in his eyes, but there was something else there, too—something like understanding.

"I'm not saying I trust you," he said finally, his voice gruff. "But... maybe you're not the man I thought you were."

I didn't say anything. I knew that was the closest thing to a concession I was going to get from him. And honestly, it was more than I'd expected.

"I'll take that," I said, a small, tight smile tugging at my lips.

Harry shook his head, but there was a faint hint of a smile on his face, too, barely there, but enough for me to see.

"I'm not saying I'm okay with this," he muttered. "But...the way you saved those people in the building... I respected that. And I could see how...look, I can't say you're the man for Madeline, but I see your point about being a good man, at least. *If* the changes you claim to have made are real."

"They are," I replied, my voice quiet.

Harry looked at me one last time, then nodded and walked toward the door. Just before he left, he turned back. "Don't screw this up, Hudson. Or I'll fucking kill you. Hell, I still might."

And then he was gone, leaving me standing there, the weight of his words pressing down on me. I took a deep breath, letting it out slowly, feeling the tension in my chest start to loosen.

It wasn't over. Not by a long shot. But it was a start.

And for now, that was enough.

Thirty-One
Madeline

The cool air of Park City should have felt refreshing, but as I stepped outside with Joanna for what was supposed to be a fun night, all I could feel was the tightness in my chest.

Something was off. I couldn't quite put my finger on it—whether it was the stress of the past few weeks catching up to me or the constant, dull ache I felt from missing Hudson—but it was there.

Joanna linked her arm with mine as we walked toward the bar, her laughter cutting through the quiet of the night. She had been such a rock for me throughout this whole ordeal, always there when I needed to vent or distract myself from the chaos back home. It was hard to believe her brother was the one actively ruining my life.

"Come on, Madeline, wake up," she teased. "You need to let loose a little. One last night out before we go back to reality."

I forced a smile, nodding. "Yeah, you're right. Let's make the most of it."

But my heart wasn't in it. As much as I wanted to enjoy this last night in Park City, my thoughts kept drifting back to Hudson, back to Miami, back to everything I had left unresolved. Every time I thought I had gotten some distance, that I had finally found my footing, something pulled me back into the emotional whirlwind.

The bar was bustling, filled with the hum of conversations and the clinking of glasses. Joanna and I found a small table near the corner, away from the crowd, and I tried to settle into the moment. But the unease I had felt earlier was still there, creeping under my skin.

Joanna ordered drinks, her eyes sparkling with excitement. She had been looking forward to this night, and I didn't want to bring her down with whatever weirdness I was feeling.

But as I leaned back in my seat, a wave of nausea hit me out of nowhere. I blinked, my vision blurring for a second.

What the hell?

"You okay?" Joanna asked, looking over her shoulder at me, noticing my sudden discomfort.

"Yeah, just... I don't know. I feel a little off," I admitted, holding my cheeks as though I could squeeze the nausea out of my face.

"Maybe you need some food. Have you eaten today?"

"I...don't think so? I don't know, you were with me. Have I?"

Joanna turned her back to the bar and looked at me strangely. She pushed a hair out of my face. "Let's get something greasy. Something that'll fill you up and soak up whatever little bug you caught."

I nodded, but before we could order, something—or rather, someone—caught my eye across the bar. My heart skipped a beat.

There he was. The man from the bar in Miami. The one who had been driving the Honda.

I froze, my breath catching in my throat. It couldn't be him, right? Not here, of all places. I must be seeing things. It had to be anxiety from all that I had been through. Then again, I had thought that about Jon and it had turned out to be him.

"Joanna," I whispered, nudging her and nodding in his direction. "Do you see him?"

Joanna followed my gaze, and when her eyes landed on him, she tilted her head. "He looks familiar. Why? Who is it?"

She looked over at me, at my face that I was sure had gone pale, and whispered again, more urgently, "Who is that?"

My heart now racing, I said, "That's the guy that was...stalking me. He drives a Honda. If that guy drives a Honda, that...that has to be him. He was showing up at Hudson's. He even hacked the alarm system. He choked me!" My voice was rising in octaves as I uncovered the fear that I had buried.

Joanna's hand tightened on her glass as she stared at the man. He was standing near the bar, talking to a few people, completely oblivious to the fact that we were watching him.

"What the fuck are you talking about?" Joanna hissed. "You didn't tell me any of this."

"I didn't want to scare you."

"Well, now I'm scared. He *choked* you?" She grabbed my arm and started fishing for money in her purse. "Let's get out of here."

"Yes! When the restaurant was sabotaged, I showed up to survey the damage, and that guy –that guy—" I couldn't help myself. I was pointing at him, trying to control the volume of my shaky voice. "...he attacked me. Hudson saved me, and he ran off, but I saw his face, and that's *him,* Joanna. We have to call the police."

"I think I recognize him," Joanna whispered, her voice hushed. She finally managed to pull a wad of cash out of her bag and slap it on the bar. "Let's go, come on."

"*Recognize him?* From *where?* How would *you* know him?" The nausea I had felt earlier returned with a vengeance, but this time, it wasn't just from stress. I felt light-headed, the room spinning slightly around me.

"Madeline?" Joanna's voice was distant, muffled.

I tried to stand, tried to shake off the dizziness, but everything went black.

***

I woke up to the sterile smell of antiseptic and the faint beeping of machines. My head was pounding, and as I blinked my eyes open, the harsh fluorescent lights of the hospital came into focus. Joanna was sitting beside me, her face etched with worry.

"Well, hey there, sleepyhead," she said, putting down a magazine she'd been reading and standing up.

"What... what happened?" I asked, my voice raspy.

"You fainted," Joanna said softly. "At the bar. I brought you to the ER."

I groaned, rubbing my temples. "Great. Just what I needed."

"The doctors ran some tests. They'll bring back the results soon. I told them that you'd been under a lot of stress, but still, just to be safe." She rested the back of her hand on my forehead. "You scared me."

"I'm sorry."

She let out a breathy chuckle, biting her bottom lip. "Don't apologize to me, Madeline. You fainted. There's nothing to be sorry for."

"No, there is, though. Because I've been ruining everything for everyone pretty solidly for months."

She grabbed one of my hands and murmured in a serious voice, "None of this is your fault. Stop that. You rest. I'm going to grab your doctor and tell him you're up."

Luckily, I didn't have to sit with my thoughts for long because she left and returned within the span of a few minutes. My doctor was close behind her, telling her she'd have to step out. "No, she can stay," I piped up.

"I really must insist I give your confidential medical information to you confidentially," the doctor said, firmly. She had a serious look on her tan face.

I nodded quietly, and Joanna slithered out of the room backward, mouthing, 'I love you.'

The doctor stood at the end of my bed with my open clipboard in front of her.

"First things first, you're completely healthy. Okay? So let's get that out of the way. Your friend seemed pretty worried."

"Okay..."

She closed the clipboard and held it to her chest. "But did you know that you're pregnant? She didn't, so I have to ask."

My heart skipped a beat. "What do you mean? Did I know...?"

Her eyes softened a bit as she repeated herself. "You're pregnant. Four weeks along, it looks like."

For a moment, the world stopped. My breath hitched, and I felt like I was floating outside of my body, watching everything from a distance. *Pregnant.* The word echoed in my mind, over and over, until it finally sank in.

I was pregnant. With Hudson's child.

"I... I can't be," I whispered, shaking my head. But deep down, I knew it was true. The nausea, the fatigue, the strange feeling I'd had for weeks... it all made sense now.

"Do you have anyone you can talk to? Do you need resources?" the doctor asked, a look of concern on her face.

"Um, I need Joanna," I whispered, shaking my head slightly.

"Joanna? Oh, the woman out – sure. I'll send her in. In the meantime, here's some pamphlets on your next steps. You have choices."

Choices. I knew what that meant. I couldn't even think about my *choices* right now.

The door creaked open and Joanna walked over to me, reaching for my hand and squeezing it gently. "Everything okay?"

"I'm pregnant," I told her numbly, staring off past her at the wall, my mind far away as I thought of my dad and what he would think. He barely forgave me, he said he would *never* forgive Hudson, and now I had to drop this bomb on him. I didn't know if I could ever repair the damage I had done.

"Whose...never mind." She stroked the back of my hand. "I know it's a lot. But we'll figure this out, okay? You're not alone."

Tears welled up in my eyes as the reality of it all crashed over me. I was carrying Hudson's baby. The man I had been trying to distance myself from, the man I had told myself I needed to forget.

But now? Now everything was different.

"I need to go to Miami," I said suddenly, my voice shaky. "I need to tell him."

Joanna nodded, her expression understanding. "So it's Hudson's."

I nodded, finally meeting her eyes as mine swam.

"Do you want me to come with you?"

I shook my head, wiping away the tears. "No. I need to do this on my own."

Joanna gave a weak smile. "I understand. You may need to do this part on your own, but you're not alone. I'm going to look into that Honda guy. I'm going to see if I can find out more about him. And we're definitely filing a report. You shouldn't have to deal with a stalker while you're dealing with...this."

This. My pregnancy is a 'this' situation indeed.

I squeezed her hand. "Thank you."

***

The flight to Miami was a blur. My mind raced with a thousand different thoughts, all tangled together in a mess of emotions I couldn't even begin to untangle. How was I supposed to tell Hudson? *How would he react? Would he be happy? Shocked? Angry?*

And what about Kenzie? How would this change things for her? She would be a big sister to a half-sister. That was a lot to put on a little girl, especially with her fears of abandonment.

What if I could never give her the relationship with her sibling that she deserved? What if she didn't get to see me as much as she wanted? How could I hurt her, too? That was the last thing I wanted to do.

I stared out the window of the plane, my hand resting on my stomach, still trying to wrap my head around the fact that I was carrying Hudson's child. I couldn't feel anything in there yet. It felt like a stomach, nothing else.

It felt surreal, like something out of a dream. Or maybe a nightmare. I wasn't sure yet.

By the time I landed in Miami, my nerves were completely shot. I hadn't even told Hudson I was coming. I wasn't ready for that conversation yet. But Kenzie... I had to see her.

Kenzie had been sending me little texts through the nanny's phone for days now, and every time my heart ached a little more. I missed her so much. Missed both of them. But Kenzie... she had wormed her way into my heart.

As I sat in the back of the cab, driving toward Hudson's house, I stared down at my phone, my fingers hovering over the keyboard. I needed to tell him. But I couldn't just blurt it out, not like this.

Hey. I'm back in Miami. I'd love to see Kenzie. She's been texting me and I miss her. Let me know if it's okay.

I hit send before I could second-guess myself. My heart pounded as I waited for a response, my stomach twisting with nerves. I told myself this was about Kenzie—that I needed to see her, to check in on her—but deep down, I knew it wasn't just about her.

It was about Hudson, too.

I missed him. God, I missed him more than I wanted to admit. And now, with this news... with our baby growing inside me... I didn't know how to feel. Part of me was terrified. The other part of me... well, I wasn't sure if it was hope or something else entirely.

My phone buzzed, and I nearly dropped it in my haste to check the message.

Of course. Come by whenever you're ready. Do you want me to send you a car?

My heart skipped a beat. His answer was simple, straightforward. But I knew Hudson. I knew he was probably as nervous as I was, even if he didn't show it. It was just like him to offer to send a car even if he was planning on calling it off.

No need, I typed back. The cab pulled up to the familiar house, and for a moment, I just sat there, staring at it. This was it. There was no turning back now.

I took a deep breath, paid the driver, and stepped out onto the driveway. As I approached the front door, my heart pounded harder in my chest. I was about to face Hudson. About to face the reality of what was happening inside me.

I knocked on the door, my hands trembling slightly, and waited, my anxiety growing like the life inside of me.

.

Thirty-Two
Hudson

I couldn't sit still. Every minute that passed felt like an eternity as I paced the length of my kitchen, staring down at my phone.

Madeline was on her way, and Kenzie was at my side, jumping up and down, but it wasn't Kenzie's excitement that had me on edge. It was the feeling in my gut that something wasn't right.

I had already hired a private investigator. It was the only thing I could think of doing after seeing that Honda parked outside of my house one too many times.

I knew the car wasn't just a coincidence. The PI had tracked down some leads, but nothing concrete yet. Whoever was behind this knew how to stay out of sight. But I couldn't shake the feeling that it was all connected—Jon, the bar, the weird calls Madeline had been get-

ting. I needed answers, but right now, all I could do was w
ait.

And waiting was the hardest part.

I glanced out the window toward the driveway, my heart
racing as I thought about Madeline coming over. It had
been weeks since I'd seen her, and every day since she left
had felt like a slow torture. I'd thought about calling her,
reaching out, but I didn't want to push. She had asked
for space, and I'd respected that. But now she was here,
coming to see Kenzie. And I was nervous as hell.

*What if she didn't want to talk to me? What if things had
changed?*

I shook my head, trying to push the doubts away. I
couldn't let myself spiral like this. Not now. Not after I
had promised her dad that I could handle anything that
came my way, that I could be a strong man for Madeline.

Just as I was about to start pacing again, I heard the soft
rumble of a car pulling up outside. My heart jumped
into my throat. She was here.

I moved toward the front door, my palms suddenly
sweaty. When I opened it, there she was—Madeline,

standing on the doorstep, looking as beautiful as ever. But something was wrong.

She was pale, her usual bright energy dimmed, and she kept glancing away from me like she didn't know what to say.

I wanted to pull her into my arms, to ask her what was going on, but I held back. "Hey," I said softly, my voice betraying how nervous I was. "Come in."

She nodded, stepping past me into the house. Her eyes scanned the room, but they didn't settle on anything. I could tell she was distracted, maybe even anxious, and that only made my nerves worse.

"Kenzie's in her room," I added, trying to keep the conversation light. "She's been talking about seeing you all week."

Madeline smiled, but it didn't reach her eyes. "I've missed her."

I watched her carefully as she moved toward the kitchen, her steps slower than usual. Something was definitely off.

I followed her, my mind racing with questions. She seemed... like she was holding something back. I was afraid of what that something might be. It had been such a rocky road to her dad finding out. I didn't know how it would feel to be dumped right after the hard thing that had happened. Not that I was anyone to her. She couldn't dump me. She could simply decide not to do whatever...*this*...was anymore.

When we reached the kitchen, she leaned against the counter, her eyes darting around the room. I couldn't take it anymore. I had to know what was going on. "Madeline," I said softly, stepping closer. "What's wrong?"

She didn't answer right away. Instead, she stared at me for a long moment, like she was trying to find the words. Her hands were trembling slightly, and that's when I couldn't hold back anymore.

I reached out, pulling her gently into my arms, and to my surprise, she let me. She leaned into me, her body soft and warm against mine, and for the first time in weeks, I felt like I could breathe again. Her breathing matched mine, a gentle ebb and flow, and I felt our heartbeats match.

"I talked to your dad," I said, my voice low. "He didn't give me his blessing."

Madeline let out a soft sigh, her head resting against my chest. "I know," she murmured. "My mom told me."

I tightened my arms around her, wanting to protect her from everything, from whatever was weighing her down. I could feel her trembling slightly, and it took everything in me not to push her to tell me what was going on. I wanted to know—needed to know—but I didn't want to force her.

"But he didn't kill me, so that's good." I looked down at her and smiled. "And he said he'd let you make a choice for yourself."

We stood there in silence for a long moment, just holding each other, and I felt the tension between us start to melt away.

Slowly, she pulled back, her eyes searching mine. "Hudson..." she began, her voice hesitant. "There's something I need to tell you."

My heart skipped a beat. She was about to say something important, something that had been weighing on her mind for weeks. I could see it in her eyes, the way they flickered with uncertainty and fear. I wanted to tell her that whatever it was, we'd figure it out together. But before she could get the words out, the doorbell rang.

I cursed under my breath, my body tensing as the moment shattered around us. Madeline blinked, her expression shifting from one of vulnerability to confusion.

I followed her toward the door, my stomach twisting with annoyance. Whoever it was, their timing couldn't have been worse.

When I opened the door, my frustration only grew. Joanna stood there, her face lit up with excitement, completely unaware that she had just interrupted something important. Madeline's best friend, always the unpredictable wild card.

"Joanna?" Madeline said, her voice laced with surprise. "What are you doing here?"

Joanna grinned, stepping inside without waiting for an invitation. "I have big news! And I couldn't wait to tell you."

Madeline glanced at me, her expression a mix of confusion and anxiety. "How did you know I was here?"

"You told me," Joanna said, her forehead wrinkled in confusion. "Plus, we share our locations, remember?"

Joanna waved her phone in the air. "You're not mad, are you?"

Madeline shook her head, though I could tell she wasn't exactly thrilled with Joanna's arrival. She was holding something back—something big—and now we were going to have to wait.

I stood there, my mind spinning, trying to piece together what had just happened. One minute, Madeline was about to tell me something important, and the next, Joanna was bursting through the door with some kind of news.

"What's this big news?" I asked, trying to keep my tone neutral, though I couldn't hide the tension in my voice.

Thirty-Three
Madeline

Joanna barely made it through the door before I knew something serious was going on. The usual spark in her eyes was replaced by something heavier, more urgent.

We walked toward Hudson's office. I could feel Hudson tense beside me, his hand brushing mine for a split second, but I was too focused on Joanna to respond. My heart was already beating too fast, and I had no idea what to expect from her.

"Joanna, what's going on?" I asked, unable to keep the anxiety from creeping into my voice. She'd come all the way to Hudson's house, and that alone told me whatever she had found wasn't good.

She glanced at me, then at Hudson, before taking a deep breath. "I figured out who the guy was—the one you saw at the club in Park City."

A cold chill washed over me. My mind immediately went back to that night, the fainting, the nausea, the blurred image of that man.

My stomach tightened, and I could feel Hudson stiffen beside me, his protective instincts kicking in. "What club? What guy?" Hudson's voice was low, controlled, but I could hear the underlying anger.

He wasn't angry at me; he was angry at himself for not being there, for having so many questions about something that was clearly important.

"Um," I swallowed and looked up at the ceiling, trying to think of how to tell the story in a way that made sense without telling him about my trip to the ER. "I went to the club with Joanna my last night in Utah and I saw the guy in the Honda."

"You saw him? And you didn't tell me?" Hudson grabbed my inner elbow and whirled me to face him. "You have to make safer decisions, Madeline! We need you safe, both of us."

"What's wrong?" Kenzie asked, from the doorway, and Hudson rushed to close the door to the office, telling her, "Nothing, baby, grown up stuff. We'll be right in there with you. Why don't you pick a movie?"

He turned back to me and growled, "You belong here with us, where I can keep an eye on you."

Joanna cleared her throat, snapping him out of it. He looked up at her and snapped the hair tie around his wrist. "I'm sorry. Go ahead, Joanna."

She pulled her phone from her pocket and started scrolling. "I know him because he's connected to Jon," she said quietly, her voice tinged with hesitation but an underlying excitement present. "It took me a while to place him, but then I remembered seeing him in some of Jon's social media posts."

I blinked, trying to process what she was saying. "Jon?" I repeated, the name leaving a bitter taste in my mouth.

Everything had been coming back to Jon lately, and part of me knew it had to be him, but I was holding out hope. It didn't make sense after I saw the man's face how it could still be connected to Jon.

Did he put a hit out on me? That guy almost fucking killed me!

If he did, this... this was a new low, even for him.

Joanna nodded, and then she handed me her phone. "Look."

Hudson and I leaned in, staring at the screen. There, clear as day, was a photo of Jon and the man from the club, standing together at a poker table, grinning like they were on top of the world. The caption read 'Vegas, baby!!!'

My heart dropped. This was the man who had been following me. The man who had been in Miami lurking in the shadows. And he was a friend of Jon's? Just some guy that Jon got drunk with in Vegas? Just a regular idiot like Jon?

"Who is he?" I asked, my voice shaky. "What's his connection to Jon?"

Joanna hesitated again, like she wasn't sure how to explain.

"His name is Mark," she said slowly. "He's a poker buddy of Jon's. Jon loves to gamble—it's kind of his thing. He can afford to lose money, but Mark... he's not in the same financial position. From what I know, Mark owes Jon a lot of money. Like, *a lot*."

Hudson cursed under his breath, taking a step back, his hands clenching into fists. I could feel the anger rolling off him in waves, but all I could do was stare at the picture. At Mark. The man who had dragged me into waters I was terrified of and choked me.

Jon had sent this guy after me? To spy on me? To sabotage Hudson's projects? Had he also been the one who had done the slideshow or was that Jon? And what did Jon have to gain from all this?

I handed the phone back to Joanna. My fingers trembled, but I wasn't afraid. I was angry. "So, Jon put him up to this because... what? He wants to ruin my life?"

Joanna frowned, her eyes softening with sympathy. "I don't know all the details yet, but I think that's part of it. Jon's ego is bruised. He hates that you're with Hudson, and he's not used to losing. I think he's using Mark to mess with you both. And since Mark owes him money, he's probably willing to do whatever Jon tells him."

I felt sick. It was now confirmed. The man I had once trusted, the man I had once loved, was now behind this entire mess. The sabotage, the vandalism, the stalking... it all came back to Jon. But what was worse was that he'd dragged other people into it, people like Mark, who were desperate enough to follow his lead.

Hudson stood rigidly beside me, his eyes locked on Joanna. "You're sure about this?" he asked, his voice rough. "You're sure Jon's behind all of it?"

Joanna nodded. "I'm sure. I've been trying to figure out why things were going wrong for you, Madeline. At first, I thought it was just bad luck, and then...I'm ashamed to say this, but I thought it was Jon, and I didn't know what to do, so I did nothing. But when we saw Mark at the club in Park City, and you said that was the guy following you...well, obviously that couldn't be Jon. I knew I recognized him, I just didn't know where from. Then, when I went through Jon's posts, everything started to click."

Hudson huffed and ran a hand through his hair. He turned as though to leave, then turned back around.

I could see the conflict in his eyes—anger, frustration, and something else. Something deeper. Guilt, maybe? The realization that I had been in danger, and he hadn't been there to stop it.

"I'm sorry, Madeline," Joanna said softly, her voice breaking through the silence. "I should have seen this sooner. I should have warned you."

I shook my head quickly. "No, Joanna, this isn't your fault. You've done more than enough by figuring this out. I just... I don't understand why Jon would go to such lengths. What does he think he's going to accomplish by sabotaging my life? By stalking me?"

Joanna's eyes flickered with guilt. "Jon has always been... complicated."

"He's not complicated, he's a psychopath!" Hudson exploded, slamming his fist against the nearby foyer wall. "Madeline, how long ago did you and this guy break up?"

"Three years ago."

"Three years ago?! My God, that's forever in your twenties! What's wrong with your brother, Joanna?!" He turned to her with rage simmering in his eyes. He looked like he blamed her for her brother.

And her eyes sinking to the ground showed that she took that blame readily. "He's used to getting what he wants, and when he doesn't, he doesn't handle it well. I think, in his mind, he believes that if he can mess with your life enough, maybe you'll come back to him. Or maybe it's just about control."

"Either way, it's sick," Hudson spat. He stepped forward, his hand reaching out for mine. I could feel the warmth of his touch, the steadiness of it, and it grounded me in that moment. "We're going to stop him," he said firmly. "Whatever he's planning, it ends now."

I nodded, trying to hold onto Hudson's words, trying to believe that we could fix this. But there was still that nagging feeling in the back of my mind. *Why had Jon escalated things to this level? Why was he so desperate to destroy everything I had built, everything Hudson and I were building together?*

As if reading my thoughts, Joanna spoke up again. "I don't think it's just about you, Madeline. He's targeting Hudson, too. You know how competitive he is. I did some digging and found out that Hudson was the one who blacklisted Jon's commercial resort project in Miami, the one that Jon was considering as potentially the peak of his career, and he's been furious ever since. He sees you two together, and it's like a double blow to his pride."

I closed my eyes, the weight of everything pressing down on me. Now it all made sense. This wasn't just about me and Jon's broken relationship. It was about Hudson, about the tangled mess of business and egos and jealousy. Jon wasn't just trying to hurt me—he was trying to destroy Hudson, too.

While I processed the news, Hudson whispered, "So it's my fault. This whole time I kept wondering, 'why now?' I knew he was a stalker, but I didn't know why he'd waited so long. And then, I thought I had made so many enemies, but I also—"

Hudson looked at me with regret on his face, the small crinkles around his mouth etched deeper, "I thought this was about you. I thought for sure Jon was behind this and this was about you. I couldn't make sense of any of it."

He wrapped me in his arms. "I'm so sorry. I can't believe my actions put your safety in jeopardy. I'll never forgive myself."

Keeping my eyes closed, I hugged him back, enjoying the embrace. In his arms, I felt like none of this mattered. I could live enclosed in his chest, and all of this would melt away.

Except it wouldn't. "Hudson, none of this is your fault. The only one at fault is Jon. He needs to learn how to handle rejection. You blacklisting that project doesn't justify this response." I snapped my eyes open. "So what do we do now?" I asked, stepping back from Hudson's embrace and looking between him and Joanna. "How do we stop him?"

Joanna sighed, running a hand through her hair. "I'm still piecing everything together, but we need to be smart about this. If Jon's willing to go this far, we can't underestimate him. I'm afraid for you, Madeline. We need to get proof, solid evidence, of what he's been doing. Once we have that, we can confront him with the law."

I felt a punch in my gut as I remembered this was her brother we were talking about. I squeezed Hudson's hand with mine and reached out with the other to grab hers. "You'd do that for me? You know he's your brother."

She nodded. "I care about Jon, but he made his bed. He has to lie in it. You're my best friend, Madeline. He can't fuck with you like this."

Hudson nodded, too, his jaw tight. "I'll talk to my PI. See if we can dig up more on Mark and his connection to Jon. But you're right—we need to be smart."

I took a deep breath, trying to steady myself. The thought of confronting Jon made my skin crawl, but I knew we had no choice. He had crossed too many lines, and now it was time to end this.

Joanna looked at me, her expression softening again. "Madeline, I want you to know that this isn't about family loyalty for me. It's about doing what's right. That is why I became a lawyer in the first place. And that is why I'm doing this now."

I gave her a small, grateful smile, but the unease in my chest didn't go away. Hudson squeezed my hand, and I leaned into him, feeling his strength, his resolve. Whatever happened next, we would face it together.

But as I stood there, holding Hudson's hand, my mind couldn't shake the feeling that this was only the beginning. Jon wasn't going to back down easily, and neither was the man he'd sent after us.

And that terrified me. Almost as much as all this happening without telling Hudson about the secret in my womb.

Thirty-Four
Hudson

We sat around the table, tension hanging heavy in the air as we plotted. We'd all watched *Encanto* with more tension in the room than anyone ever had, waiting for it to be Kenzie's bedtime.

As soon as she went to bed, Joanna laid it all out—a plan to lure Jon to Miami, to trap him into revealing what he'd been up to. I hated that it had come to this, but there was no other way. He wasn't going to stop. Not until we made him.

"I'll text him," Madeline said, her voice steady but quiet. She was calmer than I would've expected, given everything we'd just learned. But I knew this was taking a toll on her; I hated that she had to be the one to bait Jon. And I hated that she was baiting him. It disgusted me that he would, even for a second, think he had Madeline for his own.

"Are you sure you're up for this?" I asked, watching her carefully. I didn't want her doing something she wasn't ready for.

She met my gaze, her eyes clear but tired. "Yes. This is the only way. If I tell him I want to talk, that I'm willing to consider... you know, what he wants... he'll come. He won't be able to resist."

My blood boiled again at the thought of what Madeline would have to say to him, but I forced myself to keep calm. This wasn't about my pride—it was about protecting Madeline. And if this was how we had to do it, then so be it.

"All right," I said, nodding. "We'll be ready when he shows up."

Joanna nodded, pulling out her phone. "I'll be monitoring everything from the hotel. I'll text you when he's on his way, then you hit record. Don't worry about waiting until he gets here. I don't want your nerves to be going and you to forget. Once we get him talking, we'll have enough to take him down."

Madeline took a deep breath and pulled out her own phone. I could see her fingers tremble slightly as she typed out the message, but she stayed focused. I admired her strength, her resilience. This wasn't easy, but she was doing it.

"There," she said, after a moment, putting her phone down on the table. "I told him we need to talk, and that I've been thinking about what he said. He'll take the bait." I wondered if that was really all she had said. I was certain there must have been some...flair...added.

We waited in silence for a few agonizing minutes before her phone buzzed. She picked it up, glanced at the screen, and then looked up at me.

"He's coming tomorrow," she said, her voice flat. "He said he'll be in town."

I felt the tension in the room shift. It was happening. Tomorrow, we'd face Jon head-on, and this nightmare would finally be over. At least, that's what I hoped.

Joanna stood up, grabbing her bag. "I'll head back to the hotel and start putting everything in place. We'll nail him, Madeline. He won't get away with this."

Madeline nodded, but I could see the exhaustion in her eyes. She was strong, but even she had limits.

379

Once Joanna was out the door, the silence between us was thick, heavy with unspoken fears and unresolved tension.

I stood up, walking over to where Madeline sat, and reached for her hand. "Hey," I said softly. "We're going to get through this."

She looked up at me, her eyes soft but weary. "I know. I just wish... I wish it didn't have to be this way."

I pulled her into my arms, and she leaned into me, her body fitting perfectly against mine. "Me, too," I murmured against her hair. "But we'll be okay. We'll get him, and this will all be behind us."

She tilted her head up, her lips brushing my neck as she let out a soft sigh. "Will it? You won't be mad?"

"Mad?" I asked, confusion wringing my stomach. "Why would I be mad at you?"

"For introducing this guy into your life. I can't shake this feeling that this is all my fault." Her eyes were gentle, and I could see the emotion in them.

I tipped her head up to mine by her chin and brushed her cheek with my other hand. "None of this is your fault. If anything, I'm the one who added to all this by unknowingly making him my enemy in business. But I've been through worse. We'll get through it, I promise you that."

She sighed, pulling her head away from my hand and burying her face into my chest. "There will just be more. My dad, for starters."

I held onto her back, rubbing it in circles the way she had done for me many times. "He'll come around."

"Do you really think so?" she asked in my chest, her voice muffled.

I tightened my hold on her. "Yeah, I do. He's angry now, but he'll see how much I love you. He will."

Madeline nodded, but I could feel the lingering doubt in her. It had been hard enough dealing with Jon—dealing with her father's disapproval was another battle entirely. I wasn't giving up though. Not on her. Not on us.

She lifted her face to me and smiled, a soft, sad smile that made my heart ache. But then she leaned in, pressing her lips to mine, and all the worry, all the fear melted away. It was just her and me. In that moment, everything else disappeared.

I kissed her back, my hands sliding down to her waist, pulling her closer. I needed to feel her, to remind myself that she was here, with me, and that nothing—not Jon, not her father—could come between us.

She moaned softly against my mouth, her fingers threading through my hair, and I deepened the kiss, my heart pounding in my chest.

We stumbled toward the bedroom, our lips never breaking apart, the heat between us rising with every step. By the time we reached the bed, I was desperate for her, for the connection that only she could give me.

I laid her down gently, my hands exploring her body as our clothes quickly disappeared. Every touch, every kiss was a reminder of how much I loved her, how much I needed her in my life.

"Hudson," she whispered, searching my eyes for an answer to a question she hadn't asked. "I love you."

Hearing those words, in that moment, was everything. I kissed her again, slower this time, savoring the way her body responded to mine, the way we fit together so perfectly. "I love you, too, Madeline."

"It makes me sick that Jon thought you might want him back," I growled, hovering over her, my hands on either side of her face. I pressed my forehead to hers. She had nowhere to go and nothing to look at but me.

"Me, too. I don't want anyone but you, Hudson, I promise," she whispered, stretching her neck to kiss my lips.

For a moment, I kissed her back, but then I held her at bay with a hand on her sternum. "Say that you're mine."

"I'm yours." Her voice was breathy as she complied.

I lowered my mouth to her nipples and ran my tongue in circles over them. "Say it again."

She gasped out, "I'm yours, Hudson."

"That's good. You keep saying that." I grabbed her by the waist and flipped her over so that she was on her stomach. She moved to prop herself up on her hands and knees, but I pushed her back down on her stomach, crumpling her arms underneath her. "You lie there like the princess you are and take it. Your pussy and your ass are mine, right?"

"Yes, sir," she whined, her ass arched in the air as I pinned her down by her lower back.

"Say it. I'm not going to ask you again," I demanded, as I lowered my mouth to her cheeks and rubbed them with my hands, watching them jiggle underneath my fingers. Then I dove in, enjoying the way she squirmed and sighed underneath my tongue.

She moaned out, "My pussy and my ass are yours, Hudson."

"That's right," I told her, with my mouth on her ass and her ass cheeks squeezing my face, smelling her pussy even from where I was.

I slid my hand beneath her and tried to circle her clit with my finger as I ate her ass. I was rewarded with a guttural moan.

"That's right," I repeated, slower, listening to her turn into an animal beneath my hands and mouth.

I sat up on my knees and pulled her up by her waist so that she was pointing her beautiful ass at me. I poked my cockhead at her pussy, watching as it opened slightly for me, revealing a rich red. I pulled back and she moaned, "Please, Hudson."

"Please what?" I asked, pressing it against her opening, letting her entrance take me for just a second before taking it back again. "Say what you want."

"Please fuck me," she begged, her voice embarrassed and small.

"You want me to fuck you? Why's that?"

"Because I'm yours." Her voice was resolute, determined to have me inside her.

Hearing her say that did something to me, and I couldn't help myself from plunging all of my length into her. She cried out, pressing her face into the pillow, and I continued to pound inside her, forcing my entire length as far as it would go.

I ripped the pillow that she was unleashing her screams into out from under her and shoved it under her stomach. I murmured into her ear, "Hump this pillow while I take you." I laid down on top of her and fucked her with full force.

Her legs were clamped tight, squeezing me with her canal. I grunted as I felt her pushing me out. She was so wet that she was slick, and I had to use all my might to push through the barrier she made with her pulsing pussy.

She let out one long groan and went limp as I pushed inside her with my entirety, feeling an electrical current zapping through my shaft.

My balls were slapping against her, and she groaned out, "I'm going to cum. This pillow is...rubbing against me." She seemed embarrassed at the fact as if it wasn't the exact reason I told her to do it.

"That's good, baby. You should cum. You deserve it. You've been such a good girl." I held her around the middle in a hug as I used her body for my own ejaculation, letting her body control the rhythm that I followed. I moved in waves, pushing my hips against her in a swooping motion, enjoying the padding that her ass provided.

"I'm really going to—" She cut herself off with a breath that told me she was orgasming, and she started squeezing me again, cutting off circulation to my erection. I enjoyed the sensation, thrusting my cock through it, letting her ride that orgasm as long as she could, until I felt my own finally mounting and exploding.

I came quickly and deliberately. It had been so long since I'd touched Madeline. I could have cum the minute I saw her breasts again, but this had been wonderful torture to go through. When I felt her breath slowing down, I slowed my motions, too, feeling my cock deflate inside her.

We moved together, our bodies entwined, the world outside fading away. For those moments, it was just us. No Jon, no schemes, no worries. Just Madeline and me, locked in a rhythm that felt like home.

As we lay there afterward, her head resting on my chest, I stroked her hair, feeling the steady rise and fall of her breath. Everything was calm now, peaceful. Tomorrow would be a storm, but tonight, we had each other.

And that was all I needed right now.

Thirty-Five
Madeline

The weight of my secret was suffocating. Every time I thought about telling Hudson I was pregnant, a wave of anxiety pulled me underwater. I had rehearsed the words in my head a hundred times, but I couldn't bring myself to say them. Not yet. Not until Jon was out of the picture once and for all.

I stood in front of the mirror, staring at my reflection, trying to steady my breath. How could I tell Hudson that I was carrying his child when Jon was still lurking in the background, manipulating everything, trying to control my life?

No, I had to settle things with Jon first. I had to make him confess. Then, maybe I'd be able to breathe again.

The plan was set. I had made peace with Juan, the bar owner, and he was on board. He didn't believe for a second that I had anything to do with the flooding anymore, not after I showed him the truth behind the sabotage. He agreed to let Jon and me meet at the bar before it opened—neutral ground, a place where I could corner Jon and finally get him to admit what he'd done. I needed to hear it from his mouth, needed him to say it so I could take it to the police and put an end to this madness.

I grabbed my phone and checked the time. It was almost noon. Jon would be at the bar soon, and I had to be ready. I couldn't afford to let my emotions get in the way, not this time.

I closed my eyes, taking a deep breath. This wasn't just about me anymore. It was about my future. My child's future. And Hudson's. I placed my hand on my stomach, feeling the slightest flutter there, and a surge of determination washed over me.

This had to end today.

***

The bar was eerily quiet when I arrived. The usual hustle and bustle of patrons and music was missing, and the stillness only added to my nerves. Matt wasn't in yet, but the owner was, and he gave me a nod from behind the counter as I walked in, his face serious. He knew how important this was.

"Thanks again for this," I said, quietly, as I approached the bar. My voice felt shaky, but I kept my composure.

"No problem, Madeline," he replied, giving me a reassuring smile. "I hope this works out the way you need it to."

I nodded, my heart pounding in my chest. It had to work. It was my only chance to get Jon to show his true colors.

I took a seat at one of the tables near the back, my eyes darting to the entrance every few seconds. I was on edge waiting for Jon to show up, rehearsing what I would say, how I would handle him. I needed to keep my cool, no matter what he threw at me.

I'm safe, I told myself. *Hudson is waiting and watching in the parking lot. He won't let anything happen to me.*

The door creaked open, and there he was. Jon. He was wearing a button-up shirt and crisp jeans, trying to show me what a stand-up guy he was. But his smug expression gave away the demons underneath. He thought he had the upper hand. His sick little brain had convinced him that torturing me had worked and that I was running back into his arms.

My stomach turned as he made his way toward me, but I forced a smile, pretending I wasn't completely repulsed by the sight of him.

"Madeline," he said, smoothly, sitting down across from me. "I'd say I wasn't expecting this, but, well, we both always knew you'd come back to me, didn't we?"

"Did we?" I asked, my eyebrows shooting up. I folded my hands in front of me, knocking on my phone with my pinkie. It was face down and recording, and it made my heart rate spike to remember that. "Well, I guess you were right. I've been thinking about what you said, Jon. About us."

His eyes gleamed, and I could tell he thought he'd won. I could almost see the wheels turning in his head, the way he believed he had me exactly where he wanted me.

"Good," he replied, leaning back in his chair, completely at ease. "Because, Madeline, we were really good together. It was a mistake to break up. I'm glad you see that n ow."

I forced myself to smile, even though the thought of being with him again made my skin crawl. "I've been so afraid lately, and it's really...made me think of how safe I felt with you." I held back a gag, transitioning it into a smile.

Jon exhaled, a long breath, and said, "That SEAL didn't make you feel safe?"

I tilted my head. "How'd you know about him anyway?"

He shrugged. "You know I keep tabs on you, Maddie. You're important to me. I always watch out for people important to me. I never let them go."

He reached out for my hand, and I let him take it, even though it made my skin go clammy. "I need a drink. How about you?"

I shook my head, remembering the precious life inside me. "I have to work later." I giggled, to seem like otherwise, I'd consider it extremely normal to drink at this time.

"How about water?" he asked, standing up.

BABY FOR MY DAD'S SEAL BEST FRIEND

An image flashed through my mind of him spiking my drink on the way back to the table, and I shivered. "No, I'm good, thank you."

He eyed me for a moment before shrugging and walking to the bar to get himself something. He came back and slid into the booth. "So, you were saying you've been feeling unsafe."

He took a swig of his drink and leaned back, raising an eyebrow smugly. "Why's that?"

I fidgeted, interlocking my fingers and releasing them over and over. "Um, a lot of bad stuff has been happening lately."

"Is that right? Well, maybe that's the universe telling you who you need."

I took a slow breath, trying to keep my temper in check. "Maybe you're right. Maybe the universe led me back to you."

He smiled and hopped a little in his seat, jumpy. "Well, okay, not just the universe."

"What do you mean?"

393

"Well, I'm behind some of the things that reminded you how much you needed me. Only someone who really cared about you could do what I've done for you."

"That's why you've been sabotaging my life? Why you've been spying on Hudson? Why you sent that guy Mark to attack me?"

Jon's smirk faded slightly, and I could see the flicker of panic in his eyes. He hadn't expected me to bring up Hudson. "That's not—" he started, but I cut him off.

"Don't lie, Jon. I know what you've been doing. The sabotage, the vandalism, the spying. You're just jealous of what Hudson and I have. You're still the same jealous guy you always have been."

Jon's face hardened, his smug confidence cracking. He glared at me, his jaw clenched tight. "You don't understand how this works, Madeline. You think Hudson's some kind of hero? He screwed me over. He owes me."

I shook my head, my heart pounding in my chest. "Hudson doesn't owe you anything. What, because he wouldn't approve that project you wanted in Miami? You're doing all of this because you're desperate. You never valued me when we were together, and now you think you can just waltz back into my life because it's convenient for you? Because you think it'll make you look good in front of your bosses? And because you want to take out your revenge on Hudson?"

Jon's expression darkened, and for a moment, I thought he might actually lash out. Instead, he let out a bitter laugh, leaning back in his chair. "You always were too smart for your own good."

My pulse quickened. This was it. I needed to push him, to get him to admit everything.

"So, what was the plan?" I asked, crossing my arms. "You thought if you sabotaged my career, I'd come running back to you? That I'd just give up everything I've worked for and be the trophy wife you need to make partner?"

Jon shrugged, his smirk returning. "Something like that. I figured if I made things hard enough for you, you'd see that being with me was the easier option. You wouldn't have to fight so hard. I could take care of you. And it worked."

I stared at him, my blood boiling.

He really thought I'd just give up? That I'd throw away everything I had built because he made things difficult?

I leaned forward, my voice low and steady. "Is that what you think? You think your delusional plan worked? You've underestimated me, Jon, as usual. You think you can manipulate us, but you're wrong. I'm not going to let you control my life, and I'm not going to let you get away with what you've done."

Jon's eyes narrowed, and I could see the anger bubbling beneath the surface. "You think you're going to stop me, Madeline? You think you and Hudson are going to walk away from this unscathed?"

I stood up, my hands trembling with rage. "You'll have to kill me, then. Cause I'm not coming back."

He looked up at me. "I'm not going to kill you, Madeline," he said softly. "What Mark did...he panicked. Those weren't his directions. I'm sorry that happened. But you can't hate me after everything we've been through."

I looked down my nose at him, taking in the momentary look of regret on his face. "If you're sorry, apologize for everything. Tell me everything you've done to me since I've been in Miami. And apologize. Then I'll consider not hating you anymore."

He twisted his face into something inhuman – fury, regret, I wasn't sure. He looked down at his beer and then back at me. "I sabotaged the gala and set up the slideshow to present pictures of you and Hudson. I'm sorry for that. I set fire to the hotel afterward. I'm sorry for that, too. I sent Mark to stalk and harass you, but he went too far and... hurt you. I'm sorry. I'm sorry that I also sabotaged the very bar we're in. And that I started the rumors that you cheated to win that award. There. Now you have it. I'm sorry for everything, Madeline, but you have to realize—"

"I don't have to realize anything. You need help, Jon." I bent at the waist so I could be at eye level to him. "You need serious, psychological help. You should look into that. Now leave us alone, or I will take this recording to the police."

He sneered at me, standing up to meet my gaze. I glanced out the window and saw, from the parking lot, Hudson getting out of his car, slamming the door behind him.

"You were recording me? And you think *I'm* the one who lacks empathy? While I sat there pouring my heart out, you were coming up with a plan to put me away?"

I didn't flinch and responded cooly, "Actually, I came up with the plan before you poured your heart out. Like I said, you underestimate me."

He stepped closer, so that our noses were almost grazing each other, and at that moment, Hudson came busting through the front door, his eyes wild.

Jon's face twisted in fury, but I didn't care. I was done being afraid of him. I was done letting him control my life. I stepped back, ready to let Hudson do whatever he wanted to do to him.

"You've made a big mistake, Madeline," Jon spat, his voice dripping with venom.

"And just how do you plan to correct her?" Hudson asked, pushing his chest with his palms. Jon stumbled backward, catching himself on the booth.

"No, Jon," I said, my voice steady. "You're the one who made the mistake. And now you're going to pay for it."

He clawed at me with one hand, looking to steady himself, and I stepped out of the way of his grasp, hissing, "Watch out for the baby!"

Thirty-Six
Hudson

I wasn't sure that I had heard Madeline right, but when I looked over at her, she had two hands around her stomach as if she was cradling a baby. Blood rushed in my ears, and I couldn't see anything as my vision blurred.

Time slowed down, my world crashing around me as her words echoed in my head. *Baby.* She said baby.

Madeline was pregnant?

My mind spun, trying to catch up with what was happening, but it felt like I was wading through molasses. Madeline was carrying a child?

I stared at her, my body frozen, my heart beating so fast I thought it might burst. She hadn't said anything.

Was it... my child?

I couldn't even form the question, my throat too tight, my thoughts too jumbled.

Something overtook me, and I gripped the front of Jon's shirt and pulled him toward me. "You have two choices right now, Jon. You can run like the bitch that we both know you are, or you can hit someone much bigger than you, but we both know you're not touching her in front of me."

For a moment, he hesitated, his eyes darting back and forth between me and Madeline. "Let go of me," he said, licking his teeth aggressively.

"Sure, just as soon as I can see your hands." Jon raised his hands in the air, and I pushed him back by his shirt, ripping a part of the collar. He stood looking at us both with pure malice before storming out of the bar. He slammed the door behind him, and I let out a shaky breath.

Relief washed over me.

I turned to Madeline and said, "I'm sorry if I got in the way of a confession, but I'm not risking your life for that. We can handle whatever else he throws our way."

A small smile tugged at her lips. "He confessed. We did it."

I grabbed her around the waist and pulled her into me, hugging her tightly. Her small frame fit perfectly into mine, and I breathed out into her neck as I held her.

As I pulled back from hugging Madeline, the rushing in my ears started to slow down. Seeing Jon get in her face like that had terrified me and angered me. It was a shame he'd run away as fast as he did – I was looking forward to hitting him. It would have been satisfying seeing that smug smile disappear under my fist.

"Are you okay?" I asked her, and she nodded with that serene smile still plastered across her face. "And are you...?"

I didn't know how to ask it. *Are you pregnant? Is it mine? Do you love me?*

"Madeline," I whispered, my voice hoarse. "Is it true?"

She didn't say anything at first, just clung to me, her breath shaky, her eyes wide with fear and exhaustion. My heart twisted painfully in my chest. I needed to hear it from her. I needed her to tell me what she had just blurted out a moment ago.

"Hudson..." she began, her voice barely audible. "I was going to tell you. I only just found out."

I stared at her, my heart racing, my mind reeling. Relief washed over me, followed by a flood of emotions I couldn't even begin to process.

I pulled her into me again, my hand instinctively resting on her stomach, as if I could already feel the life growing inside her. She trembled slightly, and I tightened my grip, needing her to feel safe, needing her to know that I was here.

"We should go," I said, quietly, my voice steadier than I felt. "Let's go home."

***

Back at my house, the reality of everything started to sink in. Madeline sat on the edge of the couch, her hands resting in her lap, while I paced the length of the living room, my mind racing.

I didn't know where to start, what to say. There were so many things I needed to know, so many emotions I was trying to sort through. But all I could think about was the fact that Madeline was carrying my child.

I stopped pacing and turned to her, my heart pounding. "Why didn't you tell me?" I asked, softly, my voice filled with more emotion than I intended.

She looked up at me, her eyes gentle but filled with exhaustion. "I...was planning to, of course. You know I was. I wouldn't keep something like that from you. I came that day to see Kenzie and tell you. But then Joanna showed up, and we had this whole plan, and I just wanted Jon out of my life first." She looked down at her fingers, picking at her nails, afraid to meet my eyes.

I stared at the top of her head, my mind whirling. "You weren't going to keep it a secret?"

She shook her head and said, "No, Hudson. Of course not."

The weight of her words lifted something inside me. Relief flooded through me, mixing with the overwhelming love I felt for her. She hadn't been hiding it. She had just been waiting for the right moment. And now... now I knew.

I moved toward her, kneeling in front of her, my hands gently covering hers. "Madeline," I whispered, my voice thick with emotion. "You're carrying our baby."

She nodded, tears welling up in her eyes, and I felt my heart swell with a kind of happiness I hadn't felt in years. I cupped her face in my hands. My thumbs brushed away the tears that were spilling down her cheeks.

"I'm so happy," I said, my voice breaking slightly. "Madeline, I'm so happy."

She let out a soft laugh, the tension in her shoulders finally easing. "I was so scared, Hudson. I didn't know how you'd feel about it. There's been so much going on, and I know this isn't the best time. If we were afraid of how my dad would feel before, well..."

I leaned forward, dropping my head into her lap, my heart racing with the overwhelming love I felt for her. "I'm ecstatic," I whispered. "You and me... and now, a baby? This is everything I've ever wanted. I don't care about the rest. You get to be my age, you hit a few snags. It works itself out."

Her hands moved to rest on my shoulders, her fingers trembling slightly as she held on to me. "I was scared," she admitted. "I didn't want to tell you until things with Jon were settled. I couldn't handle everything at once."

I nodded, understanding completely. "You don't have to be scared anymore. Jon's gone. Joanna's sending that recording to the cops. He's out of our lives. And now, we can focus on what really matters."

I kissed her softly, my heart swelling with love and relief. She wrapped her arms around my neck, and I squeezed her around her waist, still so small, no bump yet.

For so long, I had felt like my life was spiraling out of control, like everything I loved was slipping through my fingers. And I knew she had felt it, too. Now, holding Madeline in my arms, knowing she was carrying our child, I felt like I had finally found my way back.

We sat there for a long moment, wrapped in each other's arms, the weight of everything finally starting to lift. It wasn't just about us anymore. It was about the future, about the life we were going to build together, and about the baby that was going to change everything.

Madeline leaned back slightly, her eyes searching mine. "Are you sure you're okay with this?"

I smiled, my heart full. "More than okay," I said, my voice steady. "Madeline, I love you. And now we're going to have a baby of our own. Kenzie's going to be a big sister. There's nothing more I could want."

She smiled through her tears, her fingers brushing lightly against my cheek. "I love you, too, Hudson. And I'm ready for this. For us."

I kissed her again, my heart soaring with happiness. It didn't matter what we had gone through, what obstacles we'd faced. We had each other, and now we had a future—a family—to look forward to.

And for the first time in a long time, I felt like everything was finally going to be okay.

Thirty-Seven
Madeline

The morning light filtered through the curtains, casting a soft glow over Hudson's bedroom. I lay there, wrapped in his arms, feeling his cheek against my bare breasts. His head moved up and down gently with my breasts.

The events of the previous day felt like a blur, but the weight of what we had gone through was still lingering in the air. We had faced so much, yet somehow, we had come out on the other side—together.

I traced light circles on Hudson's arm, my mind wandering to the conversation we'd had last night. His joy at finding out about the baby had been overwhelming. I hadn't known what to expect, but his reaction had made my heart swell with love and relief. For the first time in weeks, I felt like I could finally breathe.

Everything was going to be okay. We had each other, and we had a future—a family—growing inside me. I could call this place home. I could call him and Kenzie home.

Just as I was about to close my eyes and let myself drift back into the peaceful quiet, the doorbell rang, jolting me out of the moment. I frowned, glancing at Hudson, whose eyes sprang open and focused on me.

"Who the hell?" he muttered, rubbing his eyes and sitting up.

I shrugged, a sense of unease creeping into my chest. "It's a bit early for visitors." I looked at the clock. 8 a.m. "Did the nanny already take Kenzie to school?"

He nodded. "Should have, unless she's 'sick' again." He smiled a little, the smile of a dad who knows his little one is in trouble. "She's been faking it lately to stay home with me."

"Maybe she *is* sick, and the nanny got locked out?" I knew it was a leap, but thinking of who else could be at Hudson's house so early made me sick.

I looked at my phone and saw a text from Joanna: *Police picked up Jon and Mark.* Short and sweet. *So it can't be them, at least.* Hopefully, he didn't sic another gambling addict on me.

Reluctantly, we pulled ourselves out of bed, and Hudson tossed me a robe as we headed toward the door. My heart was pounding for reasons I couldn't quite explain. I wasn't expecting anyone, but something about the timing felt... off.

When Hudson opened the door, the last person I expected to see was standing there.

"Dad?" I blurted, my eyes widening in shock.

My dad stood on the doorstep, his face unreadable. I froze, my mind scrambling to understand why he was here. The last time we'd spoken, things between us had been tense—strained, to say the least. I hadn't been sure how to fix it, and now... now he was standing here, unannounced.

Hudson's body stiffened beside me, his hand instinctively brushing against mine and linking pinkies with me. "Harry," Hudson said, cautiously, his voice carefully measured. "What can we do for you?"

Dad's gaze flicked between the two of us, standing there only in our robes and, for a moment, I couldn't read his expression.

Then, he sighed. "So, this is how it's going to be? Not going to invite your old man in?" He walked in between us, turning sideways to avoid bumping us with our shoulders.

Hudson closed the door behind him and he continued to let himself in, making his way to the couch.

"Dad, what are you doing here?" I asked, padding gently into the kitchen to make myself some coffee. I didn't usually need coffee right when I woke up, but I needed something to do with my hands. Hudson sat across from my dad in a chair, leaning forward to take in whatever it was he was going to say. It had to be good if he came all this way. Or, at least, that's what I hoped for.

"Well, I got a phone call this morning," he began, his voice gruff. "From Jon."

At the mention of Jon's name, I tensed, my stomach churning. Of course, Jon had used his one phone call from the police station to stir up more trouble. He couldn't leave well enough alone, even after everything that had happened.

"What did he say?" I asked, my voice quieter than I intended.

Dad let out a dry laugh, shaking his head. "He thought he'd get me all riled up, telling me about how my daughter's pregnant... with an 'old man' like Hudson."

I winced, my hand instinctively moving to my stomach. I could only imagine the way Jon must have delivered that news, hoping to provoke Dad into some kind of reaction. I glanced at Hudson and could make out his jaw tensing. The muscles in his cheeks moved, and he ran a hand over his morning stubble.

My dad's eyes caught my hands on my stomach and closed. "So it's true."

"I—" I started.

Hudson interjected, "She's had a lot going on with Jon trying to destroy her life. We weren't keeping anything from you, I can promise you that. We would never want to keep anything from you. We respect you so much more than that. Both of us."

"Well, you can understand why that would be hard to believe," my dad quipped, looking Hudson in the eyes.

"Of course, but Dad—do you want some coffee?" I asked, sitting down next to Hudson. I felt like a teenager in trouble for sneaking out to meet my boyfriend like I might find myself grounded at the end of this conversation. He shook his head.

"Dad, this isn't like that. This is...big news."

"So you're keeping it," he said quickly. The response gutted me.

Hudson narrowed his eyes. "Of course she's – we're keeping it. Why wouldn't we? This baby is a blessing, Harry."

"Is it? As much as I'd like to think Jon has never had a good point in his entire life, you are an old man, same as me. You think you'll be around long enough to take care of this baby? Babies turn into adults, Hudson."

Hudson scoffed. "You think you have to tell me about kids? I've got one of my own, if you don't remember."

"No, I remember. It's why I waited so long to show up at your door. I've been sitting at my hotel awake for a couple of hours, but I thought I'd spare your daughter a scene."

Hudson laughed wryly. "Well, thanks so much for your consideration. How about you get the hell out of my house now? You're not welcome here to torment me and Madeline and our choices. They're just that. *Our* choices."

I expected my dad to stand up and deck Hudson right then, but to my surprise, his expression softened. He looked past Hudson and directly at me. "Are you happy with this, sugar?"

I nodded quickly, pushing my unruly hair back out of my eyes. "I'm so happy, Dad. I know it's hard to understand, but I love Hudson. He makes me feel...safe. He understands me. He's a gentleman."

He laughed a little. "Well, I don't know about that, but he certainly seems to be playing the part well for you. Maybe that's all anyone can ask of a partner – that they put their best foot forward."

I kept my eyes trained on him, my coffee growing more lukewarm by the second against my palm. "Do you remember when you told me about Mom getting pregnant right before you were shipped off? You were so scared. You said it wasn't the right time. But then do you remember what you tell me every time you tell that story?"

His expression softened, and he smiled slightly. "That no one is ready, the timing is never right, and babies are always a blessing." We all sat in silence for a moment, and he continued quietly, "I'll admit, I wasn't thrilled—"

Hudson coughed out a laugh, and my dad shot him a look before continuing, "Okay, I was fucking pissed when I first found out about the two of you," Dad said, his voice quieter now. "But after everything... after seeing how much you've both been through together, I can't stay mad. And finding out you're pregnant..."

He paused, his eyes softening as they moved to my stomach. "You're right. Or, I guess I was right. Babies are a blessing, the timing is never right, and no one is ready. I can't stay mad forever if I want to be a grandparent," he laughed.

I blinked, stunned by his words. I instantly felt a thousand knots in my shoulder breaking apart. "Dad..." I started, my throat tight with emotion. "So, you're... you're okay with this?"

Dad sighed, standing up and walking toward me on my chair. "I don't know if 'okay' is the right word. It's a lot to take in. But Madeline, you're my daughter, and I love you. And Hudson..." He looked over at Hudson, his expression hard to read. He looked...resolved. "You've been there for her in ways I couldn't be. I see that now. And I can't deny that this baby... it's going to bring us all together, whether we like it or not."

Hudson cleared his throat, his voice steady but thick with emotion. "Harry, I want you to know... I love your daughter. I'll do whatever it takes to take care of her and our baby. That's all I've ever wanted."

Dad nodded, his eyes lingering on Hudson for a moment before turning back to me. "I know you will. And I've come to terms with it. This baby... it's a new beginning for all of us."

A tear slipped down my cheek, and before I knew it, Dad had pulled me into a hug, his arms tight around me in a way that felt like he was finally letting go of all the anger, all the hurt.

"I'm sorry," he whispered into my hair. "For everything. I just want you to be happy, Madeline. That's all I've ever wanted."

I hugged him back, my heart swelling with gratitude and relief. "Thank you, Dad. That means more than you know."

When he pulled away, his eyes were a little misty, but he quickly cleared his throat. A small, reluctant smile tugged at the corners of his mouth. "Well then, I guess I'm going to be a grandfather. And your mom? She doesn't know yet but she'll be over the moon. Maybe it's time we moved closer."

The words hung in the air for a moment, and the weight of everything we'd been through—the fights, the misunderstandings, the fear—it all seemed to melt away. There was still a lot to work through, but for the first time, I felt like we were all on the same page. Like we could move forward as a family.

"Stay longer, Dad. Let's talk. We've got a lot to catch up on."

He shook his head. "I've got to get back to your mother. She's at home confused and worried out of her mind. I didn't tell her what Jon said, but she knows something's up." He reached out and shook Hudson's hand. "Take care of her while I can't. That's all I ask."

He hugged me again and walked to the door.

"I love you, Dad. Thank you."

His hand on the doorknob, he turned to look at me and said, "Call your mother."

The door closed behind him, and I glanced up at Hudson, my heart full of love and gratitude. We had come so far, faced so many obstacles, but somehow, we had made it to this moment. Together.

Call your mother. It was strange to think *I'd* be the mother that someone would be worrying sick someday.

Hudson smiled down at me, a genuinely carefree grin.

We were ready. We were ready to face it all.

Thirty-Eight
Hudson

Harry had barely left before there was another knock on the door. Lately, it had felt like my house was a rotating cast of characters.

I snapped the hair tie on my wrist and breathed deeply, my eyes closing. I tried to tap into my senses and ground myself.

I smell coffee. I feel Madeline's hands on my shoulder. I hear Madeline's voice.

"Hudson, I'll get it, okay? You take care of yourself. It's probably nothing."

She kissed my cheek, her lips so supple that it momentarily relaxed me. My breathing returned to normal as I kept my eyes closed and listened to her cross the room to the front door. She opened it and said, "Oh! Hi!"

I hazarded a peek and saw Madeline hugging Joanna. Joanna rubbed her back in small circles, and Madeline let her in, saying, "Hey, Hudson, look! It's only Joanna, no police or stalkers." She smiled hesitantly, unsure if the joke was acceptable, and I offered a weak smile in return.

I hadn't been expecting Joanna to stop by again so soon after what happened with her brother. I didn't blame her, but it seemed like a tough place to be in.

But from the look on her face, I could tell she had something big to share. She walked in with a determined energy, clutching a folder in her hand like it held the answers to everything.

Joanna greeted me with a small smile before cutting straight to the point. "I've got great news for you two, but mostly for Madeline," she said, her voice bright but steady.

She sat down on the couch where Harry had just sat and given us his blessing. *It's been a strange morning.*

"It's about the award."

Madeline blinked, readying herself, then nodded. "Okay, give it to me straight." She sat next to me and rested her hand on my upper thigh. I wrapped my arm around her, pulling her into me. We would get through this together, whatever the news ended up being.

Joanna held up the folder she'd brought, her eyes lighting up with satisfaction. "So, after Jon confessed, I looked into the emails that were shared with the award committee—the ones that made it look like you bribed the judges."

Madeline's face tensed at the mention of the emails, her hands instinctively curling into fists. I felt my chest tighten, too, just thinking about how much damage those accusations had done. She had worked so hard to build her reputation, and Jon had nearly torn it all down in an instant.

"And?" Madeline prompted, her voice tight.

Joanna's grin widened as she flipped open the folder. "They were faked. And I can prove it. The email he used is linked to his old Facebook account. Evidently, he finally started to get sloppy and forgot that just because he doesn't use it anymore doesn't mean it's gone."

For a moment, the room was silent. Madeline stared at Joanna like she hadn't heard her right, her eyes wide with shock. I could see the realization starting to dawn on her, the weight of Joanna's words slowly sinking in.

"Wait. You can prove it?" Madeline finally breathed, her voice barely above a whisper. "So I'm in the clear?"

Joanna nodded. She stood up and walked over to us, handing Madeline the folder. "It's all in there. I had everyone who was "bribed" verify the email address they received the bribes from. Jon's old Facebook page. The award is yours, fair and square. Oh, that's in there, too."

She grinned and sat back down while Madeline's eyes scanned the papers. "And for the record, no one ever thought any different. Everyone I spoke to said they thought it seemed very out of character for you."

"Really?" Madeline's eyes flickered up to Joanna, and she smiled encouragingly. She buried her face in my neck before looking more closely at the contents of the folder. Her hands trembled slightly as she turned the pages of the documents inside.

I watched her closely, feeling a sense of pride and relief as she processed the truth. She had been vindicated. All the lies Jon had spun, all the damage he'd tried to do—it was over.

"You're going to be okay," I whispered to her, kissing her cheek over and over, pulling her into my lips.

She giggled under my kisses and whispered, "I don't... I don't know what to say," her voice thick with emotion. "I thought my career was ruined."

Joanna shook her head, a soft smile playing on her lips. "Nope. Not by a long shot. You're stuck doing this now. You're going to have tons of clients."

Madeline let out a shaky breath. "Thank you." She hugged the packet to her chest. "Thank you, oh my God."

"You've been cleared of everything. That award is yours, Madeline, and no one can take it away from you."

Madeline's eyes glistened with unshed tears. "I can't believe you did this for me," she murmured, her voice barely audible. "I mean, thank you, but I can't believe you're...on my side."

Joanna waved her off. "You're my best friend, Madeline. I'll always be on your side."

"But he's your brother," she sobbed, overtaken by emotion.

Joanna stood up and crushed Madeline into a hug. "And you're closer than any sister I could ever wish for. Besides, I'm always on the side of the righteous, and unfortunately, that never happens to be my brother."

The room felt lighter after that, the heavy cloud of Jon's sabotage finally lifting. Madeline wrapped Joanna in a tight hug, and I couldn't help but feel a surge of gratitude for her. Joanna had stood by us through everything, even though Jon was her brother. She had chosen fairness, justice, and Madeline —no matter what it cost her.

"I'll let you two celebrate," Joanna said, pulling back from the hug with a wink. "I've got some work to catch up on, but I wanted you to know as soon as I found out."

Madeline nodded, wiping at her eyes as she smiled gratefully at Joanna. "I can't thank you enough, Joanna."

"Just promise me you'll keep doing what you do best," Joanna replied with a wink. "You're too damn good to let anyone hold you back. And congratulations on the baby, you two. Good job locking a woman like this down, Hudson."

With that, Joanna gave us both a quick hug before heading out, leaving the house feeling a little lighter, a little more hopeful than it had in days.

***

That night, we were lying in bed, the weight of the day slowly fading into the background. Madeline was curled up beside me, her head resting on my chest, her fingers lightly tracing patterns on my skin.

We had played board games with Kenzie and told her about the baby, gifting her a big sister basket. She was over the moon that Madeline was "daddy's girlfriend," even though I hadn't officially asked Madeline to be my girlfriend. We hadn't done labels the whole time. There was a calm between us, a sense of peace that hadn't been there in a while.

For the first time in what felt like weeks, I could see the light in her eyes again, the fire that had always drawn me to her. She was coming back to herself and seeing that calmed the internal storm that came with insecurity. I hadn't even realized how lost I had felt through all this and how much of it had to do with empathy for Madeline.

As we lay there in the quiet, her phone buzzed on the nightstand. She reached for it absentmindedly, her fingers swiping across the screen before she froze, her eyes widening.

"Hudson," she whispered, her voice full of disbelief.

I frowned, glancing down at her. "What is it?" I pet her hair in a soothing motion, feeling how tense she was.

She turned the phone toward me, a tense smile on her face. "It's from the architectural magazine... the one I submitted the Park City property to."

I sat up a little straighter, curiosity piqued. "What did they say?"

"They want to feature the property... on the cover," Madeline said, her voice breathless. "And they want to interview me for the article."

For a moment, I couldn't speak. I just stared at her, watching as the realization of what that meant slowly dawned on her. This was huge for her. The Park City property was one of the most prestigious projects she had worked on, and now it was going to be featured on the cover of one of the top architectural magazines.

"They... they want to put me on the cover," she repeated, her voice barely above a whisper.

I couldn't hold back the grin that spread across my face as I reached for her, pulling her into my arms. "Madeline, that's incredible. I'm so damn proud of you."

She let out a laugh, shaking her head in disbelief. "I can't believe it. After everything that's happened... I never thought..."

I cupped her face in my hands, my thumbs brushing away the tears that had started to well up in her eyes. "You deserve this," I said firmly. "You've worked so hard for this, Madeline. This is your moment."

She smiled up at me, her eyes shining with a mix of pride and relief. "I guess it is," she whispered.

I leaned down, pressing a gentle kiss to her lips, my heart bursting with love for her. She had been through so much, but she had come out on the other side stronger than ever. And now, she was being recognized for the incredible talent I had always known she had.

As I pulled back, I felt a surge of emotion inside me. This woman, this incredible, strong, beautiful woman, had turned my world upside down in the best possible way. And now, with everything that had happened—with Jon behind us, with the baby bringing us closer—I knew there was something I needed to ask her.

"Madeline," I said softly, my heart pounding in my chest. "I have something I need to ask you."

She looked up at me, her eyes full of curiosity. "What is it?"

I took a deep breath, my fingers brushing through her hair as I gathered my thoughts. "We've been through so much together, and I know things haven't always been easy... but I love you. More than I've ever loved anyone. And now that everything's out in the open, now that everyone knows and has given their blessings... I mean, Kenzie said something that made me realize I haven't actually asked you to be my girlfriend. I want to make this official."

Her eyes widened slightly, a soft gasp escaping her lips before smiling slightly. "Hudson..."

"I want you to be my girlfriend," I said, my voice steady and sure. "Officially. No more hiding, no more doubts. Just you and me, together. I want you to live with me. I want people to know what we are, and I want to take care of you." I pressed my palm to her stomach and awaited her answer.

She stared at me for a long moment, her eyes searching mine, and then a slow smile spread across her face.

"Yes," she whispered, her voice full of emotion. "Yes, Hudson. I want that, too."

I let out a breath I hadn't realized I was holding, my heart soaring as I pulled her into a deep, passionate kiss. This was it. This was everything I had ever wanted and more.

Madeline reached into the elastic waistband of my pajama pants and held my hardening member in her small, warm palm. She squeezed my shaft so that I could feel my blood pumping through it, constricted by her hand. Groaning, I wrapped my arms around her, my fingers spreading out on her shoulder blades. I leaned into her, gliding my cock through her fingers, pumping into her grasp.

She gasped as I did so, and her eyes, being so wide and lusty, turned me on even more. I kissed her again and let my tongue explore the inside of her mouth. Our tongues intertwined. I needed her.

My hands slipped from her back to her face, and I held her cheeks, cupping her face as I tasted her mouth. She nibbled my bottom lip, holding it in between her teeth and letting it drop. My head tipped back in a throaty growl.

"I want you," she whispered, in response to my growl, and I cupped her breasts through her thin t-shirt, feeling the form of her teardrop breasts. They were already growing, already a cup size bigger than they used to be. I knew they probably spilled out of her bra, perfect mounds, her nipples holding onto the edges of the fabric.

Her sighs filled the space between our mouths as I brushed her nipples through the thin t-shirt. Her hand snuck out of my pants and she ground against me.

With her legs wrapped in mine, I could feel the heat coming from between her thighs. I could feel the dampness of the crotch of her panties. I could feel the way she wanted me.

I reached for her ass and pulled her in even closer, letting my bulge press against her wanting clit. I knew how engorged it could get, knew how red and swollen it probably already was.

I let my hand drift between her legs, and she was quick to disentangle herself from me and open up. She hoisted one of her legs on top of mine, and I smirked at how badly she already wanted me.

My hand moved up through the bottom of her panties, and my fingers reached for her clit, touching it lightly. Instantly, she moaned gutturally, sighing, "Yes."

"Is that what you want? Do you want me or my fingers?" I asked her, between our kisses.

"All of you," she answered, kissing back between her moans, her mouth open against mine, her eyes rolling up to the ceiling. I pressed my finger harder against her clit, not moving it at all, letting it sit against her. She was so lovely when she squirmed.

Smiling, I told her, "That's a good answer, baby girl." I slipped a finger into her wanting pussy, feeling how slick she already was. When she groaned in response, I pushed it deeper, holding her still by her back. I didn't want her to wiggle away from me. She bucked her hips in the direction of my hand, trying to fuck herself against it. I kissed her open mouth as she arched her back and whimpered.

Her pussy was so tight and already squeezing me. I loved the way she felt everything. It felt like this time was different, like her body reacted to my touch even more than usual.

I moved my mouth from hers down to one of her nipples. I sucked it through her shirt and clamped down with my teeth, earning myself a small gasp. Her hands sprang to hold my head, and she tipped her head back to the ceiling. She tried to keep her mouth closed to keep the volume down. I grinned up at her with her nipple between my teeth.

She tugged at my pants, begging for more, and I rolled her over onto her back, holding her face with my hands. "Madeline, I love you. I want you to be mine more than I've ever wanted anything. You're my safe space."

"I love you, too, Hudson. I am yours. You don't have to want me. You have me." She kissed me back, and I pushed her underwear to the side to let the head of my penis touch her opening. She sighed, wrapping her arms around my neck. "Please, Hudson, take me. Show me how bad you want me."

I couldn't take it anymore. I thrust my erection inside her, feeling the way her body swallowed every inch of me, so ready for me. Her warm, tight opening was the perfect size, and I groaned loudly, sitting up on my elbows for a better angle.

We looked into each other's eyes as I pressed into her slowly and purposefully, feeling every inch as I crawled in and out of her. Every time I pushed my length into her, she bit her lip and closed her eyes. I whispered, "Keep your eyes on me," and she listened, her eyebrows arching as she tried to keep quiet. Her mouth opened slightly, her perfect bow lips in a pout, as I continued to tease her with slow motions.

I felt like I wouldn't be able to hold back much longer. Her sex appeal was too much for me, the way she opened her mouth, the sensual look in her eyes, her hard nipples pressed against my chest...I felt myself start to move faster in spite of how badly I wanted to tease her.

The base of my cock was brushing against her clit, and I could feel how swollen it was. She scrunched her nose every time, her building orgasm obvious on her face and her flushed complexion. "Are you going to cum for me, Madeline?" I murmured, kissing the corners of her mouth.

She nodded wordlessly, her mouth opening in an even wider o, her legs splaying further apart and wrapping around my waist. "Mhm. Hudson, you feel so good. I can't believe I get to have this forever."

I didn't get to respond before her breaths got heavier and slower, and then she was cumming on my cock, pulsing all around it, squeezing me so hard that it was difficult to continue to thrust into her. I pushed through, forcing her to ride out her orgasm, moving slower as it calmed down.

When she let out a deep breath and relaxed, her arms above her head and her teeth biting down on her bottom lip, I smiled at her and whispered, "Forever and ever," before I slid down to the foot of the bed to taste her.

My tongue deep inside her, I felt an overwhelming sense of peace settle over me. We had faced the worst, and we had come out stronger on the other side.

With Madeline by my side, be it in work or in bed, I knew we could face anything.

Epilogue: Madeline

ONE YEAR LATER

The evening air was warm, the soft breeze carrying the familiar sound of laughter and conversation through the open doors of the event hall.

It was hard to believe that a year had passed since everything had changed—since Hudson and I had faced the chaos that had once threatened to tear us apart.

Now, standing here on the anniversary of the SEALs' graduation, watching Hudson smile and laugh with his brothers-in-arms, it felt like a lifetime ago.

I took a deep breath, looking out at the crowd. The event was in full swing, and this year, Hudson had taken the reins of organizing it. He'd thrown himself into the planning, making sure every detail was perfect. His attention to detail, the way he cared so deeply about honoring his fellow SEALs, made my heart swell with pride. This event wasn't just a tradition—it was a celebration of survival, of brotherhood, and of everything they had been through together.

But this year, there was something else in the air. A lightness, a calm that hadn't been there before. Hudson had changed so much in the past year, his PTSD fading with each passing month. He had worked hard on himself, and the transformation was nothing short of remarkable. I could see it in the way he carried himself now—more relaxed, more at peace. The weight he had once carried on his shoulders seemed lighter, and it filled me with a sense of hope for the future.

But despite how bright a future I knew we had ahead of us, the present was already pretty good. I had quickly moved in with Hudson after realizing I was pregnant, and I hadn't regretted it for a second. It had been easy, natural, and he made a wonderful partner, having already gone through it before. He made it feel like something that was easy to conquer, something that was meant to be instead of something terrifying.

His support had allowed me the freedom and confidence to open my own interior design firm. The magazine cover and the award had opened so many doors, had gained me some local New York notoriety, and though I credited Joanna with a lot of it, Hudson was my rock through it all. I wouldn't have been able to do it without him holding me through the panic and showing me the way out of sticky situations.

I glanced over at him, watching as he knelt down to pick up our little boy, Kinsley, lifting him into his arms with ease. Kenzie wanted her baby brother's name to go with hers so she chose Kinsley among the choices we had given her.

Our son, with his chubby cheeks and wide eyes, giggled as Hudson lifted him up in the air, bringing him down fast with a grin. The sight of them together—Hudson, so strong and steady, and our son, so full of life—made my heart skip a beat. It was moments like this that reminded me just how far we'd come.

Kenzie stood beside them, smiling brightly as she watched her dad and her baby brother play. She had grown so much in the past year, and seeing her bond with Hudson and her new baby brother had been one of the most beautiful things to witness. She was a big sister now, and she took that role seriously, always looking out

for her brother, always making sure he was happy and s
afe.

Everything felt perfect.

As I walked over to join them, Hudson's eyes met mine,
and I saw something flicker in his gaze. A warmth, a
secret smile that told me he had something planned. My
heart fluttered, and I couldn't help but wonder what he
was up to.

"You look beautiful," he murmured as I reached him, his
hand sliding around my waist to pull me close. His lips
brushed against my temple, sending a shiver down my
spine.

I smiled up at him, my heart full. "You're pretty handsome yourself," I teased, leaning into his embrace. Our
son, still in his arms, reached out for me, his little hands
tugging at my hair.

As we stood there, the four of us—our little family—I
felt a deep sense of contentment settle over me. This was
everything I had ever wanted. A family, a home filled
with love, and a partner who saw me, who cherished me
for who I was.

"Are you having a good time?" I asked, my voice soft as I looked up at him. "This time last year was so insane. I can't believe how much has changed."

Hudson's smile widened, and he nodded. "I am. And that's...that change you mentioned— that's something I've been meaning to talk to you about."

Before I could ask what he meant, he handed our son to Kenzie, who took him with a giggle, apparently already knowing what was about to happen. Hudson turned to me, his eyes locking with mine, and suddenly, the world around us seemed to fade away.

"Madeline," he began, his voice low and filled with emotion. "This past year... it's been the best year of my life. You've given me so much—love, hope, a son, a mother for my daughter. A deeper friendship with my best friend." He looked over at my dad, who nodded, tears glistening in his eyes. "And I can't imagine my life without you."

My breath caught in my throat as I realized what was happening. My heart pounded, the world tilting as Hudson reached into his pocket and pulled out a small velvet box. Time seemed to slow, and in that moment, all I could see was him—this incredible man who had changed my life in ways I never could have imagined.

"I've been thinking about this for a long time," he continued, his voice steady but filled with emotion. "Probably before it was appropriate or normal." He laughed, as did the crowd that had formed around us, listening intently.

"But I waited. I waited for everything to fall into place. I want to spend the rest of my life with you, Madeline. You and our family. I want to build a future with you, one that's filled with love, laughter, and everything we've dreamed of." Tears welled up in my eyes as he dropped to one knee, holding the ring out in front of him, his eyes never leaving mine. "Will you marry me?"

The world stood still. I could hear the distant sound of laughter and conversation around us, but all I could focus on was Hudson—the man I loved, the father of my child, the man who had stood by me through everything. The tears spilled over, and I covered my mouth with my hands, overwhelmed with emotion.

"Yes," I whispered, my voice breaking. "Yes, Hudson. I'll marry you."

A cheer erupted from the crowd around us, but I barely noticed. All I could see was Hudson's smile, the joy and love in his eyes as he slipped the ring onto my finger and stood, pulling me into his arms. Kinsley giggled in Kenzie's arms, and she grinned, watching us with the same happiness that filled my heart.

I kissed Hudson, the world melting away as our lips met, sealing the promise of our future together.

"All right, all right, let me get in here, lovebirds," my dad said jokingly, offering his hand to Hudson to shake. "Hudson, we had a hard path to get here, but you make my daughter happy and you take care of her. You deserve the life you work for—" he looked over at me with a smile "—and you earned this life." Hudson shook his hand for a second before pulling my dad in for a hug. Over his shoulder, I could see tears welling in the eyes of my dad, the veteran Navy SEAL, the strongest man I'd ever met besides my fiancé.

"Stop, you're making me look bad in front of our brothers," my dad teased, pushing him away and holding his arms out to me. While my mother hugged Hudson in the background, I let my dad wrap me up in a hug only a dad can give, one that contains all the lives you've lived with him, all the heartache and the love. I melted into it and sighed as my mom smiled at me behind my dad.

This was it. This was the life I had always dreamed of, and it was more perfect than I could have ever imagined.

The End

Did you like this book? Then you'll LOVE my other book "Secret Baby For My Ex's SEAL Brother", a steamy age gap billionaire boss romance, in the "Billionaire Silver Foxes' Club" series, available to read for FREE on Kindle Unlimited here.

Here is a short description of what "Secret Baby For My Ex's SEAL Brother" is all about:

I didn't know the luscious woman I savagely devoured that night, was my brother's ex-girlfriend, and is now pregnant with my baby.

All I wanted that night was an escape from the trauma haunting me since my SEAL days...
and the mess my ex-wife had left for me and my son.

Instead, I realized it was my baby brother's freshly mint-ed ex-girlfriend I had just wildly overtaken that night...□ the one he was still in love with.

Two days later she showed up outside my office, report-ing for duty.□
Now she was walking around in my business and in my head...all the time.

I tried keeping my distance by being an absolute prick. Yet each divine taste of her sinfully curvaceous body, made me lose even more self-control.

Remembering she was off-limits got even harder when she became the only one ever to calm my panic attacks... and the only one my son ever called mommy.

And finding out I was going to be a father for the second time was all I needed to finally claim what was mine,
even if it meant redefining loyalties.

***

"Secret Baby For My Ex's SEAL Brother" is a scorching enemies to lovers, billionaire boss, age gap romance in the Billionaire Silver Foxes' Club Series. Each book is a com-

plete stand-alone with no cliffhangers and a satisfying happy ever after.

Click the link below to grab your copy of "Secret Baby For My Ex's SEAL Brother" and check out a sneak peek into this sizzling book on the next page:

https://www.amazon.com/dp/B0D1N9ZW9T

Sneak Peek Into "Secret Baby For My Ex's SEAL Brother"

Prologue: Mia

You know how they say, "when it rains it pours"?

Well, right now, it feels like a hailstorm, thunderstorm, tornado, and avalanche hit me all at once.

I chewed my lip, trying to find the right words.

"Chris, I've worked hard to get to where I am and—"

"I don't care. I'm not interested in hearing about it."

The domineering energy stifled me.

He stepped forward, towering over me.

His cologne permeated through the air, melting all sense of rationality for a brief second.

Memories of that night, how he held me in a tight, protective embrace, haunted me.

Get it together, Mia!

I slipped back, remembering the situation I was in.

I had to convince him. I rested my hands at my side as I remembered the self-help book on emotional intelligence I read the other day.

"I get it, but I'm the best employee Grant's got."

I spent years of my life balancing college and promotions in the tech world.

I started as a junior programmer but made it here because of hard work, dedication, and my mom's support.

There was no way in hell I was going to give this up because of one mistake. One very dirty mistake I couldn't stop thinking about.

Chris cleared his throat and turned towards the window.

His arm protruded slightly in the casual dress shirt he wore. *For a company billionaire, I thought he'd dress a little nicer.*

But *that* was probably part of the appeal.

He turned back towards me with a scowl.

I looked at the cold, blue eyes that stared back at me, feeling like they saw through every part of me. Almost undressing me.

Like that night.

I pulled myself out of those thoughts. It was an honest mistake. Neither of us was sober.

"I don't know why I'm even entertaining bringing you on."

"Because I told you that I have experience and—"

"You're not capable of handling my assets."

Okay, now he was just making up crap to get me out of this office.

I shook my head and smiled.

"With all due respect, you haven't even *seen* my work yet. I think you know the fact that I made it this far speaks for itself. If you at least give me a chance, I can prove it to you."

Chris grunted and turned away.

"Give me one good reason why I should?"

I bit my tongue as I held back from mentioning that night. *The man didn't even realize he was inside me till I cried out his name.*

I smiled, maintaining composure. "I've worked up the ranks in Arlington, Virginia, for the last ten years. I have the stats to back them up."

I grabbed my phone and opened up the Google sheet depicting our sales. I placed it on the table and stepped back.

"There, proof enough?"

He looked down and scoffed.

"Mere numbers don't mean a damn thing to me, Mia."

"I'm sure I could show you my production quotas for the last five years and my accolades and you would *still* not believe me. But I'm not here to prove anything. I'm here to get results."

That was the truth. This wasn't a side gig for me that I could leave at any time.

This was my life, and I treated this job like my life depended on it.

Chris stayed silent. I leaned forward and smirked.

"Got anything else? Maybe more insistence that I'm not capable?"

He furrowed his brows and sighed.

"No, I just don't think you should be here. This is a strictly professional environment and–"

"Tell me something I don't know, Chris. If anything, *you're* the one making this unprofessional."

"And you're the one walking back into my life."

His words didn't affect me.

I'd dealt with enough rude people in this field that a little bit of aggression from a guy I thought I'd never see again didn't bother me.

"We don't have to like each other, Chris. But just—"

"Get. Out."

"Come on, please be reasonable and—"

"Why should I be reasonable to the woman who broke Casey's heart?"

Seriously? He wanted to bring *that* up right now?'

"That's irrelevant to the situation here and—"

"If you have nothing else to say, then do me a favor and get out of my office. I'll be talking to Grant after this."

No words would sway this man's mind.

Of course, he would be stubborn rather than put that night behind us.

It was a week ago, but it felt like yesterday.

The memories flashed vividly despite the drunk haze.

His hands were on my body as he felt every part of me, not to mention the wanton sounds that escaped me, begging for more.

Ugh! It was so good, but I knew it would *never* happen again.

When Grant approached me with the merger, Chris was the *last* person I thought I'd see.

"Fine, but there's nobody else as capable as I am. So getting rid of me is only going to shoot yourself in the foot."

"I'm sure there's someone else Grant knows."

"No, there's not. Grant chose *me* to be his CTO for a reason. He saw my potential, and how much I contributed to the team. Hopefully, *you* will see it sometime soon."

I didn't need to listen to this crap.

Right now, we'd be in a stalemate if we continued in this direction. I knew when battles weren't worth fighting.

I walked to the door and opened it. I turned around and flashed the fakest grin I could.

"I'm looking forward to working together, Chris. Hopefully, you and I will eventually see eye to eye."

I didn't like him, and he didn't like me. Back when I dated Casey, he always ignored me.

The guy pretended like I was the equivalent of a doormat half the time.

Not to mention, he *barely* acknowledged anything good that happened between Casey and me.

His arrogance, too. The man was so full of himself and didn't care about anyone except Casey.

Even though the night in the club was a drunk-induced night of pure fun, the reality of the situation was simple.

I had recently broken up with Casey.

The last thing I needed to do was fraternize with his super close and overprotective older brother.

I pushed open the door and slipped out of there, refusing to listen to any more of Chris's crap.

But even as I closed the door, my thoughts drifted back to the way he stared.

Those animalistic, feral eyes locked onto me like a predator catching their prey. That primal energy drove me crazy, whether I liked it or not.

I knew better than to get involved, though.

If he wasn't going to work with me, then so be it.

I worked better on my own anyway.

***

One: Mia

One Week Earlier...

"Two cosmopolitans. My treat."

"But Nat—"

"I invited you out. You need to let loose. Be immature for once in your life."

I rolled my eyes. *Yeah, immaturity is why I threw away my relationship of two years.*

The bartender slid two drinks next to us. Nataly brought hers up for a toast, and I did the same.

"To a better future!"

"Right. A better future."

It had only been two weeks, but the pain was still there. I needed time.

Nataly didn't realize not everyone gets over breakups by getting drunk.

"Nataly, I don't—"

"Mia, I don't want to hear it. You're going to enjoy tonight and get your mind off things. Plus, there's, like, tons of hot guys for you to get with."

"Sure, but—"

"You broke up with him. Come on, live a little! Problems aren't solved simmering over them!"

I hated that she was right.

The liquid hit my mouth a second later. *Damn, that's good.* I downed the contents and put the glass down. I exhaled and smiled.

Nataly smiled with that same shit-eating grin she always had plastered to her face.

"Want another?"

Dammit, Nat. I knew coming here was a bad idea.

"I shouldn't—"

"Don't worry, Mia," Nataly chirped, winking. "These guys know me. And plus, you need it! Get your mind off your ex, girl."

Before I could protest, another drink sat in front of me. More and more settled, and before I knew it, my vision was a haze.

I slammed my hands on the counter and got up with a smile.

"There we go!" I cried out.

"Finally turned your brain off and forgot?"

I smiled a confident grin.

"You could say that."

Nataly giggled and gestured to the dance floor. "Then let's forget even more."

I didn't need to be told twice.

When I got up, my vision blurred. I shook my head a little, and it cleared up.

"You good Mia?"

"Yeah, I'm fine."

"Alright. Don't need you dying on me now."

"I'm not some stupid freshman anymore, Nat. I'm twenty-eight. I've been around the block before."

"Then prove it!" Nat cried out as she rushed towards the dance floor.

I followed her without a second thought.

Nat's challenging energy helped with the storm of emotions that raced through my head.

My relationship with Casey hung over me like a grim reminder. I wished it worked out, but he never changed.

He ignored every attempt to settle down, whereas I worked and grew as a person.

I climbed the corporate ladder and managed to secure a stable job with a company I liked.

The final straw, however, was when he ran off for a month to be a racecar driver. He *swore* it was just a phase, but I couldn't do it anymore.

At least for now, even though the breakup still sat fresh, I could forget for a while.

We danced together until I heard a low, tenor voice behind me.

"Mind if I cut in?"

I turned and looked at the source of the voice.

Holy shit. He was hot. Tall, dark blonde hair and a muscular frame barely contained in the shirt he wore.

"Sure. She needs it. Gotta forget that pesky ex of hers."

"Wait, Nat—"

Nataly's gone vanished into the throng of people.

I turned back to the tanned hunk, barely visible in the dim lights of the club.

We danced together, hips gyrating and our bodies pressed against each other.

Damn. *He's like crazy hot.*

My hands felt up the defined abs, and I slid my fingers under his shirt.

A feral grunt escaped him.

"Getting ahead of ourselves, are we?"

I pulled back, smiling. I probably look like a freaking idiot right now.

"Maybe. Or maybe I just want to forget."

"As do I. Came out here for the same reason."

Large hands pulled me closer. He trapped me in his embrace.

Our chests touched, and soon, eager lips met.

I moaned, opening my mouth as I felt his tongue dominate me the moment our bodies came together.

Being with this man liberated me. Having casual sex was such a rarity that it became a treat. Something new, not the same tedium that I experienced with Casey.

Sometimes, a change was all a girl needed.

The bass reverberated around us, but right now, I was spirited away into my own little world.

Drunk and desiring this man, I wrapped my arms around his shoulders.

The kisses grew wilder, and I ground my hips against him. He groaned as he reached down to grab a handful of my ass.

"You can't wait either, can you."

"Hell no. Let's get out of here."

The words were raspy, barely audible, but enough to prompt the stranger.

He pulled back and grabbed my hand. He led me through the throng of people to the nearest place we could go.

An unoccupied single-use bathroom.

He opened the door and thrust me inside.

After he locked the door, our lips were on each other again.

Quick hands made work of the lilac dress I wore.

Thank god Nat has a sense of fashion. I trusted her with the attire tonight and didn't regret a damn thing.

The dress sat somewhere in the bathroom. Not like it mattered.

His lips teased my neck with subtle licks and touches. I moaned and clenched against him.

I needed more. His large, inviting hands pulled me in and drove me crazy.

His hands draped downwards to my breasts, teasing them against his fingertips. The touches were slow but exact.

He pinched my nipples in just the right way.

His lips soon replaced his fingers as I felt his tongue flick against the nubs.

He teased me, and I clung to him. The ache burned, but I needed him inside.

While the foreplay was good, my core dripped with an ache for something big to come inside.

And judging from the feeling between my legs, there was a *very* big surprise in those pants.

I could barely keep it together. He's got me on the edge.

He tugged on the nipple a little harder, and I threw my head back.

"You have the most intoxicating moans."

Dammit, why did he sound so familiar? The thought sat there until, once again, he slid his fingers to my aching breasts.

Hungry lips nipped at my neck, sucking on the flesh. I clung to him, barely able to think straight.

I pushed against him, my juices probably smearing his pants.

Not like it mattered. The growls emitted from his lips, animalistic and wanton, shot a fire deep in me.

"Take me right now. Please."

The mystery man slid down to my sopping panties. He teased the outer lip through the outline with delicate touches.

I cried out, spreading my legs as far as I could.

"Stop fucking teasing," I begged.

He growled, and animalistic hands pulled the waistband off. They snapped, breaking apart as he pulled them off.

Damn. There goes those panties.

His fingers teased inside, touching the deepest parts of my inner core. Large and rough, I mewled, unable to fathom anything going on.

Two fingers, followed by three, entered into me.

My body was raw and needy by the time his fingers curled up all the way inside.

He teased my clit with small motions. I clenched my walls against his fingers, crying out broken, barely audible sounds.

The slick touch and sounds of my wet slit made the ache between my legs even more profound.

I could barely wait as baited breaths escaped my lips.

I grabbed his muscular shoulders.

For a second, I admired his build. He was *built,* and his taut muscles felt perfect to hold onto.

But I couldn't wait any longer, and as I felt my orgasm loom over the horizon, I practically begged him to stuff me.

Do it already. Please.

The sound of foil being unwrapped pulled me out of my thoughts.

He spread my legs apart, and for a second, we locked eyes. They were so familiar to Casey's and yet so different.

Holy shit, that's—

I recognized the man instantly. I knew him.

It was Casey's brother, Christian.

Before I could protest, he plunged inside.

All thoughts about how wrong this was silenced by his rod.

He pressed all the way to my core, and my walls clenched, sucking him all the way in.

My hands gripped his shoulders so I could feel every inch of his body.

This was so wrong but felt so right.

I couldn't pull away. Even if I wanted to get the hell off Christian, his member split me open. My body ached.

His large, robust member filled me up completely. It was like he managed to fill me up.

My hands gripped him even tighter as I held him there.

The bass from the club became just a meager thought in the distance. It didn't matter anymore.

What mattered was Christian's body, entwined with me.

I moaned and clawed at his back. *I shouldn't be doing this.*

His thrusts hit deeper than I ever felt before. Not even Casey managed to hit these spots.

I was lost in a trance, mesmerized by the feeling of this man.

He groaned and held me tighter. He didn't see anything wrong with it.

Maybe the guilt of the situation didn't bother him either. At least not enough to stop.

"Shit, Mia, I'm—"

"I am too," I cried out.

It should've been awkward, but it wasn't. Instead, it felt so different and yet so right.

Hot breaths mingled together.

I wrapped my legs even tighter around his waist. He grabbed my hips and continued thrusting inside.

After a second, he reached down and teased my clit.

I looked at him, and when our eyes met, my orgasm hit me.

"Chris—"

My fingernails tightened against his large biceps. As my vision went white, pure bliss seeped through me.

I came down from my high. *What did we do?*

Chris pulled out of me. His wide eyes looked at me, I suppose from hearing his name on my lips.

His jaw dropped, and the realization of who I was had hit him like a ton of bricks.

Shit. This wasn't what I wanted.

"Chris, I'm—"

"Fuck! This should have never happened."

He stepped back and pulled up his pants. I stood there, naked and confused.

"Chris, I don't want this to—"

"It was a mistake. Let's forget this ever happened."

I tried to form the words. It was impossible. *What have I done?*

***

Click here now to read what happens next in "Secret Baby For My Ex's SEAL Brother".

About the Author

Valencia Rose is an Indie Author who loves to create a world of love and happy ever afters for her readers to escape from the crazy times we currently live in. She loves to breathe life into sizzling hot stories revolving around Sexy Billionaires, Alpha Bosses and Dominant Playboys who will stop at nothing to achieve their happy endings with their feisty heroines, when they want and how they want.

When she is not writing, Valencia loves to play the piano and also travel with her husband and two little girls to explore fun new activities with them.

If you like sensual steamy page-turning contemporary romance books, make sure to sign up here for Valencia's Romance Book Club to receive FREE Advanced Reader Copies (ARCs), first dibs and discounts on her latest releases.

And as a new member of Valencia's Steamy Romance Book Club, you will receive a special gift from her; your very own copy of one of her steamy romance novellas, called "Bad Boy Professor".

Click on the link below to join and download your copy for FREE!

https://dl.bookfunnel.com/b08u2ku9nm

"Bad Boy Professor" is a Grumpy Billionaire Off-limits Romance. Here is a short look at what happens inside that book:

That moment you realize your hot professor is the sexy bad boy you slept with last week...

So here is what happened: I was hard on money and met this sexy tattooed playboy who claimed my body without even saying a word.

Fast forward to a week later, my smart, sexy-as-hell, but arrogant Professor walked through the class door!

I didn't know whether I should squeeze my thighs or throw up in my purse because it was him... And he recognized me too.

Next thing I knew, that first one-night stand turned into a passionate relationship. But we had to stop it because I could be expelled. He could lose his job. We could lose everything.

The problem was we couldn't keep our hands off each other. We were in way too deep.

***

Sign up now by clicking on the link below to get your FREE copy of "Bad Boy Professor":

https://dl.bookfunnel.com/b08u2ku9nm

Made in United States
North Haven, CT
03 March 2025

66405888R00283